EDGWARE ROAD

EDGWARE ROAD

YASMIN CORDERY KHAN

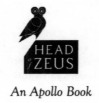

An Apollo Book

ISBN (HB): 9781801107341
ISBN (XTPB): 9781801107358
ISBN (E): 9781801107372

Typeset by Divaddict Publishing Solutions Ltd

Printed and bound in Great Britain by
CPI Group (UK) Ltd, Croydon CR0 4YY

MIX
Paper from
responsible sources
FSC® C171272
FSC
www.fsc.org

Head of Zeus Ltd
First Floor East
5–8 Hardwick Street
London EC1R 4RG

WWW.HEADOFZEUS.COM

For Markus, Adam, Leo, Amira, Jamie, Feliks and Mila

'For why is gambling a whit worse than any other method of acquiring money? How, for instance, is it worse than trade? True, out of a hundred persons, only one can win; yet what business is that of yours or of mine?'

The Gambler, Fyodor Dostoevsky

EDGWARE ROAD, LONDON

15 DECEMBER 1987

1

SHE LOOKS UP AT THE FRONT OF THE STATION BY TWISTING
herself round, turning from the pavement to the shiny red brick
arches. It says in huge black and white letters, made out of tiles:
EDGWARE ROAD. Definitely at the right stop then. She's
been here fifteen minutes and there's no sign of him and she
goes back inside the ticket hall. It's a small station; just a few
barriers opening into a narrow exit, and not many people about.
A family of Americans in matching shell suits, and a lady in a
burkha with the sparkliest shoes ever.

She can't have missed him.

She'd wanted to wear her Wham! T-shirt and Mum told her
not to, and she'd won the argument and now she's in this wind
tunnel. The cold wind whips straight into her face. And it's
kind of weird standing here, maybe she should walk around to
warm up? She has three ten-pence pieces in her pocket, in case
of emergency. There's a corner shop over there, it's basically
a little kiosk built into the wall. She's under strict orders not to
leave the station. The shop barely counts, does it? She goes in
and has a look at the rows of sweets, and settles on a KitKat for
nineteen pence.

Back in the ticket hall she unpeels the paper wrapper and

eats one of the chocolate fingers, saves the other one for later, carefully folding over the foil at the top. There's a clock fixed into the wall and if she cranes her neck she can see that it's twenty minutes past. He really is late now and the last thing she wants to do is tell her mum. He's going to arrive, full of apologies. She shouldn't have eaten half of the KitKat because he's going to take her to a burger place and she won't have an appetite.

What will she talk to him about when he arrives? School's going OK. She loves reading. She doesn't like the playtimes when the boys put down goals made from their coats and jumpers and take over the whole space. All the girls end up squeezed on the other side, not able to run around freely. The boys leap for headers and fly round like birds with their arms out behind them when they score a goal.

On Friday she'd sat down on a bench, squeezed in between two girls from her class. One of them was eating crisps out of a packet. She didn't share them. She didn't mind her not sharing because she doesn't like salt and vinegar, and she had said so.

The girl kept picking out crisps and inspecting them for dark edges.

'So why'd your mum and dad split up then?' the girl on the bench had asked. And she'd ignored her.

She's never actually thought about this question in a way that she can put into words. Maybe that's what she should ask him about. She twiddles the end of her hair round her fingers.

Still no sign of him. She should have brought a book. Her legs are getting tired and she knows she probably shouldn't sit on the floor. It looks grubby. The floor is made up of black and white checks, like a chess board, but the white tiles are chewing gum grey, so she sort of squats on her haunches.

'You alright, love?' The Tube man, ancient in a faded blue uniform with a blue turban and a long grey beard that ends in a wisp, has been watching her and now he comes out from behind his little glass kiosk, leaving the office untended, to speak to her, specially.

'Yeah, I'm OK, just waiting for my dad.' It's been drummed into her not to speak to strangers and she deliberately looks away, as if her father will turn the corner at any second. It's nice of him to check, though.

A few more minutes and she'll use that last coin in the phone box; she'll have to call Mum and tell her to pick her up early, to meet her back at Hammersmith. Never mind, she's eleven now, well into double figures. Almost a teenager, she can deal with this. What is it that Mum always says? There's worse things happen at sea.

She goes out onto the pavement, into the roar of the traffic where the flyover meets the main road. There's a red phone box a few steps from the station. The door is heavy to push open and inside it smells of wee and ashtrays. She has to stand up on tiptoe to reach the receiver. Around the edges of the phone box cards have been stuffed into the glass panes and stuck onto the doors; pictures of naked women, turning so their bums are high in the air, showing off their G strings, not really smiling. Some of the cards are trampled on the ground and she can't help standing on them, on their massive boobs, and feels bad.

The receiver is so heavy too, like a brick, and damp from other people's breath, and she steadies herself with one hand, though she doesn't want to touch anything in this phone booth.

She stands on tiptoes and dials her home number, then follows the instructions to pay when the tone sounds. Mum, she will say, she rehearses it in her mind. It's fine, he didn't come, I'm fine, I'm coming home now. Please can you pick me up at the station? She lines up her ten-pence piece carefully at the slot. Clunk, it's in the bowels of the machine. There is no ringing. Just the dialling tone. It's eaten her coin. She bangs at the telephone cradle, and sticks her fingers in the change-box below to see if the coin will roll back down. It's lost.

She rummages around in her backpack to see if there might be another ten pence in there somewhere, although she knows there won't be. She is very careful to keep any coins that come into her possession in her purse. The only other things in her bag are an apple, slightly brown, and an old copy of *Smash Hits* which she's read about seven times, and which has crinkled up. She'd better go back on the Tube to Hammersmith and then she'll find her way back from the station to home. She's pretty sure she knows the way.

The ticket in her hand has gone damp and bent so she can only feed it through the barrier by smoothing it out in the palm of her hand, like one of those cracker gifts, a red fortune-telling fish – she has one at home, you have to smooth it with your fingers, and make it curl upwards to say yes, or arch backwards to say no, like a dying fish out of water, a shining, flapping thing. Still, she can't get this ticket straight and she's starting to worry, when the man with the turban comes out of his booth again and opens the barrier for her, and waves her through without speaking to her.

PART ONE

1981 & 2003

2

THEY STOOD ALONGSIDE EACH OTHER ON THE ONE-ARMED bandits in the darkest corner of O'Connors next to the toilets. The smell of dried piss was almost masked by the fog of cigarette smoke, which hung low in the pub.

Khalid had known Imran for about three months.

It was about eleven thirty in the morning and they were the only punters. Brian was quiet that morning, still half-cut. He wiped last night's sticky beer residue from the tables, and pulled chairs down from the tabletops with a bang.

'Bar's open,' he mumbled, not to them, or anyone else, slinging his tea towel over his shoulder. 'Still at it, fellas?'

The two of them worked like factory workers, hands fluttering on the square buttons, feeding back the coins when they tumbled down. The tangy smell of copper and nickel rose up from the money, held by a thousand hands.

They ignored Brian, they were used to his complaints and the way he invited them in before opening time and then always felt let down by their choices, as if they didn't drink enough. And once they'd been thrown off the machines by a navvy, who came in and told them to shove off out of his way. Khalid liked Irish pubs in any case. You could usually find someone to stand you a drink in O'Connors, or in the Rose of Tralee further down the road. In Khalid's view, Sufism and Catholicism had a lot in common. Imran knew his views on the subject and was mostly in agreement. The Irish and the Asians, their own little people in a sea of imperial bastards.

Pissing their money away. That's what Suzie called it, and Khalid knew that she was wrong. It was only coins, never notes. And the sudden lighting up of the screen, and the cash pouring out. It was beautiful. The way that chance could hurl you up and bring you back down on your feet, five pounds richer, ten pounds richer. The rattle of money pouring out, like rapid gunshot. There was a new machine on the far side of the bar that asked for answers to general knowledge questions, like *Mastermind*, and some of the other regulars believed you could fiddle it, if you played it enough times, and could recall who did what to Marilyn Monroe. Khalid found it dull. You would never beat that kind of machine. Everyone knew the house always won. Only chance was pure. He didn't need to know he was clever, he just needed to know that he could beat the odds.

Imran got it. He was the same.

Khalid and Imran came straight here after their shift, straight down the Central Line from Marble Arch to Shepherd's Bush. They were still wearing their white shirts and black suit trousers, their bow-ties folded in their pockets. Imran had dark stubble, which burgeoned on his chin during the night shift. He always looked undone by the morning, with his shirt riding up over his belt, whereas Khalid was as pristine as he had been the previous evening. Just that night he'd been mistaken for a punter by one of his own colleagues, and he couldn't say he wasn't pleased. He could have been a diplomat from the High Commission or the rakish son of a high roller, out on the town with the family chequebook.

London was a grid of pubs of varying quality for Khalid – the type of fruit machines, the likelihood of a win, the warmth of the place. They should have both been sleeping, and there were women, children – they knew vaguely – in the back of their minds, waiting for them, somewhere, complaining that they hadn't returned. The night shift did things to you. Sometimes they came off it buzzing and they had to have a flutter, to do something to burn off the energy. Sleep didn't appeal. Khalid wasn't the only one, lots of them felt like that after the casino closed. And after all, he'd seen these players walking away with pockets full, thousands, screeched away by their chauffeurs in the morning light; why shouldn't he have his own little go?

'What you going to do if it closes?' Imran had a habit of talking while he played. Khalid found it threw his concentration off to chat, but he didn't want to be rude to his friend. And Imran was anxious, always seeing the risks round the corner, never the opportunities.

'Face that when it comes to it.' The lights flashed dull blue, the machine played a quiet jingle. Jingle – jingle – better luck next time. He fed in another coin.

The club was under review by the Gaming Board. It was in the High Court and all over the papers like a bad rash. There was a rumour of dodginess, a whiff of malpractice. The sheen was coming off the most fashionable place in town, and Hugh Hefner was on the defensive. Not that it stopped the stars – they were still coming. But Khalid could feel that the wind had changed direction. The glitter was coming unstuck.

'I'll be shafted,' said Imran. 'Got to think of something else. I want to be my own man, you know?'

'What about the Windies?' Khalid tutted under his breath as the machine gulped down more coins. The rumour was that, if Playboy closed, there would be jobs for loyal staff in other locations, like Florida, maybe even the Bahamas. 'The club there is going to be on the beachfront, bhai. They're building it out of an old plantation house. All the Hollywood stars take their holidays there.' Khalid had told Suzie all about it. They had laughed together about wearing floaty white clothes, drinking out of coconuts with long straws. They had whispered about how much Alia would like the beach. She was only four and hadn't seen the sea yet. It would be a good place to grow up. 'Bastard machine.' Another loss. Khalid slid in more money, eyeing Imran briefly to see if he'd noticed his damage. 'Good cricket. All year round.' He pulled down the lever of the bandit with his right arm.

Suzie liked the idea of monsoons, and Christmas in the warmth. She had started looking at bikinis in catalogues. She had circled two; a yellow one and a fancier one, with frills, big blue spots on cream. It will suit them. A fresh start, a good time to move on from the grime of London. Khalid could see the upside.

'I'll believe it when I see it.' Imran had a little win. The machine flashed orange and red, the cher-ching of the coins rolling down. 'Lownes, Hefner – I think their days are over, Khalid. I think it's time to make it on your own. Under your own steam. Ladies in pom-pom tails and ears, it's not going to last, is it?'

Imran had a sort of morose look about him, for someone who

had just made five pounds from a machine. He put the money in his pocket as if he was about to go. A pang of anxiety raced through Khalid. He needed a win before he could step out into the day, before he could even contemplate sleep.

'Don't go yet, bhai.' He called Imran brother and he looked the part. Imran, the younger, shorter one, with his pockmarked skin and skinny frame. There would never be any competition between them. A brother, nonetheless. It amused Khalid the way they walked in sync, and patted each other on the back. They weren't related at all – they only met at the club a few months ago when Imran walked up to his roulette table, in the middle of a game, looking for the floor manager. 'That's me,' Khalid said and Imran nodded, and then he started sticking close.

Sometimes it occurred to Khalid that his mother would be appalled that he hung out with such men. Imran's father probably had a bullock cart back home. They never talked about it, and it was all so different at Playboy. They had black friends, Chinese friends, working the blackjack tables and pouring martinis. You could change your name and run away from your roots. Tony – their mate on the Playboy cloakroom – had ditched his slave-owner name by deed poll, was pleased as punch about it. He was Tony King now. It wasn't the same as Karachi; things rolled differently.

The machines had fallen silent.

'Want something for that?' Brian offered from behind the bar where he was stacking pint glasses. He changed a fiver for Khalid. He didn't really mind if they didn't drink, as long as they kept playing.

And sometimes they did drink, too.

'Never quit while you're ahead.' Khalid went straight back to the machines and gave half of it to Imran, sliding the coins into the warmth of his palm.

'OK, just one more.' They both pressed down their levers at the same time.

The reels started to turn again behind the glass screen, apples, plums, dollar signs, in a chain, and there was an order to the pattern: red, orange, blue, green, which Khalid could anticipate. It looked random, spinning into a fruity blur. But if you saw it often enough you knew where the win might be. There was a slight element of skill, which gave a beauty to it that he couldn't explain.

'I met this Mr Gupta,' Imran says, 'Gujarati. He's got plans, got paisa, he actually got a loan from some new bank... he's starting up a chain, three chemist shops already in Harrow, two in Wembley.'

'Go on.' He wanted Imran to keep talking so he could concentrate on when to press the buttons.

'Thinking of going to work for him — says he'll teach me — how to develop photographs. Says he'll send me on a course, even.'

'Not the same as being your own man, though, is it?'

'Proper hours, and I'll see my boys. Anyway, I like cameras, all that stuff.' Imran glanced across at Khalid. It was almost as if he was asking his permission to leave the club. He couldn't deny him. They were all passing in the night. Most of them flitted in and out like bats.

KHALID DIDN'T LIKE TO THINK OF HIMSELF AS A COMPANY MAN, though he was wearing the cufflinks with the little bunny logo, he dressed the part and he had never said a bad word about the club or the owners. It was a well-paid job, as jobs went, and there had been a time when everyone was talking about Playboy. They still were – just for the wrong reasons.

And Khalid is a good croupier. Nobody quibbles when he's on duty.

His job is to be there in the background, almost invisible, holding the whole place together in the palm of his hand, like a little god, staying out of the errors of men's ways – it's not for him to say. He has to have their absolute trust, to hold their complete respect. He never shares in the joys of winning or commiserates when they blow it all. He never smiles or, God forbid, laughs. He takes it seriously and doesn't let his concentration show.

He must know over a hundred regulars by name.

He can do the sums. A lot of the odds are ingrained in his memory.

Good evening, Lord Ashbury.

Good to have you with us, Monsieur Boustani.

Place your bets please, gentlemen.

The world comes to his floor. He's seen grown men break down in sobs. He's seen silly, tipsy show-offs with the women they want to impress, and dedicated believers with their notebooks, who think they've found the system to beat the house. Well-known celebrities – rock stars, footballers – skulk in wearing dark glasses, even wigs, and he's seen Harley Street's finest heart surgeon study the deftness of his own hands. Khalid's hands are always on show, thin nimble fingers, nails neatly pared back and immaculately clean.

And they like him for his discretion and tact. They like the

15

transparency on the table and the way that he never coughs or slips up or asks the same question twice. He never turns his back or hides his actions. They don't think much more about him than that. That is enough.

'I want to try my own thing. Playboy's just…' Imran wrinkled his nose as if he'd smelled something sour. 'It wasn't part of my plan.'

IT WASN'T KHALID'S PLAN WHEN HE CAME TO LONDON EITHER. His entry visa had said college student. He had enrolled at Imperial College to study mechanical engineering. MEng (Hons). That was the plan.

That was what his parents wanted. It was expected of him and he'd gone along with the scheme, always knowing deep inside him that he didn't intend to conform; that the pathway marked out in hope, in his father's study, was a simplification of the way life twisted and uncoiled.

London was expensive; he hadn't really had to deal with money much before, and soon he discovered what he described to himself as the cash-flow problem. He took a couple of loans from drinking mates for textbooks, for LPs. He had started putting a punt on the horses at lunchtimes, just a flutter, when the allowance from his mother was running dry. It had soon become clear that the trickle from home wouldn't allow him to live like other young people in London, drinking and dancing in Soho, and wearing interesting clothes.

The idea had occurred to him to try to earn some cash.

Someone mentioned to him that Playboy was hiring.

It wasn't straightforward; he'd had to do a maths test, long divisions, he'd rattled them off, and he'd been asked to stand upright in the middle of the room, examined as if he were a prize beast. Victor Lownes himself circled him, inspected him slowly, front, back and sides. The famed London boss, with a name like a lounge or a yawn, in his black polo neck, looking like he'd just got out of bed. He nodded, and said, 'Well hello, charmer,' in his New York murmur, 'welcome to Playboy.' They didn't want anyone old or ugly. And they liked the internationals because the club was a meeting place for the world, as Lownes had put it, so Khalid was a perfect fit.

And then life really started. His life at night was dazzling, and the university students around him, and his lecturers, soon seemed tired. Scruffy in their moth-chewed jumpers and their cords. They were waiting in an ante-room, whereas life was fizzing all around him at Playboy. And who wanted to spend all that time learning tiny details to be regurgitated, just to get a salary in some anonymous firm of civil engineers, building multi-storey car parks, when you'd seen the kinds of money that could be made and lost in a night on Hyde Park Corner, in the blink of an eye?

He had dragged himself into college after the night shifts, and more and more he found himself sleeping through his alarm clock, missing a deadline to submit an assignment. He was at a loss about what to talk about with his classmates when he did manage to attend a lecture.

It was a company that treated its staff well, located at the best address in London. A state-of-the-art tower, ten storeys tall, overlooking Hyde Park, the Dorchester on one side and the Hyde Park Hotel on the other. They had a canteen to be envied and legendary Christmas parties. He was promoted to

Gaming Inspector and was making £8,500 a year by the end of 1978. That was the year he made an annual bonus and put down a deposit on an upper floor flat on the Queen Caroline estate. He had chosen Hammersmith because of the Piccadilly Line.

He looked at his hands on the fruit machine, how he offered them to the table with the palms up and rotated them at the wrist, palms down.

He resisted the temptation to make any of it theatrical. There were croupiers that made a show out of it, but it wasn't his style. Far better if he went unnoticed, was just part of the backdrop to the game.

Women could be a problem. The ones on the arms of rich men could be tricksy, especially if they weren't playing. Too much time to look him up and down, already bored before they even crossed the threshold of the club. And they noticed his long fingers, and the deftness with which he dealt out, and they liked the sheen of his jet-black hair and the hand-tied bow-tie, and his dimples. Their eyes bore into him, willing him to drop his concentration, to look in their direction, so that they could flaunt something, a cigarette holder or an engagement ring. Sometimes they tried to whisper to him, and to ask him where he was from. He's learned how to keep his eyes down, and to think of the numbers, to just concentrate harder.

'It's fine with me, Imran, you should give the photography a go. If that's what you want, if Hasina says so too. You're missing out on a chance. Think of the life, my friend. The Bahamas, blow me down. Come and see us on the beach. Take Hasina on a proper holiday. Show her the world.'

'She can't swim,' said Imran.

Brian was studying them, watching them with his arms

18

folded, a look of pity from across the bar. 'Hair of the dog, fellas?'

Imran shook his head. He had no stomach for alcohol; it always ended badly.

'How's Suzie?'

'She'll be worrying.' Khalid slipped another handful of coins into the machine.

Imran did the same, and the fruit began to whirl again.

'Let's get back home, shouldn't we?'

KHALID WAS ON THE WAY. HE SHOULD HAVE BEEN HOME FIVE hours earlier. It was past lunchtime. The excuses ran through his head, like tunes that he had played too many times. Better not to say anything. She hated excuses, especially, she said, when they didn't make logical sense. She had made that very clear. He was walking along King Street towards the Hammersmith end. Home in fifteen minutes. He just had to walk down a small row of shops, and turn two corners, past the greengrocers, the dry cleaners and the bookies.

He took it all in, the long panels of glass revealed the shopkeepers, counting change, exchanging words with customers. The old ladies with their headscarves, pulling along trolleys, and the trays piled outside the greengrocer, lined with fake grass, dull potatoes and a few hints of springtime, greens and cabbages. The butcher's racks of beef, fat, bald chickens, and whole flanks suspended from meat hooks, the owner glaring out in his bloody apron as a Rasta laughed with his friend outside, his braids streaming from his crocheted tam. It was all alright. He wasn't in his element but he was alright here. He crossed at the zebra crossing by the newsagents, where the lollipop lady chivvied a group of children over in the other direction, with hair dripping from swimming, and the Easter eggs, stacked like shoeboxes in the window, decorated with fluffy yellow chickens. And his mind flickered to home; it was his choice to be here, this and not the heat and dust. He had wanted things wrapped in layers of plastic, factory fresh. He had wanted modern stuff, people in shoes, temperate weather, sliced white bread. It had all been his choice.

A neighbour with a child about Alia's age was talking outside the post office, with another mother with a buggy. She didn't notice him, or at least didn't greet him. He strode past the shops. He could swear he wasn't looking at the chalkboard with the odds pasted up outside.

Someone ran into William Hill. The way the man was trotting, half-running, flat cap in hand, suggested something starting. It might be a big one? The windows of the bookies were frosted, so it was impossible to see in, as if something distasteful or adult happened inside. He just allowed himself a glance at the board. Newmarket. The names – that's what grabbed him – Raider, Pizarro, Brave Knight. He knew this shop well – in his pocket he had one of the stubby undersized biros that you could pick up for free. He had made promises not to go in there again, to Suzie, to himself. He'd even said to Imran the other day, 'It's a mug's game,' parroting one of Suzie's phrases, but he wasn't feeling it in his heart.

It wasn't as if he'd been trying to hide it.

He had left newspapers on the table, with names circled in red biro, all asterisks and loops and underlining. He'd tried to explain it to her. She didn't want to hear. It's all some kind of

20

divination, trying to figure out the underlying logics. 'There's a complete order, a complex pattern,' he'd said, thinking of the embroidered borders his mother used to sew. 'You might even call it divine.' She'd looked puzzled, as if she was trying hard to understand. 'It's all about probability.' He wanted her to understand that it wasn't just chance. He was finding a way to befriend probability. He'd topped maths at school without much effort, he could add up quicker in his head than anyone he'd ever met, surely that counted for something? When none of those arguments had worked he had said, 'It's just a way to use up loose change.'

Loose change drags your jacket pockets out of shape. He'd broken even at O'Connors, and the money was blazing like a fire in his coat. He could see two animals in his mind. One was a stallion, raring to go, chomping. The other was like a tired ox on a dried-out field, weak and ageing, too feeble for the plough strapped to its back. In other words, there was no choice at all.

Plastic multi-coloured streamers hung down over the doorway, keeping out flies, shielding the mysteries within. He found himself crossing the threshold of the shop, opening into its secret world. Cigarette smoke pooled near the ceiling, and it reeked of male sweat. It was full in there, men standing up, others perched on high stools. A big race. The walls were tacked with paper lists of horses, jockeys' names and the starting prices. They all knew him. It was like finding extended family behind the curtain. One old boy doffed his cap. Just a quick look, he told himself.

3

STAY AWAY FROM THE PUB, HE SAID TO HIMSELF. HE WASN'T going to piss this one away, or start buying rounds for all and sundry. One thousand pounds sterling, and on a bog-standard, nothing horse in the middle of the week. English Prince – by a neck, like a born winner, he would remember that name. He hadn't cheered or even clapped his hands, he had swallowed the joy. He had straightened his spine and composed his face, cool as a cucumber, buttoned his jacket and collected the winnings. Everyone knew that if Pat gave you an envelope it was a good one. He wasn't telling. His body was alive with the race, the surge of it at the finishing post. He walked out of that shop elated, feeling like a man, a man who was going to walk home with his head held high and carry his wife into bed. He wasn't going to screw this up.

Outside, things were brighter; drawn in primary colours, like one of Alia's paintings – yellow daffodils in pots he hadn't noticed earlier, the tomato red of the number 94 as it rolled past, the paintbox blue of the sky. His body was awake to the world in a way that felt dull before. He ran his finger along a low wall, just to feel the rough brick surface on his fingertips.

He turned away from the shops, raised his collar against the spring breeze, and made off in the direction of home. He took a longer route on a footpath round the back, a detour away from Fulham Palace Road, down the side of the industrial estate, tucked under the flyover, feeling the need for this crisp April air.

He passed the garage on the corner, set back from the pavement on a side-street, which he'd never really spotted before, and it was there, sitting on the forecourt. A gold Datsun. Parked behind several other cars, a card freshly scribbled and propped in the windscreen, the same black numerals as the grocers. He moved closer to it so that he could read the price. Almost new, two previous owners, shining like a gemstone in the sun. Almost perfect condition, you could tell just looking at it, a little marvel. Cream seats, built-in radio, flashy.

This was the sort of thing you should do with a win, rather than frittering it in the machines. It would be an investment. He saw himself driving to work, returning earlier from shifts at the club. They would be able to take Alia out, they could go out together on Sundays for excursions and call on friends.

'A lot of folks don't like Jap cars.' The dealer approached, coming out of the office, with an earnest air, wiping his hands on the side of his trousers. He was wearing a red ruffled tux, as if he might be off to a disco later that evening, heading up town.

'What's not to like?' said Khalid, without taking his eyes off the car.

'Every Tom, Dick and Harry had an uncle in Burma. We've got to move with the times, though. World changing, ain't it?' The man was younger than Khalid, and keen. He might be saying something about Khalid, the way that he looked at him, eyeing his suit in mutual regard.

'Electronic ignition?' Khalid asked.

The man shook his hand with respect. His name was Danny. Khalid felt there was some understanding between them, the man was honest, and he could hear a tinny tune he liked coming out from the office. The singer's high voice imploring, *Ring my bell.*

IT TOOK THEM A WHILE TO MOVE THE OTHER CARS OUT OF THE way so that Danny could extricate the Datsun and roll it out onto the driveway. Khalid's test drive was perfunctory, an unobservant lap around the block. It was his. He'd already made his mind up by that point, and Danny knew it too.

The paperwork didn't take long, and he watched the salesman write out the duplicates with concentration, before ripping off the top copy with a smile. He brought out notes from the envelope, warm from his inside pocket, peeling off twenties. They shook on it, and Danny pumped his hand, genuinely pleased for him. He recognized a man on the up. 'Not going to regret this one, mate. Solid little runaround.'

Khalid drove the car to the toyshop on the corner of Stamford Brook, which was full of fancy German brands and soft toys with leather tags in their ears to prove their heritage. He hadn't been in there since the week Alia was born. He bought the largest teddy bear he could find, a giant, golden thing, as solid as a bolster, with a green satin bow round its neck, probably about the same size as Alia herself. He propped it in the passenger seat.

When he arrived in their street, he turned the corner beeping the horn and the woman from upstairs, a meddler from the estate committee in a prim headscarf, looked out from a window

and frowned at the car, disapprovingly. For a moment there was
no sign of them, so he beeped again, and on the second floor
the nets were pushed aside, the sliding door opened, and he
saw Suzie, and behind her, the serious little face of his daughter
peering down at him from their balcony. It took them a few
seconds to piece it all together, to work out where he was and
that he was the one making the racket. Suzie laughed and he
heard the racing of footsteps, amplified, as they rushed down
the stairs and opened the door onto the street.

He rolled down the window.

'Ma'am, your carriage awaits.'

'Khalid, you didn't?' He could see that she was pleased and
suspicious at the same time.

'My ship came in.'

'Newmarket, was it?' She tried to pull a disapproving face
but couldn't wipe the smile away.

'Twenty to one. English Prince. I had the measure of him.'

Alia tried to reach up to him through the car window. She
was too small to even reach the edge of the door and he rolled
the window lower with the handle, so that the glass retracted
completely. He lifted up the heavy teddy bear to show her.

He stepped out to let Suzie sit behind the wheel, and settled
in the passenger seat with Alia on his lap and the teddy jammed
between his legs and the gear stick. Suzie turned the key in the
ignition, moved into first, and they lurched forward a little and
began to drive, gently forward, then faster and into second gear.
Suzie flicked on the windscreen wipers by mistake and they all
laughed, thrilled by the car, and by how easy it was to turn
things on and off. Alia kept fiddling with the radio but Khalid
didn't tell her off. They drove slowly around the block, up and

down the tarmac, in front of the four parallel buildings on the site, like dignitaries visiting their estate.

THE QUEEN CAROLINE WAS ONLY A FEW YEARS OLD, ALL BUILT out of the same pale bricks interspersed with white cladding and balconies, only stretching four storeys up, respectable housing on council land. If they stood on tiptoes on their balcony they could see the Thames and the bridge running over to Barnes and the green southern edges of London. The trees dotted around the estate were saplings, and empty flats quickly filled with young families that Suzie often recognized from playgroups and nursery school. Children were out on their tricycles or skipping on the shared grass in front. Few people on the Queen Caroline owned cars and it was a lap of honour. They wanted to be seen, and Khalid leaned his elbow out the window and closed his eyes, as the spring air washed over him and he reclined his seat, and the tiredness seeped into his body.

Suzie kept repeating the name of the horse, and going over the others in the race, the facts of the win, and the way that she had known that something good was going to happen this month, convinced that it marked the turning of the tide and a new run of good luck for Khalid.

'You've been working so hard, Kal, you deserved a lucky break.' She had a way of making random things fit into patterns.

They turned at a mini-roundabout, back towards their block.

'I always tell you, there's no such thing as luck. You make it yourself.'

He had been testing her patience lately. She would have felt furious if he'd come back having lost. There would have been swearing and sulking, making him sleep on the sofa. Not a look-in for days. In fact, he probably wouldn't have told her at all. He didn't want to think about that now, and pushed it away.

'Bahamas is really on the cards. I talked to Lambert about it today,' Khalid looked up at her, seeking her enthusiasm.

She smiled, an inscrutable, opaque smile as if that would be another lucky windfall, falling from the heavens. 'Well, that will be something else.'

God, she was nice-looking.

'I'm going to make it happen,' he said solemnly, patting her thin thigh as she changed gear.

A lot of men envied him, as if he was a cat who'd got the cream. She was modelling for a fashion house on the King's Road when he met her, but her beauty was not the point. Khalid liked the way she looked, but it wasn't her sexiness, it was her innocence, as if life hadn't touched her or hurt her, her belief in general that things could be trusted. Suzie left her purse on tables in pubs and restaurants, she never locked anything – 'I've never had anything stolen,' she would say with a shrug when he got annoyed. Once a café owner had run after her with her change down the street. She used to go to the cinema by herself when she should have been at school, slipping into the back once the film had started.

And since she had the baby, she'd been happier than not, most of the time – apart from their rows, about him getting in late and this and that with money and so on – she seemed content. She was glad to quit work and settle into the flat; she filled her days up easily, without a fuss, playing with Alia, making drawings with crayons and reading fashion magazines. And she seemed willing, about the new plan to move; he thought she was happy, following him to this island they were heading towards. Not like Imran and his wife, stuck in their ways.

He'd had a lot of sex in his life. It hadn't been hard for him to find women. As a teenager he had a good time with the daughter of his father's old retainer back in Sind. She had been seventeen and he was sixteen and she was plump with hair down to her backside and she used to ask him to teach her some English words afterwards while he helped fix her scarf. And there were other girls on the land, willing, one or two of them married young to old farmhands who knew or didn't care or turned a blind eye because they had to because he was the landlord's eldest, and those young wives had taught him little things that he'd never imagined before. Sometimes he wondered what might have happened if any of those girls had got pregnant. They might have done, but he would never have come to hear of it. His mother would have been angry. There were a couple of aunties who pinched his cheeks and called him naughty boy.

And there had been other women. One girl he had gone crazy over who wouldn't go to bed with him; a student at the medical school in Karachi, very determined, she wanted marriage or nothing. She had strung him along. She'd been hitched to an engineer from Lahore. It was a good match for her, people said. And once he got to London – wow – it had been a good time, the late 1960s. A great time. He played his exoticism for all it was worth. He could be anything they wanted – Sicilian, or an Eastern prince. Bunny girls, models, an heiress to a supermarket chain for one night only. He had lost count, it had all got blurry.

AND THEN SUZIE. SHE'D BEEN IN THE CLUB ONE NIGHT ON THE arm of some rich rugby player. She said later he wasn't her boyfriend although it seemed unlikely, a big jock from Cape Town. He couldn't hold his drink, and had started trying to pick a fight because he wanted to use his rands or something on the table, instead of just going to the cashier and buying chips. Suzie said she'd been impressed by how calm Khalid was, not a flicker. He dealt with the bruiser and guided him away from the floor, he was stumbling. The bugger was built like a brick shithouse, heavy and legless, and he was escorted off the property and the bouncers managed him into a taxi. And just ever so slightly aware of her there, the whole time, embarrassed, watching on in his peripheral vision, in a purple mini-dress, lost without anyone to stick to. And he helped Suzie get a taxi and she looked at him, and she saw he was kind, and she said, 'Let's meet up in the daytime,' as if she'd had enough of going out after dark. She had scribbled her number on the back of a card inside the taxi, while the driver sat with the engine running.

That had been seven years earlier, and that was pretty much it.

They pulled up at the kerbside outside their front door and she put on the handbrake and leaned across and kissed him on the cheek, and he felt the heat from her breath, and Alia squeezed between their bodies.

'Well, this was meant to be.' She made it all fit together, she could smooth away any cracks between the joints.

That night, Suzie tiptoed to their bedroom, and pulled Alia's door closed. That was a good sign.

She clicked on the bedside lamp, with its frilly beige shade, and wriggled out of her jeans and lay on the bed face down in her boyish knickers, with her rosy little nipples squashed against the duvet cover. Her skin had this amazing sheen to it, like the cream on a bottle of gold top. She pretended to be flicking through *Cosmopolitan*, making a mock serious face, but really she was watching him undress. It was at least twenty hours since he had last slept, but the fatigue acted as a kind of comforting blanket, in which his thoughts were dulled and his body was slipping between one world and another. He stripped, very carefully and slowly, in the light of the bedside lamp, folding everything along the seams and leaving it on a chair.

His eyelids were drawing down, heavy as metal shutters, but he didn't fight them. Then he lay down beside her and stroked her back.

She slid herself over him, so he was pressed up tight against her and he slipped even further into a languid haze, powerless, somehow pulled into her orbit. They heard a child's cough and slight cry through the muffled plasterboard of the wall. She paused, and they both listened, in a kind of anxious stillness. Nothing more. The flat reclaimed the air, its usual low-level noises, the burr of the twin-tub spinning frantically in the kitchen, and she muttered something like a worry which he brushed away from her face. And then he felt her forgetting too, and heard her breathing quicken, and everything was alright, almost despite herself, because of him.

THE NEXT MORNING KHALID HAD THE DAY OFF, AND HE WENT downstairs in his dressing gown and threw open the curtains to another clear spring day. 'Let's go to Kew Gardens,' he declared, 'for a picnic.'

It was unusual for them to take an outing, like playing at being adults, at doing the things that parents did. Suzie and Alia fell in with his plans. Suzie found an old wicker basket at the back of the airing cupboard, and did her best with whatever she could find in the fridge: apples, chunks of cheddar – and found a rug specked with dried leaves from the previous year, some spare metal cutlery, a bat and ball. She tugged Alia into a smock and sun hat. They drove out from Hammersmith in the Datsun, along the Great West Road and curled round the Hogarth Roundabout. The radio played Radio 1 and Khalid let Suzie drive. He preferred to be driven. He squinted out at the mammoth grey gasholders and the choked traffic, and was glad to be crossing the river.

'It'll be good to leave all this, won't it?' He looked across to her frowning face, as she negotiated between the kerb and the side of a delivery van. He watched for some sign of assurance.

'London's still home, Khalid,' she said, as if it wasn't something they should talk about today.

AT KEW, THEY AMBLED FOR A LONG TIME, AIMLESSLY, PAST THE Pagoda, inside the great palm houses with their thick, humid air, along the wide avenue leading to the sloping riverbank. Alia hurtled after ducks and geese, and Khalid had brought his Kodak and took photos of his daughter and wife and asked a passer-by to take a family portrait of them posing by multi-coloured tulips. They stood for a long time on a miniature bridge, looking down at the river below them, and Suzie taught Alia to throw twigs down and race them, and Alia shouted with pleasure as her mother's stick snagged on a bigger branch.

Many other families were out too and a man in unfashionable jeans with too much fat pushing up over the waistband stared at them and prodded his wife as they approached. It was as if he recognized them, as if they might be film stars. Khalid and Suzie both had sunglasses on, and they had a worldly ease about them, their lean bodies hinting at celebrity. The other families looked so ordinary, with pale, washed-out faces after the winter, and their kids all wearing sludge-coloured clothes. Khalid was used to them being stared at and sometimes he thought it was because of her being white, and him being Asian, and all that, but today it might have been just because they looked so bloody good together.

They found a space on a lawn, with crocuses pushing up around it, and spread out the blanket, and Suzie kicked off her shoes. She began to comb and plait Alia's long hair, and twisted it into bunches on either side of her head.

Khalid lay on his back, resting his head on his hands, and stared up at the sky and at the vapour trails from planes coming and going from Heathrow, spotting the tailfins, guessing them as they came lower and into view – Air France, British Airways, Pan-Am, Air India – double lines of white that lingered far longer than he expected. Eventually, they started to shimmer apart and merge with the clouds.

These were his tracks. His father had watched the railways spanning his district, linking his town to the world, shipping out cotton and bringing in new things – bicycles and typewriters. Calligraphy had given way to typeface, the palanquins lay empty in outhouses, as people took to the rails.

Khalid had the planes. Criss-crossing as lightly as shooting stars, held aloft by something human but unfathomable, each one holding three hundred little dreams and hopes of arrival. There was so much comfort in living under those flight paths. It was a constant reminder to him that the rest of the world was there.

He ran his fingers through the new grass, and felt the earth beneath him and breathed out, audibly.

'Delta, that one.'

'That's TWA, isn't it?' Suzie played the game too, joining his thoughts. 'All the way from America.'

'We'll take you, Alia, the Empire State, the Statue of Liberty.' Suzie tried to anticipate his dreams, to talk of these places as if she had already sauntered along Fifth Avenue swinging a handbag. It was like she was trying to make up for not committing earlier, for not enthusing about the Bahamas.

Alia didn't reply. She was concentrating, threading a daisy stem into the tiny fissure made in another stem by her small round fingernail. Khalid saw her clearly, in all her solemn loveliness, and reached for his camera.

'I want to take you to Pakistan.'

Suzie looked up. 'Khalid, do you? You've never said that before.'

Even as he said it, he knew it was a terrible idea.

It just wouldn't work. His cousins would be charming, wrapping Suzie up in clothes and jewellery and taking care of her, and whispering in his ear about her prettiness, spoiling Alia with everything she asked for. But there was something that he'd find too difficult, pulling him in two directions. It wasn't their fault. Just the artifice, pretending again that he belonged there, when things had moved on so much. This was his life now. He had created something that couldn't be exported.

His mother called every week from Karachi to ask him about the family, and sometimes he put Alia on the phone. It was all kind of excruciating because of the language. The incantation of the same words, Mashallah, Khuda Hafiz, and his little girl's blank expressions when she heard Urdu, which made him guilty for not teaching her more, and not knowing quite who this grandmother was or where the voice came from. The worst was when Alia held the phone away from her ear with a scrunched-up nose and refused to speak at all.

His mother cried sometimes, self-pityingly, about the way that they'd all left and how she had to face her sister's grandchildren every other day, and it was a grief she was just starting to adjust to. It was hard to imagine her being so fierce once.

GOD, HIS FATHER HAD WHACKED HIM. AFTER THE MOVE FROM India, they didn't know how to deal with these kids of theirs who were starting to go their own way and, as they had got bigger, wearing nylon shirts and listening to American records. Suzie had seen the photograph of Khalid's younger sister, with her skirt up above her knees, in big sunglasses, palm trees behind her, looking like, as she had said, 'quite a girl', and the chance freedoms of the white house where the family all lived with more space than in that old place, but without a courtyard, without a village. And the maulvis would call round and mutter. His father often had cases, and Khalid would stay out later until after sunset. It became harder for his father to slap Khalid as he grew into a six-footer, and sprouted a moustache. But they would both yell at him, for what? He had never known the answer, perhaps it was buried in that line between a generation, and in a line across a map, which cut off the courtly ways, the old ways, from the son?

One month in the 1960s there had been a development fair in Karachi. White tents had appeared on the maidan with pictures of new plans and schemes, blueprints of a great irrigation work and barrage, and visions of concrete blocks springing up around the city, on grids so people wouldn't get lost and with power and water. Khalid milled around with his crowd until his friends had had enough, and he stayed on alone, ambling up and down. PIA had a recruitment stall, where flight attendants stood in their Pierre Cardin uniforms, and a map of the world was marked with string and drawing pins, showing the flight routes spanning out from Karachi like a shooting star. And next to that there was an American tent, with tins of cold beer in fridges with the brand name Coors and the sound of blues coming from a radio. Some guy in an airline uniform had sat down with him, and he had told him he should be an engineer and described his family back in Illinois, and topped up his glass, and when he got home his mother had smacked him hard across the face and he had submitted to it, barely felt it, because his mind was so full of the taste of that day. The chance of building a new world, but not the way his parents had built their new world.

Recently, he had got Alia to learn the names of the world leaders, the ones that mattered. Who is the president of America? 'Ronald Reagan.' What is the capital of West Germany? 'Bonn.' Who is the Prime Minister of Great Britain?' 'Mrs T.' It sounded improbable from the mouth of a four year old, it was a party-trick. Their friends would gather round, the air thick with the smoke from their cigarettes and heads cocked back, laughing at the touching sight, the recitation of the precocious child, before she was packed off to bed in her pyjamas in the midst of the party noises. Khalid didn't care if it seemed like he was showing off. But he never asked about Pakistan.

'Tell me about it – about your house there,' Suzie said.

'Well, the first house, I don't remember very well, that was in India. That was the grand one.'

They flew by a flimsy turbo-prop because his father had connections, the excitement of that as a kid, the delays and waiting and fuss about luggage, then the thrill of going up into the air above everything. And did he see them below? Those who walked. He was never sure. The endless trudging columns, the bewildered, the displaced. People arriving with their bundles and stories, they were everywhere and yet they were unexplained. The versions he had heard later were censored, tidied up, deemed unsuitable for his young ears.

Sometimes, as a kid, he'd missed the old house and the former servants and they came to him in dreams, carrying in platters to the table, but when he peeked underneath there was nothing on them, or worse, once, maggots. The old place, a branch that had been broken off and replanted.

'Another year. We should sort Bahamas out first. One thing at a time.'

Suzie looked disappointed. She collected a pile of petals and twigs next to her and started to arrange them, like a bird, as if she could create some order in the random materials around her.

'Imran's got plans, hasn't he, if the club closes?' Her eyes were down on the ground.

Suzie had followed all the press, in the *Daily Mail* and the *Evening Standard*, and, although she'd tried to get enthusiastic about the Caribbean, she had made new friends in Hammersmith and was full of praise for Alia's nursery school, and filling the place with little things she'd picked up at charity shops. She had brought home a few of those paint tester cards recently, with their fancy labels for emulsion, as good as racehorse names.

'It's all hot air.'

'Is it going to close, though?'

KHALID COULDN'T PRETEND. THERE HAD BEEN OMENS OF AN empire crumbling. The London club had been losing out to competitors over the last few years, ever since the end of the decade. Victor Lownes, so the rumours said, had taken a dirty road. He had gone after Ladbrokes, feeding information to the British Gaming Board. Victor had given the prosecutors all sorts of juicy bits and pieces, until Ladbrokes had lost its gaming licence. It had pushed out the competition for a while, but some of those things could only be known by someone on the inside, and the more the police had learned about what was going on at Ladbrokes, and the insider dealing, and the blackmail, and the bad debts and the cover-ups, the more they had started to think about Playboy itself. And the more questions they had started to ask, the more they had come in wanting to have a good look at the books.

'Leave it, Suze. I don't want to talk about work today.'

As he lay there on the grass, Khalid felt the call of something in his body, an itch. He needed to get back to the bookies, to a casino, or to a fruit machine. It was, by any standards, a poor deal, exchanging these riches for a game. It was not something that he could control or direct. It was no more or less complicated than thirst, just like needing a drink of water. If you looked into it you might learn all the complicated biological reasons that the human body needed liquid, Khalid reasoned, and the ways that water plays an essential part in human equilibrium. But most people just had the feeling, and if they were dehydrating then there was no way they could be messed with. He was thirsty. He started to pull things out of the picnic bag.

'I forgot to tell you. Imran called. I think I'll head out with him tonight.'

4

She had to get the number 5 bus down the Cowley Road back to her flat, because she was too drunk to ride her bike. She would pick it up before teaching a tutorial in the morning. She'd been at a college dinner and had bundled her black gown, synthetic and unwieldy, into a carrier bag that was splitting at the sides, as she got off the bus. Twenty metres under lamplight to her front door, she was trying to stuff it back into the bag.

Her flatmate Stefan was already inside; she could see him through the thin curtains which opened onto the ground floor room, the lamplight from within outlining him with a halo. The curtain wasn't quite long enough so she had a clear view of his lower half. He was wearing tracksuit bottoms, with bare feet, and held an unlit cigarette in his thumb and forefinger, poised like a pen. She guessed he was listening to music, although all she could hear was the low buzz of evening traffic coming from the main road, the whine of motorbikes, drifting into their scruffy terraced street, and a deeper bass note, from the Zodiac, where the student club night was getting started.

She walked up the pathway through the low rusty gate, past the wheelie bins which nobody had bothered to take round the back. She leaned across and rapped on the window, not making the effort to search for her keys in her backpack. Stefan moved his long pale feet and made towards the front door, and she soon heard him rattling the latch and the chain. Once inside, the flat was oppressively tiny and there was nowhere to go, to escape Stefan or the conversation, so she joined him in the front room and sat on the sofa. It exuded old smoke, years of abuse covered with a woven throw.

Stefan offered her the cigarette that he'd been holding, awkwardly, proffering cheap matches that wouldn't work. She refused. He wasn't the ministering sort, despite coming from a long line of Lutheran pastors, and she flopped down on the armchair, unzipped her boots and eased her feet out. 'Give me a sip of that, though,' she said, taking a glug from his can of beer.

'Did you mind me asking you those things earlier?' he said. 'Want to talk about it?'

She wasn't seriously annoyed with Stefan, just in the usual way that she was always irritated with him. His pants on the floor of the bathroom, his dirty dishes left congealing on summer days, so that bluebottles once hatched in their shared kitchen. As a postdoctoral engineer from Stockholm, an inventor apprentice, he did something in the laboratories of Oxford to do with cars – he believed they could run on electricity, drive themselves one day. She'd never doubted his cleverness. His English was word-perfect though thickly accented and he found it infuriating when people spoke to him slowly and gesticulated, which Alia never did. Otherwise, he was cheerful and direct by nature. She had found him by placing an advertisement for the spare room, and she had quizzed three others. He was the sensible choice – she had steered clear of anyone she might end up in bed with.

Alia was a fixed-term lecturer in English Literature, that meant she was not old enough or good enough or plain lucky enough to stay forever. The author of two good papers in highly regarded peer-reviewed journals, yet despite the gown, the letters after her name, the hours of life poured away in libraries, and the way she had scrambled and clutched on to reach this supposed pinnacle, she could never imagine herself as a don. She didn't fit in Oxford and she couldn't pretend to, and after a few months of trying she had decided to just treat it like any old job. This was her strategy for survival.

There were other academics around – a lot of them young – some of them scraping to get by like her, plagued with worries about what they wrote and doubting their decisions. Walking lop-sided with heavy totes filled with vegetables, from the Co-op on the Cowley Road, or looking worried at the traffic lights with an empty kid's seat on the back of a bike.

There were other ones too. People from country houses in Sussex or Hampshire, who holidayed in Tuscany, who knew at least someone in their family who had strolled down the path before them: piano lessons, high marks in finals, a fellowship, slipping into the Victorian living rooms in Jericho, wearing middle-aged clothes and glasses prematurely. The ones with a library at home with wooden floorboards.

And there were the internationals, like Stefan. He might settle somewhere in a cutting-edge laboratory one day, but he didn't care where, as long as there was an interesting prototype or a multi-million-euro project. He was happy to learn a few languages, try some different cities on for size in the meantime, skating across the surface of the city.

The big question of Alia's life was where she fitted in.

Though recently she had been starting to think it might be *if* she could fit in.

And now this, this raking up, almost comically, of things so past, so buried.

Her father's death had become simply a fraction of her past, a slice of kaleidoscopic material that rarely fell into focus, part of her curriculum vitae. Just a particle, Stefan would have said.

'No, I didn't mind you asking, I just haven't given it much thought.'

1987. Books from 1987 were becoming classics on the syllabus. If you talked about it, you sounded nostalgic – reminiscing about the time before mobile phones, before the internet. Her dead father was grieved, gone, from a lost century.

She couldn't even piece him together anymore. She could picture the face of Kurt Cobain or Richard Nixon much better, and they kept cropping up on late night documentaries; she had seen far more photographs of them. Her own father has been on a perpetual slide backwards into fragments. He was almost disintegrated for her; purple balloons at a birthday party when she was two or three, the memory of odd quirks – the handkerchief over his head in the rain – he hated the rain – or the way he slid his arms into a suit jacket. They took it to the dry cleaners for him, and there was a bow-tie in the pocket.

Nothing.

And now someone wanted to talk about it again?

Stefan sat on the floor and drew out the paper to roll another cigarette. He was respectful towards Alia – she was older than him, and senior, in the university scheme of things – and he wanted to work her out; although he didn't exactly fancy her, he found her intriguing. She recognized this.

'WELL, WHAT CAN I SAY? HE VANISHED. HE'D BEEN LIVING IN A rented office off the Edgware Road – sleeping next to the desk, using the bathrooms. My mother didn't know. No one used the word homeless because that wasn't what he was – it wasn't how he wanted to be seen. Only remember him in a suit. Smart, polished shoes, clean shaven. And then he wasn't there anymore.'

'Didn't you look for his friends?' Stefan, like everyone she had ever met who had grown up comfortably, always made things sound simpler than they were.

'Well, I was eleven, I didn't know anyone, I didn't know where to start. Mum hadn't been to the office where he lived, I'd been – to see him on my visiting days – I didn't even know the address. It was just somewhere off the Edgware Road, and where to start in London? It was like a needle in a haystack. And it was all kind of out of my hands, I was concentrating on school. I just heard things second-hand. No news, she'd say. She was miserable about it. I think she had... a lot of sympathy for him... despite everything.'

'Didn't they put out something on Interpol or something like that?'

'Interpol? The thing is, Stefan, people go missing all the time, and unless they are little children, or beautiful women, or obviously murdered, no one bats an eyelid. Some people want to go missing.'

'And did your dad?'

'I don't know. I guess I began to believe that he did. And then he turned up, in the water, in Portsmouth, his body had washed up on a beach. And we never quite knew the full story, what had happened in between.'

'So how did he die?'

'The coroner gave an open verdict. He'd probably had a heart attack or something – his relatives were always talking about stents and beta blockers. His body had just sort of ended up in the wrong place, and that was how we kind of lost him.'

'Sounds kind of careless.'

'Thanks, Stefan – wouldn't happen to you, right?'

He shrugged. 'And didn't you think about it, or worry about it? What happened?'

Stefan was living up to his reputation for bluntness.

'I got to grips with it. He probably died of a heart attack, we grieved him, tucked him away.' Alia folded her hands, in a sort of religious gesture. Even as she tried to explain it all, in factual terms, in ways that made sense, she could see the holes in the story, the things that could be tidied over in the mind that, once voiced, sounded illogical.

'So there must be a grave somewhere?'

'Put like that, yes.'

'So do you go there? Where is it?'

It was something she had pushed under the waterline. She was too embarrassed to admit she didn't know the address.

'Somewhere in London.'

Asking would have been awkward, and she was just a kid. She had just been once, on a very grey day. Electricity pylons looming, closer than she'd ever stood to them before. Not much else.

'Look, I was very young.'

'Jesus, you've got issues.'

'Thanks, Stefan. I can work some things out for myself.'

He could be so insensitive, although some part of her also

welcomed the frankness, the black and white way he saw her existence. He liked clear answers, without the patience for muddiness.

Why hadn't she been? She could have found out the address. Her mother wouldn't have minded. She'd always been too busy, there were GCSEs, and then A levels, endless exams, and all the absorption with crushes, and time wasted on chasing after hopeless boys. And there was life, and the business of getting on with it, which had seemed more interesting than death. And most of the time she had been broke – any money she got together was for going out at the weekends, not train fares to misery lane.

'And now you're planning on going to Pakistan? That's wild. Listen, I'm going to get back early tomorrow, get some pizza in. We're going to have an epic board game session.' He was definitely not suggesting it would be the two of them. He always had friends round, they seemed to mushroom in their flat. Geeks.

There had been enough interrogation. This was as far as she wanted to go. Perhaps she would make sure she worked late the next day.

SHE DID REMEMBER MORE. OF COURSE SHE DID. IT WASN'T quite as simple as she made it sound to Stefan. The version she had rehearsed and delivered to curious friends was polished. It didn't allow for the uncertainties.

Her last visit to him; he had met her at Edgware Road station and there was bright sun glaring into the ticket hall as she emerged on the stairs, out of the greyness below.

He had taken her backpack and kissed her formally on the cheeks. They walked back along the street, towards the office, along the market stalls of toys and fake gold, and cafés where men sucked on shisha pipes watching the passing trade.

He'd walked faster than usual, with a brisk step, and he'd talked, rapidly, urgently as they walked, his hands in the pockets of his overcoat. About a deal, about something major that was happening for him.

'It's happening this time, Alia. It's going to be different.'

'Right, Dad.' She was almost a teenager, trying out sarcasm. The worst kind. She looked down at her feet and her DM boots with trailing laces.

'No, I mean it, this time, it's my time, there's no loose ends, I'm right in the middle of it.'

'What do you want me to say, Dad?' She'd learned grown-up phrases, too mature for her years, from listening intently to her mother.

'Don't you want to know more about it? I'm not meant to say a word, not a word. I trust you, Alia – I can tell you if you want?'

'I don't want.'

The silence of that moment. Later she would rake over it.

'OK, let's go and get a Coke, there's a new place on the corner, the owner's a friend.'

And they'd ended up in the usual kind of place, with bleached tabletops and deep fried chicken nuggets, and some friend of a friend of her father's, in a similar suit, who called her habibi and shook Khalid's hand for many seconds, and gave them cold Cokes for free, with straws.

WHAT PEOPLE HAD TOLD HER, WHAT SUZIE HAD LEARNED, AND passed on, in pieces, over the days and months, was that Khalid was in the water for a few hours, perhaps a night. He was washed up on the Solent, when the tide receded, on a grey beach.

Everyone had been at pains to tell her that he couldn't have been in the water for long. She had never understood how that followed, or why it mattered. If she thought about it later, they were saying he hadn't decomposed, he was still recognizably himself. He was in a suit, a tie still around his neck, and Suzie, who hadn't even seen the body, said something softly like he looked like he was sleeping, his eyes were closed, there wasn't a mark on him.

She knew it wasn't the truth, because people kept trying to make her feel better.

The coroner had said he could have been dead before he entered the water. Entered – as if it was a diving competition – not thrown in, discarded, pushed over the edge. In her dreams she had seen mermaids and pirates, forcing him from a plank, refusing to save him. Khalid had emerged despite them, he had found his way to the beach. Nobody could say how he had ended up in the water.

She knew she was being shielded and she had submitted to it. Being hurried to a friend's house for tea, before a police visit. Watching her mother pulling on stockings, and a black dress that she hardly ever wore, for the inquest. An open verdict.

Her mother had attempted to smooth the edges, to make it a complete story, a tale with a beginning and an end. Alia was an attentive eleven year old, and the questions proliferated; the sounds in her head became too dissonant, jarring, until it became easier just to block out the memory, to invent a one-liner which could be used, easily, without too much thought whenever anyone asked about him. My father drowned in the Solent. People didn't press for details after that and she let it lie, as tangled as bladderwrack or gutweed, beneath the surface.

THE NEXT MORNING ONCE SHE GOT TO COLLEGE, WHEN SHE climbed to the top of the staircase, two first-year students were waiting for her outside her study. She had interviewed them when they applied the previous winter, when they looked more like children. Sitting on the window ledge, they fell silent as soon as they saw her. Maggie, over-confident and always wearing bright colours, in a wacky handknitted scarf. She wrote a lot for university newspapers – Alia could already see her as a hack on a national. Maggie would do all the talking today, and Alia was grateful for that.

After some fumbling with keys, they ducked under the low wooden beam and stood in her room. The undergraduates settled into chairs, scrabbled in their bags, bringing out notepads and pencils, and she gathered some papers from her desk.

This room was possibly the only thing Alia had ever looked after. It had thick inset medieval windows, and hundreds of books arranged meticulously from floor to ceiling on one side. They weren't hers – they belonged to the man, a professor, who usually occupied this study but who had been seconded to edit a folio for two years. There was a green velvet chaise longue just wide enough for two undergraduates. On another side she had hung, tentatively, a small painting that belonged to her, an abstract oil that she had bought in France. It wasn't a good painting, but it looked right on that space on the wall. It was a mirage. In nine months she would have to return the office to its real owner.

'So, tell me about Elsinore...'

At the end of the hour, as she stood and moved towards the window, replacing a book on the shelf, the other student left and she expected Maggie to gather her things and leave too, but she lingered, taking longer than necessary.

'Please can I have a word with you?' she said, apparently to the chair.

How old these students could look. She was wearing something too long and oversized for her body.

'What's up, Maggie?' She thought about offering her a coffee, and guessed that she'd refuse in any case – it would be too informal, a breach of what they expected of each other.

'My parents are separating.'

Alia knew a little about her background from the admissions form and phrases that Maggie had dropped now and then, and dredged up the memory: a country cottage in Suffolk with vegetables grown in the garden, her mother perhaps a GP, the father a hospital consultant. Maggie came from one of the best girls' schools in the country – a day school – and she had talked about her older sister, studying medicine at Imperial.

'I'm sorry to hear that, that must be tough. It's tough at any age.'

'So I think it will probably affect my work a bit. I might not be able to get my essay in for Wednesday.'

She said a little more, once she'd begun. Her mother was very upset, not behaving normally, didn't see it coming, her father had moved out shockingly fast and was already talking about divorce. The word came out uncertainly, like a rude word that she hadn't encountered before.

'OK, that's fine, we can arrange an extension. You can have two more weeks, it's not a problem.'

Maggie nodded gratefully, gathered up her stuff and left; the old oak door swung decisively behind her.

The parents like bookends at the end of the table, the Christmases as regular and predictable as the Sunday lunches, and now her world was all shattered. They should have had it out when she was small, not played it all those years, just waiting to get her installed in Oxford. That would have been the braver thing to do.

The loss of a father. Alia could see the hospital consultant – she met him once, now she remembers, at a college fundraiser, in pinstripe – he'll be meeting Maggie for awkward lunches in good restaurants. Introducing, tentatively, his junior-doctor-turned-lover.

Alia's seen it before, with her own friends, with other students.

The father will be there for her, nonetheless. He will call her and give her advice on job applications and mortgages, and he'll make sure she's always comfortable, and worry about her when he hasn't heard from her, and walk her down the aisle and do – what do fathers do? What do normal fathers do? Alia drew a blank. She had no idea what their relationship was like, what it would be like, irritated with herself for presuming to know, for daring to think it. She ripped up some scrap paper on her desk, squeezed it into a ball and hurled it, missed, kicked her wastepaper bin in frustration. She never was a good shot. What a presumption.

ALIA'S PHONE VIBRATED JUMPILY ON THE DESK IN FRONT OF
her. It was her mother.

'Alia, how are you?'

'Fine, Mum. I'm just in college.' She spoke in a half-whisper
and looked anxiously to the door in case her next students were
already milling outside.

'Working on something new?'

'Kind of. Got a class now, though.'

'Didn't you call me earlier?'

'I thought I might come out and see you for a few days.'

'Darling, that would be lovely. We'd love that.' She could
hear her mother gesticulating and making hand signals to
Milton. Excited, positive ones, but hand signals. He was easy-
going, though, and he would be pleased to see her too, if it made
Suzie happy.

'We've cleaned the pool. It's just what you need.'

'I've had a look at the Easyjet flights and there's a cheap one
that gets into Toulouse at ten o'clock in the evening. I could
make it a long weekend. Could you come and pick me up?'

'Well, you could get a taxi. We'll give you the money. Then
you'll be independent, no waiting around.' One of the worst
verbs in her mother's dictionary was to mollycoddle.

'Those drivers can never find the farm.' The last driver,
swearing in the dark as they turned onto a cart-track.

Alia's voice was becoming strained from the hoarse
whispering. She didn't say more because she didn't want to have
an argument with her mother right then, and was conscious of
the cost of the call, and the students now definitely audible on
the other side of the door. It was important that they started off
on good terms.

'You'll be fine, darling.'

'OK, Mum. I'll call when I reach the airport. And, there's something else... you know I'm planning a trip to Pakistan... I'm getting cold feet... I thought maybe we should talk first before I go.'

'Wonderful. We can always talk. We'll see you when we see you. Milton says hi too.'

5

'THEY'RE JUST PROVING POWELL RIGHT.' KHALID PLACED AN
arm on Imran's smaller shoulder in a protective way. They both
had their collars turned up against the wind as they stepped out
onto the pavement, past the man selling the *Standard*. A group
of punks emerged from the subway ahead of them, in their kilts
and charcoaled eyes. The massive screens on Piccadilly Circus
were doing their dusk show, Philips hi-fis, *simply years ahead*,
and Fuji film and Sanyo, *technology at your fingertips*. Khalid
was close enough to see each separate, vertical, fluorescent bulb
that made up the screens, and cabs beetled around the bend as
they crossed, and the buses kept going, streaming one after the
other, dispatch riders racing on the last jobs of the day. They
turned down Piccadilly and past Fortnum's where a porter in
tails had started bolting the doors on one side, a sign their shift
would soon be starting.

'Didn't take it lying down for once, did they though?' Imran
retorted.

There were some things that they all took for granted, that
didn't have to be spelled out. The pigs were fascist, the whites
always got a better deal, you could only rely on brothers when
push came to shove. All of that just came as standard. But riots

had been kicking off in Brixton in a new way. Milk bottles, wicks soaked in meths. The buses had all been diverted, going south of Lambeth. Khalid wasn't sure he liked it. England wasn't the worst place in the world – the way Imran went on, you'd think it was a military state. Always wanting to bite the hand that fed him.

'Maybe you should be more... grateful, bhai.'

'For what?'

'This country, it's given you a lot. You've got a nice house, school for your kids.'

'Try telling Tony that.'

'It's better if you're Asian.'

Imran rolled his eyes and wouldn't take the bait. He had started wearing a badge on his jacket recently that said Pak Means Pure. He'd tell anyone who asked about the meaning behind it. He'd had to remove it for work but he always made sure he pinned it on again afterwards, and it had started to get on Khalid's nerves, although he couldn't say why.

'Got to fight your corner, Khalid. Times are changing.'

On the corner of Dover Street, a gang of men in suits from the City, laughing hysterically, filled the street with their bulk and their double-breasted swagger. One was holding a half-full bottle of champagne, and wiped the back of his hand across his nose ostentatiously. 'Too many divs about,' said Imran.

The money was certainly something else in those days. It had bubbled up all around them; now it was always moving so fast from hand to hand, from bank to bank. Traders showed off with their electronic calculators as big as books as they walked along the pavement. No one thought anymore about the quality of a fountain pen, the satisfaction of a wind-up watch, the sweetness of a pretty girl. And in the club the punters grabbed at their chips and spoke to him like he was a waiter and traded the names of strippers, these bankers from the City, stiff with cocaine. It was all just more, more, more.

They hurried under the covered walkway in front of the twinkling Ritz, with its inviting-forbidding façade, the revolving doors designed to thresh out the rich from the poor. They walked faster, along the fringe of Green Park and towards the Wellington Arch, without saying that shift-time was approaching.

When they got closer to the stage door, just off Hyde Park Corner, they could see the grey shapes in the street lamps, a cluster standing there with placards. Clearly distinguishable, a small gang under the ornamental trees, huddled on the lane at the back of Curzon Street.

'Bloody hell, not again,' sighed Imran.

'Just keep walking,' Khalid said.

A small group of women, about a dozen this time, but they made it difficult for them to squeeze past, because they were all braced near the door, wrapped up in scarves and woollen coats, with their arms linked, and shouting. Imran slipped ahead of him and weaved his way through and Khalid said excuse me and pulled in his arms, and tried not to touch them as he pushed through the tunnel of sheepskin and shouting faces and sign boards.

Exploitation. Real women don't wear bunny tails. If you want meat go to the butchers.

'Why do you work here? Why do you exploit women?' A moon-faced woman, about Suzie's age, in a padded denim jacket, smiled at him broadly as if life was all a joke, as if he was a joke, her teeth very white in the lamplight.

'Excuse me, madam,' he said. He had his hand on the handle of the stage door.

Who do these women think they are, he thought, so educated and so scruffy, acting as if their way is the only way? They've never seen inside a club like this, they can't imagine what it's like to work night shifts.

She blocked his path. 'So you think it's OK for grown women to dress up as animals?'

It had never crossed his mind. It was the strangest question.

'Excuse me, I'm sorry, but I don't have the answer to your questions and I don't run this place.'

Once he got inside he sighed and clocked in for his shift, punching the beige cardboard ticket with his name typed on it into the metal time recorder attached to the wall in the entrance.

When he went into the club that night he noticed things, the way the tread of some of the carpet had worn down. And empty tables. Some of the new City guys didn't want this kind of place anymore. They still wanted girls, but they wanted them cheap and fast and brazen, not to sit and listen to a piano man, with a cocktail, and to flirt. They wanted it all, here and now. They drank white wine, instead, from giant goblets like baubles, or asked for Sex on the Beach.

That was the very same day that he saw him.

It wasn't uncommon at Playboy – a man with a perfect suit, minders in shades, a car parked outside on the double yellow, the chauffeur in a peaked cap. Everyone had seen the ladies in Knightsbridge with their Gucci bags and the flash of gold brocade under the hem. Everyone had seen these guys. Nothing special.

Khalid had witnessed it before. The whales like old Aziz,

a prince from Dubai, who had sat there with a long, sad face, like a bloodhound, and slapped down more counters, and had shrugged as he gave up the cost of a racing horse, a racing car, without flickering an eyelid; and pulled the same face when he had won, when the ball came bouncing into the red pocket, as if it was all the same to him if he won or lost, if he lived or died, as if life had cheated him already.

Aziz had sent one of the bunnies a ruby, free floating, it was said, not fixed in a setting or embedded in a ring. And she didn't know what to do with this big blood-red thing, so stupendous and daft that she thought she'd attract trouble if she took it to a jeweller or an auction, so she'd ended up keeping it in her bedroom drawer, in among her knickers.

They came and went, these men with no purpose because everything had been sucked out of life, every resolution and ambition, because their refineries spewed money faster than they could burn it. The crude curse, Tony called it.

So there he was, the Saudi, on a Tuesday night. Baby-faced with a black moustache, about fifty, in a dinner jacket and lustrous white shirt. The usual huddle of bodyguards and hangers-on. What made K stand out?

It wasn't the money, though he certainly had that. It was his pure joy. The laughter lines around his eyes, the absolute pleasure he was taking in joining the game. He had an impish look. A man so rich he could float above anyone's opinion, unbothered about his height – titchy – surely under five foot, no hint of a tiny stacked heel on his polished shoe – and unworried about his hair, thinning in black strands and pasted across his bald head. Khalid had seen rock stars, the men anxious about their status, with a touch of make-up or plastic surgery, sugary tans, petrified by ageing, looking to women to make them bigger. There was none of that with K.

K just stood there, in his beautiful dinner jacket and white shirt, with his cheeks flushed as rose petals, his black moustache shiny and trimmed, acting like he'd just come out of a Turkish bath, giggling and having the most tremendous fun. And everyone rotated around him. He was like everyone's favourite uncle.

He was the most secure-looking man Khalid had ever seen.

'You know who that is?' said Tony, sliding up to him and talking ever so softly under his breath. Croupiers, like hotel concierges, can talk barely moving their lips.

'No. Who is he?'

He had dimples in perfect symmetry. He handed an aide the pashmina shawl he was wearing and the young man laid it down very carefully on the stool next to him, like a sleeping dog or a small pet that must be kept close.

Usually men act with sincerity at the roulette table. In Khalid's experience, this was how men stood around the game. This man was unusual in his glee, rare in his inability to take it seriously.

He willed the man to beckon him over. He imagined his hand, gesturing to him, with an order or a request. He would do it, whatever he wanted, of course. He would stand by his side and soak up some of these rays, for in the smokiness of the club, the man radiated sunlight.

K moved over to the blackjack table. He started to play, and soon he was having a terrible night, bust after bust. He played diligently, paid attention, stayed amused by the way his cards turned, by the sudden flush at the end. He wasn't humble at all, he was poking fun at fate. In the end, he took heavy losses.

'Did you hear what I said?' Khalid finally noticed that Tony was still talking. 'He's Khashoggi. He's Adnan fucking Khashoggi.'

A man hovering on the edge of myth. And there he was, on Khalid's floor.

One of his posse, the guardian of the pashmina, was a young kid with a close-trimmed goatee and drainpipe trousers, utterly familiar, in his way. Khalid had seen his type a thousand times. A Bollywood film extra, one of the dancers in a crowd scene. Lithe hips. He was a runner, a coat carrier, ready to go, lining up everything Khashoggi wanted. He was standing at the side of the room, looking on, waiting, a little bored.

'Does Mr Khashoggi need anything? Anything we can do?' Khalid approached the boy and stood next to him near the wall in the shadows of the gaming tables.

'No, he's fine, he's having a good time.'

'That's good, we can all relax then.'

The boy fidgeted nonetheless, moving from one leg to another.

He would have usually left it at that. But there was something that meant he couldn't let go that night; he was pulled inexorably towards this little gaming party.

'Aap Pakistan hai?' the kid said.

'Ji.' Khalid nodded nonchalantly although his heart was jogging in his chest. Just to stand this near to Khashoggi and to speak to one of his own. He wanted to ask, 'Is he really the wealthiest man in the world?' Even in this place, in this palace of big spenders, no one could say for sure if it was true or not. There was a time when he would have asked the question, but he tamped down the thrill in his blood.

'Aap kaha se hai?'

'Bombay. Well, first Lucknow. I got myself to Bombay, then London.' The boy looked proud. He had achieved something, just to be here.

'Folks?'

'Ah, you know...'

Khalid could tell from the rough Urdu that he'd switched to, and his skinny limbs, that he was probably from a village. He could have been a street kid. Without saying anymore, they had a shared understanding, the taste of certain sweets and the cadences of certain poetry, the hard bunk on a railway sleeper carriage, owning one suitcase, fights and objections, oceans crossed, the courage summoned to wake up in a strange place. Khalid understood him perfectly.

'Mr K picked me up.' He had a bright face with an echo of Khashoggi in it, very faint, definitely a mimicry of the smile, the cheeriness.

Khalid raised an eyebrow.

'Not like that, boys aren't his thing, I can tell you that much. Ladies only.'

The way he drawled laydeez made Khalid smile.

'He found me, I was working tables in a hotel in Bombay, the Taj, you know?' He did a little flick of his wrist as if he was carrying a tray aloft. '... and he took me under his wing.'

'How's the work?'

'It is heaven. It is pure heaven. You cannot dream of the things I have seen.' He was showing off a bit now, warming up. 'Yachts, hidden princesses, fighting falcons, fountains made out of chocolate. You name it. What that man does, what he owns. And the gifts he gives us.' He told him about that afternoon:

there had been a party in Richmond, swans carved out of ice, their backs hollowed out and filled in with caviar. 'Caviar, this size.' He made his hands round, as big as a tin of Christmas biscuits, and said kav-ee-ar, a new word in his vocabulary. He had slurped some off a spoon, and found it disgusting. But that wasn't the point.

The boy looked over towards K, who was muttering merrily to the man at his side about his losses. Khalid had never taken his eyes off him. 'My name's Lucky. Can you believe that?'

'I'm Khalid. You'll stay with him?'

'He's got plans for me, he's educating me. He trusts me. It's because I've always been with him since – I was twelve, thirteen.' Lucky rolled back his sleeve. He showed him a little tattoo on his forearm, the A and K intertwined like a family crest. 'The thing you have to understand about Mr K is that he wants to have a good time, and he wants everyone around him to have a good time. That's all. It's simple. Get some laydeez for him, a Page Three, yah, some girl he's spotted at a beach, bring him something before he's hungry, get him something to perk him up, tell him a joke – he can't stand misery. So as long as we keep him happy, sab thik hai.'

Lucky considered Khalid, as if he had just remembered that he'd been warned about this sort of chat, and had been told to watch his mouth. He switched to English. 'So what about you? What's your interest?' He pulled out a penknife with a sharp edge and started peeling at the corner of a nail, carving a spiky cuticle.

'I run this floor. We look out for important clients. See if we can do them little favours, you know, make them comfortable.'

'Bring more champagne then,' Lucky said, with an imperious little flick of his hand.

By THE TIME KHALID HAD ORDERED A WORK-SHY JUNIOR waiter to go to the bar and instruct the barman, and then waited for far too long for the heavy silver bucket to roll up on a trolley, with its iced Dom Perignon and frosted crystal glasses, Khashoggi had gone. The blackjack table was empty.

The dash of disappointment, physically. As he moved towards the group at the door, he just saw Khashoggi's back, as he turned on his heel, and the fawn-coloured coat gently layered on his shoulders, leather gloves sliding onto his hands. Khashoggi patted Lucky on the head, like a patronized son.

They all swept out of the room, heading for the red staircase which led downstairs in a theatrical curve, the steps spaced out at intervals, steps too shallow to walk at speed. Lucky was at the rear of the group.

'Wait.' Did Khalid call it out loud? He didn't know afterwards.

THE PASHMINA WAS LYING THERE, ABANDONED AND FORGOTTEN. His movements were swift, assured as a cricketer on the boundary. Khalid grabbed it in one hand and made for the lift. If the lift was already rising to his floor's level, he stood a chance.

The little row of numerals lit up in turn, ascending, 2, 3, 4. Blinking, the gaps between them longer and longer. The doors slid open and he entered the gilded cage.

Alone inside, as he descended, he pressed the scarf to his nose, guiltily, and caught the aroma of discreet cologne and expensive restaurants. A glimpse in the gold-edged mirrors, floor to ceiling, of the pashmina held at his neck.

The doors sprung open at exactly the right time, and he stood at the foot of the stairs, waiting in the foyer.

Two minders walked slightly ahead of Khashoggi, hands pushed under their jackets, on reflex. They recognized Khalid from the gaming floor and relaxed their grip on their guns, although they stared at him as if he was about to do something stupid. Khashoggi pretended not to notice Khalid, and continued his airy descent, placing his dainty buffed shoes one after the other on the crimson carpet.

'Khashoggi-ji,' Khalid said, with complete seriousness, and he looked him in the eye in that way that he had been taught to greet elders by his father. 'You've forgotten this.'

'Silly old puss.' Khashoggi laughed, turning to make sure that everyone heard him. He gave Lucky the very slightest frown, and it was apparent to everyone on those stairs who had been the culprit. 'You're a croupier?' Khashoggi asked.

'Yes. Sir.' Khalid did a funny little involuntary bow, the same way he'd seen Japanese businessmen on the gaming floor. 'Khalid Quraishi, sir.'

Khashoggi made the slightest inflection of his mouth. The he opened a silver cardholder, and extracted his business card, and gave it to Lucky who had caught up with his master. The cortege moved on in its stately way, as if this was just another little piece of the world Khashoggi was inspecting, or collecting.

Lucky passed the card onwards to Khalid, slipping it to him stealthily as if it was illicit. 'Quraishi Sahib, give us a bell.' Lucky giggled as if untroubled by his own mistakes, and shook his hips on the stairs as he followed the rear of the group and they all disappeared around the corner. The boy should have been a dancer.

KHALID'S JOURNEY THAT MORNING WAS BACK HOME ON THE Piccadilly Line from Hyde Park Corner, wearing his black tie. He was on the first tube heading west, away from the centre of London, like a gentleman returning from an A-list party. His mind switched from focus to fogginess as the train emerged from its grey tunnel, the gradient of the land rising, the carriage gently emerging overground. The dawn sun struck the windows as the new day broke. He looked at the card and turned it over in his fingers. It was blazingly white against the nicotine colour of the worn moquette. The letters of K's name had been engraved in a simple, elegant typeface. Adnan Khashoggi Esq. had three telephone numbers but no job description. And Khalid didn't know another thing about him.

6

THEY HAD BEEN LYING ON SUN-LOUNGERS NEAR THE POOL ALL morning, in the March sun. Suzie was wearing a yellow bikini and flicking through a magazine.

The day was pleasant, but not ideal for sunbathing, and the experience of lounging was becoming frustrating to Alia, like a pale imitation of a real holiday. Her mother insisted on every possible ray. Restless, laying down her paperback on the flagstones beneath, Alia decided to swim.

In the deep end, she scudded upright, treading water, letting the warmth wash over her, watching her toes dissolving and reforming beneath her. Milton never stinted on the pool heating. From here she could see the white shutters pushed back against the old limestone bricks of the house, the trailing yellow rose almost touching the second floor, her mother dragging the loungers forward so that they were fully in the little wedge of sunlight available.

The place was completely isolated. It looked out onto a large fourteenth-century church, which was locked and barely used, and beyond that there were wide fields sown with sunflowers and maize. The whole place smelled of dried lavender. There was no connection to anyone within miles and not a single object from Alia's childhood.

Suzie had met Milton when Alia was a teenager, when Alia had already built her own thick web of friendships. Alia was only casually connected to them by that time. She went home from the grammar school simply to eat and sleep, and everything important happened between friends, so Milton hadn't impinged much on her life. He was a retired American banker, from the East Coast, solidly democrat, and long widowed. A few years ago Suzie had rented out the place in Hammersmith, and they had made a new home together, moving to Villeneuve-sur-Lot just after Alia left home for university.

Alia liked Milton; for his patience with her mother, for his genuine and quite well-informed questions about her research. He spent many hours cleaning the pool and listening to Voice of America on his radio, and today he had cleared off upstairs to do paperwork, which was his way of making sure that Alia had some time together with her mother. Very good at zoning out from Suzie and tuning in when necessary. He had never made any emotional claims on Alia and never expected much in return.

She returned from the swim shivering, wrapped in two thick, beach towels. She shook out her wet hair and placed one of the towels around her shoulders before she settled herself again on the damp lounger.

'Nice swim?' Suzie still had her eyes closed behind her sunglasses, and she pointed her toes unconsciously, and flexed them, so that her legs became tauter and longer.

'I wanted to ask you about Dad. We've talked about him so little.'

'OK, then, what do you want to know?' Suzie didn't move – she'd been expecting it and avoiding it – and stayed very still.

Alia rolled onto her side towards her, so that she was looking directly at her mother. 'Well, what happened – what happened when he died?'

'Oh, come on... you know all about that, don't you?'

'Well, sort of... I have questions... about where he was living, what he was doing...'

'I never tried to keep anything from you, Alia.'

'I'm not accusing you of that. I've just got curious lately, with all these emails from the cousins starting, and now I'm actually thinking of going to Karachi, you know, and that got me interested.'

Suzie closed her magazine, sat up on her lounger and pushed her Dolce & Gabbana shades up onto her head so that she could look her daughter clearly in the eye.

'Well, the police came to the door that night. It was just after Christmas, 1987, and they said that a body had been found in the water in Portsmouth, and they had reason to believe it was him.'

'And how did they *know* it was him?'

'I don't actually know, they found something on him, his wallet or something... Why are you asking me all this now?'

Alia remembered clearly – it was one of the few things she did recall from the time – that his wallet had been found on his body. A kind policeman had shown it to her. Opening it up, he had showed her the little clear window on the inner pocket. It had a school picture of Alia in it, pulpy and faded, still definitely her, in her red school jumper.

'That was it... there was no address... no stuff... I had nothing to go on. I didn't identify him – Uncle Wasim went – he came over from the States. I couldn't face it. I wanted to remember him in all his handsome finery.'

'And then what happened?'

'Well, they had to make sure it wasn't anything suspicious, so there was an autopsy – they couldn't find any signs of injuries, no signs of "foul play" – that's what they always say, isn't it? And the coroner ruled that it was an accident.'

'He must have had a bank account or some paperwork somewhere?'

'If there was, it should have been yours. And that makes me angry, especially when I see you living in that place. I mean, it's a student digs, isn't it?'

'You mean my home?'

'And I think what should be yours... I mean, he never paid a penny of maintenance, it was all before they set up the child support. Nowadays men can't get away with that, they'd have them by the balls... it was the eighties.'

She sighed and looked down at her polished toenails. 'We can't stay here long.' The sun had ducked behind a solid cloud again and had stayed there, stubbornly. The fine dark hair on Alia's arms was standing up, the skin puckered with goosebumps. She was shivering but she didn't want to move.

'Where did he live?'

'I don't know where he was living, what he was doing, what he was up to. You know how it was – I'd get a call out of the blue and he'd suggest a tube station and off you went – I worry now, were you too young for that? Going off on the Tube by yourself. I hope I haven't messed you up doing that?'

'No,' Alia said honestly. 'I liked being allowed out by myself.' Her memories of those times were of the Tube: the bristle of the seat fabric against her bare legs. Counting the number of stations along the line before she had to get off.

'And you'd have a burger, or have a walk around somewhere – see some sights in London.'

'Didn't you ask him for an address?'

'He was lost, Alia. I don't think he had a permanent address at all. He was always staying with friends, here, there and everywhere, always the finest parts of London: Green Park, Marble Arch. I was just pleased that he was still in touch, still taking an interest in you, some of the time, because a lot of those men – I mean, you know at that time, when people got divorced in the seventies, in the eighties – a lot of the men just took off, weren't seen for dust. Didn't want to know. He trusted that I took care of you, and that was enough for him.'

'But, what I've never understood was what was he doing all that time?'

'Wheeler-dealing? Who knows? Well...' she hesitated. 'I can say it to you now – I did sometimes wonder if he was killed. I just had a hunch. I never wanted to tell you when you were smaller – it would just upset you and I never had any evidence. Of course he wasn't. I'm being silly. It was just too odd – the way his body was found washed up in Portsmouth of all places – I mean, why the hell would Khalid ever go to a dump like Portsmouth? It was hard enough to get him out of West London. And nobody could tell me anything – I had so many questions myself. And the thing you have to understand is everyone was grieving too – I had to deal with all of them

71

weeping and asking me questions that I couldn't answer myself. And the police were completely uninterested. Useless. He was just a Paki to them.'

'A very lost one,' said Alia, and she didn't know if she was laughing because of the shock of what her mother had just said to her.

SUZIE SWUNG HER LEGS OFF THE LOUNGER, AND STARTED TO slide her feet into her rubber pool shoes. 'Do you want to come into town later? Look at the market? We could have lunch at Le Petit Marais?'

Alia pictured the cosy bistro and the maître'd welcoming Suzie back, the padded booths, and the elegant wide plates. The view over the cobblestoned square and the Romanesque church. It was an olive branch, tentatively held. Alia shrugged. Her mind was still in London.

Her father was made of the underground, and he belonged on the Tube. He smelt of the London dust that clogs your nostrils, not unpleasant but thick and inescapable. She couldn't think of him separately from the platforms or ticket-halls, and more and more, when she thought of him at all, it was as if he was the dust in the Tube, the ash that coats the place. He was only a sound in her mind now and then, like a train arriving, quickly and then departing again, like the back of a man in an overcoat, the doors closing behind him.

Suzie stood with her towels all tightly bundled up, worried that she was leaving her daughter empty-handed. 'There was something, though; there is something I can give you. Come on, it's in the studio.'

Suzie's studio was an old converted barn on the far side of the garden, close to the pool. An oil-burner in one corner – so she could use the studio in summer or winter – and a sofa with a pink patchwork quilt on it, with a small stove. It was bigger than Alia's whole flat. A large pinboard on one side covered in postcards from galleries around the world, and along the windowsills, pots of brushes, rags, palettes and lumps of clay in sacks. The studio's windows had a view to the sunflower fields. Alia suspected Suzie still smoked now and then in there, furtively, well away from Milton, though she'd never seen any signs.

Suzie had described it as her growth phase, the time after Khalid. She'd met a lot of women who had finished with bad men, wrong-uns, men who'd gone AWOL, died of drink, or fallen off the wagon. Alia remembered opening the door to them in Hammersmith, women who had started coming over at all hours, bringing books about yoga and positive thinking and white wine, and bad casseroles in crusty pans, and their howls of laughter when she was trying to get to sleep. How she'd strained her ears until they hurt trying to hear what they said about their orgasms one night. Being left with their weird kids at their houses on a Sunday afternoon, while the women talked urgently about self-realization, and wrote each other affirmations on slips of paper. One of the new friends was a psychotherapist and she'd met up with Suzie for sessions, from which her mother would come back smiling, with mascara smudged under her eyes. And that was the time she'd started to get serious about art and enrolled in evening classes, and had this idea about getting people to express their feelings in paint.

Suzie dabbled back in London. She'd organised a series of workshops in a community centre and Alia had lost track once she left home herself, though once Suzie got seriously involved with Milton the whole thing went professional, and they started calling the people who came over to paint pictures 'clients'. She had a business card now and a website and a diary with bookings from people who came from Paris or from London, and stayed for a few nights and immersed themselves in residential weekends. She charged a lot for it, hundreds, and Alia was never quite sure what happened in the studio, or what mysteries were resolved.

'It's looking great in here, Mum.' She meant it.

Suzie blushed, pleased to have the recognition. 'It's a long way from London.'

Suzie had wrapped a long silk kaftan over her bikini, which skimmed the floor, and she had a scarf tied round her head. She could carry it off; she had the air of a faded rock star, with tanned skin and eyebrows plucked into quizzical bows. Still noticed in restaurants. She rubbed coconut oil from a jar into her palms, massaging her own hands. 'So are you looking after yourself?'

Alia glanced down at her nails, ragged, bitten at the edges. 'Yeah, I'm fine.'

'You know it's important to care for yourself.'

Suzie appraised her like a painting.

'You're much more powerful than you think you are, Alia, you don't need to hide yourself away.'

'I'm fine, Mum, I've got a lot going on.'

'All those people you work with, all stuck with their heads in the clouds, hearts closed like fists. Their bodies are closed.'

God, don't let her get started on sex, thought Alia.

Suzie had moved a long way since her twenties. She wore it like a badge of pride and she was waiting for her daughter to move on too, as if they could grow like plants, keep shedding skins and rising up, like beanstalks.

'How's that engineer you live with?'

'Oh, Stefan. He's fine.'

'Too left-brained, though, isn't he?'

Alia wasn't in the mood to defend him.

'Yeah, he's completely lacking in empathy,' she said, speaking the language that her mother appreciated.

'And how's the work going? You were working on a piece of writing, weren't you?'

'Yeah, an article, it's about Shakespeare and numismatics... coins... I don't know... it's stalled, it's not quite gelling.' The subject sounded both pompous and irrelevant once Alia said it aloud.

'You probably needed a holiday, some time in the sun.'

Alia flicked through the stack of canvasses lined up against the wall of the studio. Some clients took their paintings home with them, wrapped up in brown paper. A lot left them behind, having exorcised whatever ghosts they arrived with. They probably didn't want their families to see them. Suzie felt bad about destroying the paintings; she couldn't bring herself to do it, and so the pile just kept growing. Each one is a story, she said. So on one side of the studio, there was a stash, in blues, and greens and pinks, a kind of archive of other people's pain.

Alia hadn't looked at them for a long time. She reached out to leaf through them. Some were big, a metre wide, tacked onto wooden frames, others made on smaller cuts of wood or cardboard. A lot of them were swirling nonsense, big gloopy paint wheels, but some illustrated something quite well. The jagged broken hearts, and tiny babies that looked like dolls, left on shelves, in buckets. The big black clouds of depression that people painted hovering over their heads.

It's a way, her mother said, to reach the things that people can't say, or don't know they want to say. You couldn't call any of them works of art. They were brave, these people who came here and paid loads of money to pour their hearts out in paint, who had a go at this innermost expression. It struck her, for the first time, that she had never seen her mother's paintings. And she'd never made any herself. Suzie had never asked her. The way Suzie listened to others for hours on end, and the way her daughter kept her own silence, while between them Khalid floated.

Her mother was pulling out bits and pieces from a wooden chest. 'Here it is. You can have it.' She slid the gold cube, heavy and surprisingly cold, into her palm. It was a gold Ronson, the sort that people used to refill with lighter fluid in the 1970s, the way they used to refill pens with ink, when people still gave lighters as gifts and inviting someone to smoke wasn't tilting them towards the grave.

It was exactly the type of lighter her father used. She could see his thumb on the metal wheel, striking it, his head dipping down to light a cigarette and his chin lifting above her, to throw out the pool of smoke.

'Yes, it's his sort of thing.' Even as she said it, she could feel his hand inside hers, clasping this chunky piece of gold, claiming it. 'Yeah, it's his.'

'Look, there's an inscription.'

In cursive, earnest swirls, his name *Khalid Quraishi* and then, *with appreciation, K.*

'Any idea who K was?'

There was something anxious in the question, and Alia saw for the first time that the failure to know had been a failing for her mother too, unresolved.

'And there's this as well.'

She held the passport in her hands. It was issued in 1980. A thick blue card cover, with a little cut-away window for the owner's name. The pages stamped and signed, but pristine, not well thumbed. Inside, the photograph was in colour, but with the tone and quality of the 1970s.

'It was another age.'

Khalid looked out steadily. His shirt collar was oversized and heavily starched. His thick black hair combed and quiffed, and he was optimistic, in a state of hope, as if presenting himself for duty. A man on his way somewhere.

She looked in the back of the passport. There wasn't much evidence of travel. No colourful visa stamps, or papers glued in. One simple US immigration stamp, showing that long stay in New Jersey. She turned the rest of the blank, watermarked pages through her fingers. It didn't mean much. There wasn't much else to note. His signature wasn't even flamboyant. It gave nothing away, the neat, educated hand. The product of an expensive school in Murree, where the Houses still bore the names of the original English housemasters, where the boys had been forced to wear their jackets buttoned up, under the harsh summer sun.

There were questions forming, swirling, in Alia's mind about how a well-dressed man with something gold and solid in his pocket could be outlived by his lighter.

Where do you find a lost father? In the mirror, in the sweep of an arched eyebrow, in the sheen of hair? In the echo of a phrase that comes in the night, passed on and learned. In the flick and smell of a lighter which he held to light the cigars of men wealthier than himself?

She knew that her mother had wept. Once the body was discovered. The soft click on the bathroom door. A squall line which descended on the horizon.

Suzie's grief had manifested in strange decisions. She'd bought a huge bunch of lilies one day, shedding indecent amounts of pollen, and was embarrassed when she couldn't find a vase large enough to hold them, so they ended up in a washing-up bowl by the sink. A sudden impulse to buy tickets to places they would never normally go; the Holiday on Ice Show at Alexandra Palace, intended to cheer them both up. She had worn peculiar clothes that year. A black dress, a pair of plain court shoes, only brought out on formal occasions and ceremonies: funerals, school parents' evenings, a coroner's verdict. Odd long skirts, with gatherings and flounces and pockets, mourning weeds.

And now this. It was daft, Alia told herself, nothing had changed. Just a useless old passport, with which he hardly ever travelled and which didn't mean anything then or now. Why should it change anything in her life? This collision with the image of Khalid had disturbed her peace. It collapsed the days between then and now. There had been something left behind, something that never went into the sea, reaching back to her across the expanses of water and time. So much that she had been hiding from, turning her own face away from, swum urgently before her eyes. A man in the water, calling to be wrenched out.

She returned to Oxford after the weekend. On Monday, she held more undergraduate tutorials on early modern tragedies in the morning. She cycled back up the Cowley Road in the afternoon and sat down in her flat, on the floor, with the lighter in her hand. It was weighing on her. All day it had sat in her backpack, cold among everything warm, nestled with the receipts and pencils.

When he disappeared, they didn't have the internet.

She started to search around, on her laptop, using the university library systems, and genealogical sites which she could access using her campus ID. Tracking down references and dates. Khalid's name coming up on the screen, firstly a telephone directory from the early 1970s, the address where she was born on the Queen Caroline. A marriage certificate for the marriage to her mother – at Hammersmith register office – they married in the daytime, on a weekday. Cheaper. He had listed his job as croupier. He was still at the Playboy Club then, running the roulette tables and working night shifts.

The bedroom dark in the daytime with heavy curtains pulled right across and last night's clothes draped on a chair. The bow-tie, the shirt with little mother of pearl buttons. The full ashtray next to the bed.

Stefan came in at eleven and she was still there, sitting on the floor in the dark, lit only by the street lamps outside and the glow from her screen. She was rooted to the floor, the rest of her body dulled, her pupils popping in the dark, and her fingers manically scrawling through lists.

'It's so crazy but I never thought to do this before now. I've got this lighter and I want to know what happened, how he vanished. I need to know.'

'Take it easy,' he said and went into the kitchen and put some water on the hob to boil. She didn't notice the time; she scrawled and scrawled, through histories of casinos, of clubs, of pictures of bunny girls wiggling their bums, and stories of money laundering, and details of Playboy's major clients. It didn't lead her anywhere, to anything.

She cracked into her new email account. She had only just started to use it a few months ago, warily trying it out. She had kept things anonymous; just Alia Q. Nonetheless, one cousin from Pakistan had found her address and sent family greetings, some techie in Dubai, who had started putting everyone in touch. There was a complex mailing list growing of Quraishis which had spiralled since she last looked at her messages.

She was related to all of them in one way or another and their streams of birthday greetings and loving messages and prayers. Photographs were sometimes attached to the emails, of perfect newborns and family weddings showing women dripping with embroidery, which took minutes at a time to download. The make-up so thick that it made it hard to see who was who, even once the picture appeared on the screen. A few of them were living in the Middle East, most in Karachi and Lahore. Last month her cousin, Nadima, had attached an old picture and sent it just to her. It was heavily pixelated but definitely her father in black and white, holding an old-fashioned telephone against his ear, styled like a film star. And there had been another one of him in a posed group, taken many years ago, of young men, in waistcoats and curled slippers, posing for another wedding. And then her grandmother had written a little note, plaintively into cyberspace, come and see us my dear, we haven't forgotten you, we pray for you.

Stefan returned with a bowl of pasta, a spoon, a dollop of pesto from a jar that he had picked up at the corner shop. It was a major effort on his part, almost heroic.

'God, I'm going to do it, I'm going to book this ticket to Karachi.'

'When did you last go?'

'Never been. I know my grandmother, and a few cousins. They came to London every now and then, when I was a kid, through Heathrow, for weddings, for shopping. In bursts. One of them was at a boarding school here.'

'You've never been?'

'I know that's hard to believe if everyone in your family comes from one Swedish village.'

She didn't mean to be unkind. In any case, she could be sharp with Stefan.

'You must go.' He was delighted for her and didn't take offence at all. 'Which terminal? I'll drop you off.'

'Where should I stay?'

'Get a hotel, bang in the centre.'

She would like it that way. She imagined for a moment trawling the streets alone, browsing cloth markets and food stalls, sightseeing at the museums, returning to a clean, anonymous hotel room.

It could never be like that. She was going to have to alert the relatives. 'I mean, that's the whole point, isn't it?'

The next morning, before she joined a college meeting, she sent a brief message on the email list, announcing her arrival dates in Karachi. She played it all down. She wrote, 'I want to see the country and I've been meaning to for many years.'

Within hours welcoming parties were already mustering. Her grandmother called her on her mobile phone in the middle of the graduate teaching committee meeting, probably at horrible expense, and Alia excused herself from the room to speak to her. Daadi handed over to her cousin Nadima, who was embarrassed but insistent: Alia must come and sleep in their house. There was absolutely no question of a single woman putting up at the Marriot. It wasn't safe, it wasn't right, it just wasn't done. She was one of them. Alia felt herself falling into the warm, tight embrace of family after a very long time, and it wasn't entirely comfortable.

7

A BUNCH OF MEN HAD BURST IN, FULL UNIFORM, ABOUT ELEVEN o'clock on a Wednesday night in September, switched on the lights and made all the bleary-eyed punters sit up. A bunny called Carly had dropped the tray she was carrying from the shock of it, and the cocktails and tiny matchstick parasols went flying all over a customer. The raid was done for the papers, that's what they all believed; it had to look as if there was an urgent problem and something serious to close down, an overnight shut-down, rather than just the steady flow of black money which was always dripping through a casino, like a leaky roof. The policemen carried out crates of paperwork from the upstairs office, and they took away a few people to question. One policeman put his hand on one of the girls' bums, as he steered her out of the second floor bar, and Tony shouted out, 'Pigs!' 'Watch yourself, kaffir,' the policeman called back without missing a beat.

Rumours had been sprouting like weeds between the pavement cracks. The club opened the next night, and the next, and a missive came from Hefner, which was read out to them by Lownes himself, who had, the rumour went, flown in from LA that morning.

Languid and unbothered, standing on the stage at the front of the disco on the first floor, that Saturday afternoon, while the employees all crowded quietly onto the silent chequered dancefloor. He had cracked a little smirk, while smoothing down his black hair. 'I'm the bunny King of Britain, folks, and I ain't got no intention of being anything else. So you just carry on. Steady as she goes.' Lownes looked down on them from the stage, in his black cashmere polo neck, two women in satin corsets standing on either side of him with their arms looped under his, like crutches.

Khalid didn't like the man much, if he was honest. His mansion had been photographed so many times, so they'd all read about the waterbeds and the silk sheets and the jacuzzi and the fridge crammed with champagne and live crabs – for some reason, always crabs. People said Victor Lownes was a showman and he had seen it as his job to keep Playboy in the papers. He had become unseemly. That day he looked crippled – too many poppers, perhaps. Somehow the women still adored him – the money helped. And that floppy hair. Suzie had a soft spot for Victor, which made Khalid feel queasy watching the man being helped down off the stage. She always spoke up in his defence because when he was a child he'd killed a friend in a hunting accident. 'They'd probably just been mucking around. Imagine what that does to you, blowing your best friend's head off.' He had been camping in the Everglades with their fathers and uncles and his pistol had gone off. The other boy was twelve too. Nobody quite knew what had happened, and Khalid wasn't even sure if it was true.

Lownes stumbled out towards the stage door and one of the backstage staff closed the purple velvet curtains, as if they were clearing up after him. The rest of the staff began to disperse, going back to their floors. A few murmured quietly about what Victor had just said. What would Khalid do if the club closed? Imran knew a doorman at the Grosvenor Victoria who might find him an opening as a croupier there, but there were so many people out looking for work. Ten per cent was the latest number. Could they manage on the dole? The number pierced him, making the reality sharp. How long could they manage without a salary, with the payments due on the mortgage on the first of every month? Two months maximum, if he put away a little bit and tried not to spend the rest at the bookies. Like a decent man would do. Which he knew, even as he thought it, he would not do and that he was not even slightly motivated to do. Suzie had never offered to get a job, although she'd worked all the time until Alia was born. It would be wrong to ask her, like trying to separate a calf from its mother, almost unnatural, that's how she made it feel.

She read all day while Alia was playing. The two of them didn't seem to go anywhere, they just stayed in the flat, the girl with her Stickle Bricks or crayons and Suzie reading. She barely ate anything, bowls of breakfast cereal and crackers mostly. Suzie ate around the edges of the day, shopping bags came and went, he knew she cooked for Alia. She might not have been eating proper meals at all.

That evening, once Alia was in bed, they were both on the settee, both smoking simultaneously so that the wisps from their cigarettes climbed up in parallel spirals. She drew her knees underneath her and she read and smoked, hungrily, indiscriminately, with no sense of who the author was or if the book was considered a classic or not. He might think she was skipping pages if he didn't know her better. Some of the books were about famous murders, others about history. Yesterday she had been absorbed in something about the Wall Street Crash.

It was another one of those things that made her unobtainable. He couldn't disguise that it was a waste of time.

'Nearly finished that one?'

She frowned when she read, looking far more serious than she intended. The bars on the gas fire glowed auburn and it gave off a slightly sickening aroma, liked warmed plastic.

'You spend all day with other men,' he laughed, trying to get her to look up. He meant it, in a way. Then he asked the question. 'Suze, may I suggest that you think about getting a job? I don't like to ask, but I think we will need the money.' He tried to keep it amicable, smiling, as if he was suggesting a jaunt out to the park. Even as he said it, he congratulated himself on his self-control.

She looked up over the top of the book and flicked the long ash, teetering on the end of her fag, expertly into the ashtray. 'Pardon?'

'A job, working, you know... how you liked modelling... not that, something else...'

She put the book down slowly, propping a beer mat inside it as bookmark. Charles and Di smiled from a coffee mug, entwined in a loveheart. The whole city was still in a froth about the wedding, although he didn't understand why she'd bought that thing, as if she was signalling something that he couldn't decode.

'Well, where exactly? What would you expect me to *do*?' There was a chill in her voice, and her blue eyes looked at him with an accusation of betrayal.

He knew he shouldn't be asking her; all the mess with the cash was his fault, and he had made promises to her – lavish, silken promises – and he had meant them. He still meant them. It hurt him because in his heart he knew she was too good to be working shifts with those ordinary women behind the tills, wearing synthetic jackets, and those awful hairnets. In his heart, he agreed with her.

'And anyway, half the world is out looking for work. Haven't you seen the jobless figures?'

He noticed her legs curled up on the sofa, as she unfolded them and pointed her toes, like a ballet dancer warming up. She was too gentle to be caught up in the common world, she belonged to a different stage. That's what he had promised her.

'Just to tide us over, while I set things right again. I just think – if the club closes, then things might be difficult for a while.'

'Khalid, I don't have any qualifications. And what about Alia? Who will look after her?' She had beliefs about women sending their children off to be looked after as if they were left luggage, as if anybody could give her daughter the attention that she could.

He'd heard all this before and he was ready for it.

'Well, she'll be at nursery school in the daytime, maybe you could make enquiries about a few hours a day, just in school hours?'

The image in his mind of what she might actually do hadn't formed, and he wasn't exactly sure of what she could do. He realized with a sudden clarity that he didn't want her to be seen out in public doing anything menial, like waitressing or standing behind the till at Budgens.

'Oh yes, it's so easy, isn't it? My hardworking husband, when have you ever got your hands dirty doing any sort of job, and do you know what it's like to stand on your feet all day, with customers trailing past you? I just can't do it, Khalid. I'm not cut out for it.' Her voice rose, and he saw their security slipping out of the window as if it was an errant street cat. He could actually see those things – security, stability, wealth – slipping away.

IMRAN HAD STARTED HIS JOB AT THE CHEMISTS, DEVELOPING photos. He'd been working for the Gujarati fellow, Gupta, for about three months. Risky to quit Playboy back in the summer, but Khalid didn't say anything then, and now he could admit his friend had probably made the right decision.

'Developing photos is incredible,' Imran said to Khalid. 'What people get up to. Incredible. Why don't you set yourself up in some business?' Khalid drained the dregs of a pint and considered putting some of his last coins in the juke box.

They hadn't wanted to get off the machines but a young builder in rigger boots, with his hard hat slung over his arm, was standing too close behind them, jingling the coins in his pockets, waiting his turn. Khalid felt the emptiness at the end of his glass, after the final gulp of liquid.

It turned out Gupta wasn't paying as much as he'd suggested that he might. It was cash in hand, but Gupta docked it every month for damaged photographic paper, and despite Imran's enthusiasm, there was something screwed about the whole set-up. Imran had taken the plunge and started his own business on the side. 'I am going to laminate,' he declared – the idea was to print pictures onto mugs, coasters and ceramic plates that people could hang from wires on their walls. It was new technology. He'd shown Khalid a sample, and Khalid had doubted it would make him money. But Imran already had a few orders, for family portraits, one couple even wanted a picture of their speckled Dalmatian, and several babies. 'Babies are always coming along,' said Imran, 'that's the beauty of it.' He offered to come and photograph Alia, for free of course. 'Be your own man, a free man, none of that clocking in, clocking out. Your own master. That club owes you nothing, you owe that club nothing. Keeping you up like an owl, all night, you know what they call ullus, I'll start calling you ullu. Don't you like the sunlight on your face?'

Imran had a packed lunch in his bag prepared by Hasina – roti, channa – but he hadn't touched it. He didn't want to piss off the landlord with the smell, with eating something that he hadn't paid for.

HE ARRIVED AT THE FLAT THE NEXT SUNDAY MORNING WITH heavy black boxes of equipment. Suzie was pleased with the suggestion and she'd curled her hair in advance with heated rollers, and put on a funny-looking outfit, a boiler suit, she called it, electric blue with a zip up the front. 'There was a builder wearing one of those in the pub the other day,' Khalid said, helping Imran carry in his camera-stands and pale umbrellas from his car into the room.

'It looks different on a woman,' she said, and blew him a kiss.

'Very graceful,' he muttered, and even he didn't know if he was being sarcastic.

Imran arranged them around the settee, and spent what

seemed like a daft amount of time to Khalid arranging Alia's hair over her shoulders and trying out his professional banter. Alia sat patiently on her mother's knee while the scene was assembled around her. When they were finally ready, Khalid stood up, straight and serious with his arms rigidly by his sides.

'So any tips for the race this afternoon?' Imran said as he fiddled one more time with a light meter. He had a habit of saying the wrong thing when he felt under pressure.

'Can't go wrong with Shergar,' Khalid muttered, as if Suzie couldn't hear. He stayed straight and kept his hands in his pockets, the way he had sat on them as a child when he had erred, which prevented them reaching for his wallet. He had been tempted by Newmarket, but he was steering clear. Suzie smiled in a phony way, and when he cast her a sideways glance he had the sense that this little family portrait was freezing them in an undesirable permanence, and that this wasn't how he'd have chosen to arrange them at all, but then again, he reassured himself, from his angle he didn't get a proper look at the way it was all organised; he couldn't see the whole picture.

They were all relieved when the photos were taken and relaxed back into themselves, like the pressure had been released on an inflatable mattress. Suzie ran her hand through her curls and Alia jumped away and went to find a colouring book and felt-tips.

Despite what Khalid had expected, it turned out to be one of those Sunday afternoons when good things collided without planning. Suzie said to Imran, 'Why don't you get Hasina over, we'd love to see the twins, nice for Alia too.' Then out of the blue, Tony rang because he was at a loose end, and he wasn't far from Hammersmith as the crow flew and he was thinking of a cheeky half down the Tralee. 'Come over,' Khalid said, 'we're having people round.' And before long the house was full. The room was crammed, there was just enough space if the women sat on the sofa, with children occasionally on their knees and laps, and the men bunched near the fridge, and Tony never came empty-handed, he brought a six-pack and Hasina put a tub full of parathas layered in kitchen paper on the table.

Khalid put some LPs on – old stuff that he liked when he was growing up – Elvis, Buddy Holly – and the new Diana Ross album – and two of the men lifted the coffee table out of the way, and Alia and the twins did funny dance routines, and tugged the hands of the adults to get them to dance too. Eventually they got hold of Khalid and yanked him towards them, and he did his hipshake and then he lifted up the kids one by one and twirled them round, and they kept begging him to do it again.

HE WAS JUST THE RIGHT AMOUNT OF PLASTERED. AND SUZIE looked bloody lovely sitting there, with her hair all pinned up and the boiler suit which now slid off one shoulder, mysteriously transformed, and when she got up to go into the kitchen, he followed her. He couldn't help himself, and she was a bit embarrassed and laughed. She stood against the cabinets and he pressed up against her, so that the cutlery drawer rattled. He could feel her wanting him back and they kissed in the corner, near the cupboard, like teenagers, with their friends just feet away.

'Don't worry, Suzie. Don't worry about working,' he said as she half pushed him away, half reached for him again, playfully, and ran her fingers over his chin, his five o'clock shadow.

HE WENT HOME WITH HIS PAY CHEQUE AT THE END OF OCTOBER as usual, tucked in the inner pocket of his suit jacket. Half of it was spent on the bills, shopping on King Street, petrol for the car. Suzie insisted on a new dress for Alia because she was going to a friend's birthday party, and chose a candy-striped dress with thick netting underneath.

The other half was spirited into the night, in Khalid's pockets, slipping through his fingers. Lots of it went on the horses, wads upon wads. Each one was so close, coming in fourth, stumbling at a hurdle, thinking of one name and then changing his mind at the final second, to back the loser.

He raged against losing, and then dismissed his choices, berated his failure to select the right one. It had always been the way.

His first visit to the Karachi Race Club had been when he was about fourteen.

It was in the middle of the city in those days; the British had carved out a big sweep of land near the railway station, shovelled on desert sand, imported the finest Arabians. 'The families over there own most of this damn country,' Khalid's father tutored him, making a gesture to the boxes where you could see faces from the newspapers, holding up little binoculars, their family-trees so tangled with the Muslim League, and the Mughals, and the Prophet, and with each other, that it was a wonder that they didn't float rather than walk. Khalid wasn't sure if he heard admiration in his father's voice and examined his stern face to gauge his mood, nodding to show his understanding.

And that was when he had asked – or the idea had first appealed to him – he had some money left over from Eid.

He wanted to put all of the money on; it wasn't a lot but the horse was at 10/1 and he was excited about it, like something good was about to happen. He felt for the notes folded in the pocket of his trousers. Those days he had been growing fast, something was stretching inside him. He stood close to his father's height; from a distance they looked like two men watching the races together in their dark overcoats, not father and son. A friend of his father's came over, another landowner, and he shook the boy's hand too, with seriousness, as if he was someone to be considered. And when he had moved away, Khalid asked about the bet, and his father said no. He didn't even say it, just made a sharp slice of his hand through the air, which closed down the discussion, as it always did. Then emitted a familiar sniff of disgust.

The horse was behind after the second furlong, but he recovered and pipped the rest of them. Phenomenal. Khalid willed him on as he crossed the finishing line, and the horses galloped again in his mind, and he knew that he could have won, and if he had won he would have come away with a thousand rupees. He made a promise to himself that he would never miss the chance to win again.

That winter in London, although he kept that hope inside himself, sometimes he hated the money, he wanted to burn it, rip it, scrunch it. One night he did that, stumbling, outside the bookies, into the back of the supermarket, past the dead rows of trollies, onto the tarmac and into the mocking cold. He held up a twenty, and put a match to it, in the dark, just to see the strange colour of the flame, and he laughed to himself in the empty car park.

A FEW DAYS LATER, IMRAN CAME OVER, BEAMING AND KIND AT the door. It was already dark outside and there were a few fireworks going off sporadically, haphazardly, on the other side of the estate. He stood on the step with a Kashmiri scarf wound around his neck and he walked straight in without an invitation, wiping his feet vigorously on the mat. He couldn't wait to show them how it had turned out. 'Royal Doulton,' he said, theatrically unwrapping the plate from its bubblewrap right there in the hallway. Under the harsh wattage of the electric bulb, their faces glowed in the middle of it, their hair crenellated at the edges.

Khalid thought the plate was a horrid thing but he said, 'Very nice, bhai.' If that was being your own master, he would stay at the club until the final hour. 'Don't take your coat off,' he ordered Imran. 'Let's get out of here.'

'Got lolly?' Imran looked cautiously at Khalid, uncertain who was paying for their evening.

'We'll manage,' he said, and followed his friend out into the dark, and the barking of the pets, frightened by the random firecrackers.

8

THE DEPARTURE LOUNGE IN DUBAI WAS FULL OF SINGLE MEN, IN string vests and football club strips, and khaki trousers, some with bundles of goods tied close with string, some with blankets draped over their shoulders. They wore expensive-looking trainers, Nikes and Adidas. Some of the men slept in the lounge with their feet resting on their suitcases. Some of them had cardboard carrier bags with thick cord handles, gifts for the relatives back home. Stuff that had been earned over many hours, and hard won. Electrical equipment mostly, and designer gear, phones and handbags. She had never seen so few women on a plane. These men could have been boarding a bus in a small town bus station, rather than catching an international flight.

They all climbed down the stairs, jostling to get to the gate, and squeezed themselves into the gangway, waiting to board. Alia was ignored – these men had seen a lot, on building sites, and although they had never been inside Dubai's shopping malls, they were not going to stare or want to talk to her. They were tired and wanted to get home and had had enough of rich women.

On this leg of the journey the airline staff gave up on the

pretence of service: first class was empty. The workers were herded on board, their packages shoved into lockers, the lights dipped and an air hostess, in thick black eyeliner, caught Alia's eye and raised her eyebrows across the aisle, as she insisted a man sit down and turn off his phone, and lifted up his seatbelt for him with an exaggerated motion: is this what I took this job for, her look said, having to care for this riff-raff?

It was morning when they reached Karachi and the bus raced out to meet them. It swept round in an arc across the tarmac. The air was hot already and dust particles twinkled in the air, and Alia was energized even through her own leaden jet lag.

This was where her father's journey had started. He had made this flight in reverse, setting out from this place, and now she had followed him home, to try to piece things together, and to join the dots.

AN AMERICAN WOMAN IN A CREAM TROUSER SUIT, AHEAD OF Alia in the line, spoke to the passport official in crisp, confident Urdu. Alia could see the navy passport with a golden eagle embossed on the front.

'Asalam Alikum,' said the man in an olive green uniform at the desk without looking up, and Alia gave, on reflex, the answer, 'Wailikum Salaam,' fiddling with the end of the scarf that she'd thrown round her neck in an imitation of modesty.

'Why are you in Pakistan?'

'Family,' she said.

The officer brought down the stamp, the resounding happy sound, a thwack of ink on passport.

As she wheeled her case through to the other side of the barrier — where the families stood among the taxi drivers with cardboard signs written in marker pen, in English, Chinese, Urdu, scanning the faces and rushing forward to unburden their relatives of their packages and suitcases, to embrace them and to kiss them on the cheeks — she saw Nadima.

Nadima was taller than most of the crowd around her, and distinguished by the quality of her simple, well cut kameez, and by the languid posture of someone who never needed to rush. She held a pair of sunglasses in her hand and a BlackBerry, which she looked up from studying. Her hair was rod-straight, gleaming.

Alia knew her better than any of the other relatives, because Nadima's sixth form was spent at a boarding school in Surrey. Alia had visited her twice when she was a university student in London herself, just a few years older, and pitied her cousin's Sundays, the chapel services and cross-country runs.

Once she had even taken her out from the school on a weekend; they had got the train into Waterloo from the small country station, and drunk mocktails in Soho, and Alia showed her a favourite record shop, where they kept the best stuff in the basement. Nadima had spoken to her earnestly about her A level revision tactics, with no passion for the subjects she was studying, and asked if they could see Buckingham Palace and Madame Tussauds, and Alia realized that day how differently they both viewed their futures.

'Darling,' she said, kissing Alia, 'it's so good that you've come, and everyone is so pleased.' She whisked her away, but didn't take her case, and Alia struggled to weave across the concourse, to keep up with her cousin, as porters with trollies and grave-looking soldiers in starched khaki cut across at right angles. Alia was aware of the sweat pooling under her arms, showing against her shirt.

The car stood directly outside, an old Suzuki slung low to the ground; a young policeman was trying to move it on and arguing with the driver, swiping in front of the windscreen with a baton. Nadima didn't look at him, but slid into the back seat and gave firm instructions to the driver to go. The windows in the back were blacked out with curtain fabric. 'Kidnappings, you know.' Nadima shrugged, as she tugged at the corner of the curtain to make sure it was closed, and told the driver to turn down the fuzzy radio, the static of broken Urdu chatter.

'My goodness, you've never been here, Karachi is wonderful, I can't wait to show you *everything*, it's too short, you're only here for five days, can't you stay longer? Daadiji is so sad that you're only here five days. And everyone is so excited to meet you. They are all waiting.' There were no hairs on Nadima's arms. She had been waxed to perfection. Alia felt ashamed of her own flaws, the hair on her arms, too thick and visible in the sunlight.

'I'm sorry, it's all I can manage,' Alia lied.

She strained to see out of the window, catching a glimpse through the windscreen. They sped along a fast road away from the airport, and then drifted into thick, hazy lanes of traffic. Two-wheelers weaving across in front, alongside the car, buses crammed with standing passengers, arms slung out of the windows and army jeeps careering with soldiers standing up. A camel passed the car with heavy sacks hanging on either side of its hump, tinsel strung around its neck. Men wearing beige, as if they could merge into the desert that lay beyond the city's distant edges.

Nadima looked at her.

'It's different here. You have to be careful. I used to get so ripped off when I moved back – they could tell I'd been abroad, the traders in the market, it was terrible. You'll have to watch them like a hawk.' Then Nadima added quickly, as if to confirm how she'd conquered the city, 'It's home now.'

Nadima had weighed up going to university and had moved back home when she was eighteen and quickly married a man her parents had picked out. The whirlwind, a big confected romance, six months of intensive wedding planning. Farrukh was handsome in a muscular way, with pecs built up at the gym, and his family wealth was compounded by his job in an investment bank. Nadima fancied him, and marriage was the only way to get it on.

And it had worked, in its way. They had three children, and Nadima dabbled with designing embroideries for a couture boutique owned by an old family friend. Alia had already seen photographs of the house, ornate balconies, the ostentatious roses tended by several gardeners.

Alia could hardly see out of the car, within its shroud, but she peered past the driver, to the billboards, posters of serious men and political pledges, and the Urdu swirls that she tried to untangle. The letters didn't quite cohere. The sounds on the radio conveyed the rhythm of something familiar, something comforting. The sound of her father on the telephone.

Nadima reminisced about England. 'The blossom, it must be all those colours now, and I used to love that time of year, and the cakes, the scones, remember that time you took me to London?'

They both recognized their difference and held it at arm's length, avoiding the possibility of envy, although it wasn't lost on either of them. Alia, slogging and working with no foundations, no property, but the freedom of a bird, the freedom to travel for five days across the world, and Nadima's alternative, the security of the family path.

They turned into a long dusty avenue. High walls and electric gates lining the road on either side, interspersed with palm trees. No pedestrians at all in this part of town, eerily empty, as if the rest of the city had been swept away. As if there had been some decree or eviction. The car slowed near one of the high gates; a security guard with a rifle slumped against his legs was sitting outside a sentry box on a white plastic chair, his head bound with a white sheet, to keep sweat and insects from his brow.

He jumped up and fussed with the gates, the rods and bolts of metal clanking as they slid apart.

'So, are you ready?' Nadima asked her. 'Daadi will have got quite a crowd already.'

Alia quickly checked her make-up in a hand mirror which Nadima handed her and scraped her fingers through her hair, ineffectually. These women had standards. As she moved to collect her luggage from the boot, Nadima gestured to the guard, making it plain that she wouldn't need to carry anything by herself from now on.

Inside the reception room was vast, with cherubs carved on the ceiling, and a thick mahogany staircase curving down from the upper floor, reminding her of the fantasy sets that Bollywood families inhabited, and the expectant faces of her relatives. Some she knew well from over the years, and visits to London, and others who were too young or distant to be familiar. Aunties with sticks and uncles seated in armchairs, and children running from one end of the huge room to another, feet clattering on marble floors, past the table loaded with kebabs, and small sandwiches and crystal bowls of sweet kheer.

Several people embraced her at the same time, right inside the entrance of the door, so she was crushed in the folds of their shalwar kameez and saris, and the smell of musky perfume. The soft silk against her skin took her back to a time when she was a small girl, when she was folded like this in their laps. Her cheeks were squeezed, her earrings inspected, a finger traced over the tip of her nose. 'So like him, so like him, the same mouth, the same eyes.' The murmur went up and rippled across the room, and one cousin said, 'He was a real prankster. Always playing tricks on us when we were children.' It was like a chorus, Khalid's lament.

She made her way to her grandmother, seated in a high-backed armchair. Far more frail than the last time she saw her, her thick hair dyed and pulled into a black chignon, with pencilled eyebrows and the demeanour of a Mughal matriarch. 'Beti,' her Daadi said, and smiled as the weak tears of the elderly filled the ducts of her eyes. She folded her into her, so that Alia's head was tucked in against her warm, crushed silk-covered bosom. She held her hand tightly with her long, thin fingers freighted with gold and diamond rings.

There was an understanding between them.

She'd always adored her as a small girl, when she came to London appearing without much forewarning, with suitcases loaded with dolls and massive bags of gooey sweets, and there was an affinity between them, something in some shared aspect of their appearance.

'Mashallah, thank God you're well, you're here. This is your home, beti. You are always welcome here.'

'Thank you.'

'Don't leave us again, alright?'

'I want to talk to you.'

'We will have time later. Now, go and meet your family.'

To the rest, she was Khalid's girl. No one here was interested in her as an individual – not in her PhD research, or her next deadline, or her daily worries. They didn't want to listen to her account of the journey. Of course, they needed to know that she was healthy and well clothed. But they cared about her because she was part of their line, their tribe, and she was the living link to the man who was her father, who they loved, and for this reason they would do anything for her and in this there was something unconditional and anonymous. She could have been anyone, but because she was his, she mattered. She was their lost property.

Someone put a plate in her hand, unrealistically loaded with food, and Alia worried about the sauce slipping onto her shirt. A shy younger cousin asked for a photograph with her and remained staring at her afterwards.

'Do you like the food?'

'Can you speak Urdu?'

'Do you recognize me?'

'Do you know who I am?'

Different groups swelled and dispersed around her. The whole room interconnected, interwoven, like plant roots.

She was finding it hard to breathe, the names merging into

one another, fearing for her pronunciation. All the knowledge in this room was on their side – aunts who knew all her parents' secrets, who recounted her father's birth, who worried about her own faith, who estimated her weight.

'Come and sit over here,' Nadima commanded from across the room, saving her, and making a space on the couch. Alia squeezed in beside her.

'I told you it could be a bit overwhelming. When you haven't seen people for a while.'

'I can't believe we're related to all these people.'

'It's an art form, knowing how to handle them.' She barely touched the others, as if she had placed a protective shield around herself.

'Over there, she's my husband's aunt.' Nadima sighed, wanting to say more.

'What has she done?'

'Oh, nothing really. She just says things to my mother-in-law – why do I work, why I don't have more sons. Unhelpful comments about my kids.'

Nadima went on, talking quietly under her breath. Her youngest son, long-legged and too large to be held snug, tried to wriggle onto her lap in any case and jiggled his mother's bangles. Her two daughters, almost teenagers, were starting up dance routines with their cousins on the far side of the room. Alia didn't know anyone the same age with such grown-up children, didn't know how to talk to the boy, or what would interest him.

'Your kids are so tall.'

'None of your friends have children yet?'

Alia shook her head.

'We have help, though, remember.' Nadima gestured to the domestic staff. 'Some things are simpler here.'

A large family was hard work, Nadima implied. A lot of people to steer and mop up after, and a lot of potential offences and remembered jibes. Nadima had spent a lot of energy on the people in this room, on this whole cocktail of personalities and sensitivities.

Although her cousin was still aloof, there was something more open about her than Alia had first realized. She understood that she could give her something too, that Nadima had been looking forward to having someone she could be candid with.

IN THE EVENING, AFTER THE GUESTS HAD KISSED HER AGAIN, and embraced her again, and the servants had carried out the empty dishes and the plates and collected the crumpled linen napkins to launder, Daadi called Alia into her bedroom on the first floor.

She was lying on the bed, still dressed, her bare feet with their painted gold toenails resting on satin-covered bolsters. A woman who usually helped in the kitchen was massaging her grandmother's lower legs with the same rhythmic movement that she used to make the roti. She sent the servant away, imperiously, and rolled down her trouser legs, and the woman left without a murmur, closing the door behind her softly.

Daadi patted the massive bed, beckoning Alia to sit close to her, and gripped her hand as if she would like to keep her here, not let her fly away like so many others. 'Darling, it fills my heart to see you.'

'I'm so pleased to be here, Daadiji.'

A vast television screen was showing a loud soap opera in the corner of the room. A woman in thick eyeliner wept and clung to a man to try to stop him from leaving, to go where – the city? Dubai? America? Who knew where? – and loud synthesizer music reverberated around the bedroom. Daadi clicked it off with the remote control from her bed.

They sat in comfortable silence for a moment.

'My heart was broken, Alia. The shock, such a young man, with his life ahead of him.'

She began to cry, tears rolling down her cheeks.

'I'm sorry, darling, it makes me so happy to see you. You are so like him and it brings back so many memories. His father was so strict and he used to come to me, he would sit with me for hours. I didn't mind if he was naughty, you know, he was my son.'

'Daadiji, where was he living when he died?' She had only five days, she had to get somewhere. She needed the grit.

'May God have mercy on us, we didn't take proper care of him, he shouldn't have been alone in London, he wanted to come back to Karachi.'

Her speech was a mixture of reminiscence and prayer.

'Did he ever come back?'

'He never came back. He called me that week – the week he died, you know – and he said, I am coming back and I'm bringing so many presents for everyone. I should have…'

Daadi looked up at her. 'Pass me a tissue, darling. Do you want some tea?'

Alia passed her the box of tissues and pressed on. 'What happened, Daadiji?'

'He wanted to tell me something. And I said no, Alia. I said no, because I didn't want to be mixed up in any funny business, I have Nadima to think about, and the house here, we are respectable people, I didn't want to get into that business.'

'What business?'

'He didn't say, he just said he would return everything ten times over. That was the last thing that he said to me. Ten times over.'

Alia had heard it before, the promises of imminent abundance, and the bounty that would follow. The jackpot moment that never quite came. Jackpot – the pile of cash, building up, in a tottering heap, ready for the grab. But it could also mean a predicament, a mess. Getting into it, getting out of it.

'And did you speak to him again?'

'The next thing I knew we got the phone call from your mother in London, saying he was dead and there was an autopsy. And we were having a wedding here, my nephew, so many had come over, from Dubai, from Lahore, and we thought we can't tell everyone and make the guests miserable, there had been a lot of expense, so we kept it a secret among ourselves. We would creep away and cry in the bathrooms, so red our eyes were, you can see in all the wedding photographs, our eyes are full of tears.'

She started rummaging to find the albums of the wedding.

'And did you have an address for him?'

'Of course, I have it here somewhere.' Slipped inside the thick pages of a massive quilted wedding album, almost too heavy to lift, and tucked in the back behind the pages of rows upon rows of obligatory family set-pieces, of women in gold, and so many intricate outfits, was a small scribbled scrap, in biro with phone numbers and an address: c/o S. Wadia, 323 Church Street, W2.

Daadi handed it to Alia, gently, and patted the top of her hand. 'What's the point of going over it all again, darling? Better to leave it alone.'

Alia said nothing. Her grandmother looked at her intently, and brushed a strand of her hair away from her face, to see it more clearly. 'Alia, do you pray for him?'

'Yes, I do.' Alia was not sure if she was telling the truth or not.

When does thinking about someone become prayer? A hell of a burden, keeping the memory of the dead alive, trying to do them justice, remembering their faces, what they liked and didn't like. So easy to let them down. The slippage into anecdote, and forgetting their preferences. How much sugar did he like in his tea? Did he even like going to weddings?

Daadi dabbed her eyes with the tissue. 'Children must pray for their parents, to help them reach paradise. Please promise me you'll pray for him.'

9

THE NEXT DAY DAADI SUGGESTED TO NADIMA THAT SHE TAKE Alia to the beach. A family from the Karachi Race Club, from grandfather's days, were planning on stopping by, and Nadima understood, reading between the lines, that they were not to be trusted, that they might make little snipes about Alia, ask about her faith, her mixed-up-ness, and her unmarried state. She was an easy target and they had a reputation for sticking their nose in. Gradations of judgement, little sensitivities; the way one or two girls saw her skin as a challenge.

'She's so fair because she has an English mother, isn't she?' one cousin had muttered, over a plate of dessert, as if Alia was somehow cheating the system.

'You girls go down to Clifton. Nadima, take Alia for an iced coffee. Have a look at the mall.' Their grandmother pressed rupees on them, pushing the notes expertly into their hands.

The driver said he would wait by the car, and they walked down from the sea-wall, taking off their sandals at the side of the beach, a vast, long ridge of yellow sand, curving around the south of the city, on the brink of the Arabian Sea. Great container ships with their coloured cargos – like children's blocks – criss-crossed on the horizon. The high-rise towers and the crammed roads never quite receded from view, but the noise of the traffic was replaced with the crash of the waves. Cooler air whipped up their scarves, high waves forming into the shape of fins as they crested, as if they might hide sharks.

A trinket seller approached them with his Sindhi treasures woven from pink and navy blue threads, key rings, wall hangings, embroidered with a thousand little mirrors, glinting in the sunlight. Nadima waved him away with a smile, and he smiled back.

The sea was a leveller.

THEY WALKED TOGETHER ALONG THE LINE OF THE BEACH, LIKE all the others, meandering. A group of students were messing around with their arms around each other, taking pictures and laughing. A coy newly-wed couple, still decked in tinsel garlands, were holding hands.

'So haven't you met someone yet?'

All the meetings, and meetings was the right word – like interviews or business lunches – where she had been stuck with inappropriate men, the unwise email messages, the photographs that misrepresented the awkwardness, the dumpiness, and there had been one, a lawyer with a broken heart and young children.

'I was on one of these new dating sites for a while but I haven't renewed my subscription. It's a challenge to meet someone like that.'

'Aren't you living with a man?'

'Oh yeah – Stefan.' Alia laughed out loud; she hadn't thought of him since she left Oxford. She hadn't put him in that category. 'It's not like that.'

Nadima, shedding some of her aloofness and returning to a younger self, curious with innocence, like a sixth former in a dorm-room, said, 'Daadiji would love to fix you up.'

'Aren't I beyond the pale?'

'It's amazing what she can do.'

All the stories that are known but hardly spoken of in these concentric circles of family; the divorcees who have been matched up again, and a probably pregnant relative in Lahore who had a betrothal arranged just in the nick of time. So it's not too late for her yet, she's not yet too degenerate, or too morally dubious.

For a slender moment there was something appealing about falling on the family's matchmaking skills, and trying out something new. An introduction to a Karachi businessman or an investment banker in London, probably suave, charming, undoubtedly better dressed than any man she could meet in Oxford.

'It wouldn't end well,' Alia said. She had swum too far from this shore. It was never hers in the first place. He would have been raised to expect something else, something worthy. 'I don't think it's for me. I'm going to have to work it out on my own. Anyway, I'm so busy at work.'

Being busy didn't have much currency in Karachi. Who wouldn't choose leisure? You only had to drive out of the city, into the village, to see what toil meant. And there was something noble in taking minutes to think about the weft of a fabric for a dress, to ponder all day the forks in the road, to spend all day not making any choices at all.

'I wonder why my father left here?' Alia looked out to the sea.

Nadima collected some fluted white shells in a half-hearted sort of way. 'Everyone said he wanted to make a fortune, and then return. He'd fallen out with his father – he wanted to prove something to him – stand on his own two feet. Daadiji used to tell this story about the night he left: there was a fight, cruel words spoken, and he never had a rupee from his father after that. It was his mother who used to wire him the money to London. You know his father, I never met him, he had a reputation, a bit of a hard guy – I don't know the details, though.'

Nadima might have been rowing back, trying not to be disrespectful to the dead.

'You should speak to Uncle Wasim. We're meeting him for dinner tomorrow. He was close to Khalid-uncle, he'll know more. You have to be a bit careful, though – nobody wants to speak ill of those who have passed.'

And that meant that they couldn't speak much about Khalid at all.

THE ALL-YOU-COULD-EAT FOOD HALL WAS CAVERNOUS, WITH different hot buffets arranged around the sides and men in white chefs' hats serving up pizza, Chinese and pilaus in steaming vats and piles of naan breads. Sizzling hot plates and rotating skewers of meat stretched up to the ceiling. The tables were big enough to accommodate families of twelve, sixteen or more, and although it was ten o'clock at night, there were babies in high chairs being spooned food by their grandparents, and children hopping and twirling to the live musicians at one end of the restaurant. Outside expensive cars were still pulling up, offloading women in heels and dazzling suits, which reflected in the mirrors. The exterior was festooned with fairy lights, and two security guards with rifles stood on either side of the door.

Alia had been given so many clothes to choose from. One of the servants on the landing outside her room ironed and ironed, so there were firm seams in her trousers, in the sleeve lines of her long silk blouse. Every piece of clothing looked as if it had been embroidered for hundreds of hours, with delicate swirls and beading. There must be sleepless women somewhere, who never stopped stitching. 'Try these,' Nadima had said, handing her a pair of rhinestone-encrusted shoes. She had run a line of kohl under her eyes. They took a group photo before they left the house. 'One of us,' an aunt had muttered, approvingly.

Uncle Wasim would meet them all at the restaurant, and Alia had been briefed about him by Nadima. Two daughters, in their early twenties, one studying to be an orthodontist, the other had set up a consultancy, and their mother had died of cancer the previous year. 'Wasim misses her terribly, it's such a shame you never met him before,' Nadima said. 'He was always the life and soul of the party.' They were travelling into town specially to meet Alia.

He was a big, genial man, large shoulders, taller than anyone else she had met, with a thick moustache and a baseball cap. He gripped her tightly in an embrace, and patted her hard on the back with his huge hands. 'Khalid was like a brother to me, we got up to all sorts. And how proud he would have been of you.'

Alia liked him immediately and sat herself opposite him at the far end of the table.

He reminisced a little, telling her how stylish her mother and father had looked together, recalled a photograph of them in Kew Gardens, when Alia was a baby, and he sent his best to Suzie. People were at pains, Alia noticed, to show that they wished her mother no ill, that there were no hard feelings about the divorce.

He had admired Khalid when they were boys – Khalid was a couple of years older – and he'd somehow got hold of a little red tin of Brylcreem and showed him how to scrape it out into his palm and quiff his hair. They had lived together for a few years, and had shared a bedroom, when Khalid fought with his own father and things had got uncomfortable for him, and Wasim's family had let a favoured nephew stay with them instead.

'We were only a few streets away in any case, our doors were open,' Uncle Wasim said. 'We were all part of the same family. I brought you photos, I found these, the time he was staying with me in Newark.'

Khalid looked happy in them, shirt open at the neck, playing pool in a big room with Wasim – they posed with pool cues like staffs in their hands.

Some of them were risqué, beer bottles in hands, and there was even a blonde woman in one of them in tight-fitting trousers and bouffant hair, the ex-wife of one of their friends.

What was he trying to tell her? To show how far Khalid had travelled, how far he was from this life in Karachi?

'We went into business together for a while. We stuck at it. Khalid-bhai was really keen. Then he drifted away, he had found something else.'

The memory, walking along in the rain on a London street with Khalid.

He explained to her what the deal was, why they were excited. Outside the smog from the cars, sliding into grey puddles, and the black hems of the ladies were soaking through the rain. He unfolded a silk handkerchief and laid it out across his head and she had laughed. He hated the rain.

'We've been developing these cards, it's a secret, so you mustn't say anything to anyone, OK? This will make us very rich. You dial in this number – look.'

They ducked out of the rain and into a doorway of a fine hotel. The doorman in a top hat inched backwards to make room for Khalid in his suit; maybe the handkerchief on head thing added to the rich look. He took out a card, with a silver panel at the front like a scratch-card, and took a small coin to rub away at it, to reveal a long, unmemorable number.

'You dial this in before you dial your number, or the number you want to call, and then you can call anywhere in the world for five pence. Not five pence a minute, just a one-off payment, a single payment of five pence.' People couldn't speak to their parents in Egypt, in Lagos, in Istanbul, he told her, and they wanted to speak for a long time, unhurried, and to put their children on the phone. He said he was linking people. Alia had imagined women with the receiver tucked under their chin, kneading dough while they chatted, real conversations, not just the same old birthday greetings. Now people wouldn't have to worry how long they spent talking. Five pence times a thousand, times ten thousand. It would add up.

The cards were not very interesting. If it had been up to her, she would have printed pictures on them of nice animals or endangered species, like dolphins or tigers.

The waiter brought another dish of kebabs to their table.

'And do you know what he was doing? Towards the end? What his business was?' Alia asked, picking at a corner of bread with her newly lacquered nails.

'He tried to get me involved and I said I didn't want to know. I didn't want to be caught up, I'm not a risk-taker. I'd had my daughters by then.' Wasim looked at his plate, assessing it for what was still missing.

And he had me, Alia thought.

'But no idea at all?'

'It was something to do with BCCI.'

'What's that?'

Uncle Wasim boomed with laughter, a glimpse of the jester, the younger man in his laugh.

'The bank! The Bank of Commerce and Credit International. It was huge, it was into everything. He was doing something for Abedi, I think. Well, everyone was doing something for Abedi. But he got involved. Khalid-bhai was serious about it.' He broke off some bread and mopped up some of the gravy on his plate with a twist of his wrist.

'Who was Abedi?'

'He was the man behind BCCI. His wife was a cousin of the man who our Nana worked with in India. Came from Lucknow, before Independence. Abedi's father was at the court of the Nawab of Oudh. They had a bit of land.'

Alia couldn't keep up with these networks of the family imagination. The strange routes of offspring, used as explanatory factors. There were too many names, too many criss-crossing wires.

'Abedi set up the bank – you see, at that time there were no big third world banks – we all had to rely on the West if we wanted to do transactions – so Abedi said, "I want to give them a run for their money" and he did, literally, he was tremendously successful – a giant. It was a world class bank, it just grew so fast – we couldn't believe it. Branches in every country. People feel proud about that here. He's a hero for many folks. He did a lot for Pakistan – donated so much, he set up engineering institutes, the best hospitals – even the place where my wife had her chemo – all down to his charity. But the world wanted to bring him down, and they did.'

'What was the connection with my dad? Was he working for the BCCI, for this Abedi?'

'It was all a long time ago, Alia. It's complicated. Khalid-bhai was living on the Edgware Road the last time I saw him, after he'd stopped working for the casinos; he was living with a fellow called Sammy. A clever fellow – Khalid liked Sammy a lot, and trusted him. They were paired together to do a deal – maybe it was for Abedi, perhaps for someone else. I think that went wrong and he lost a lot of money.'

'I didn't know that there was money involved.'

'There's always money involved.' He slurped heartily on a straw. 'We always thought that Khalid-bhai died because of that – may Allah have mercy on him – the stress must have been incredible, trying to do a deal, losing thousands, he could never handle the pressure. You see, your father was trying to do the right thing. It must have put a strain on his heart.'

TWO DAYS LATER SHE WAS LEAVING KARACHI BEFORE DAWN. She looked out of the window into the grey courtyard, and the driver was waiting, wrapped in a woollen balaclava, with a blanket worn like a shawl as if it was freezing outside, revving the car and banging about to let her know it was time to go. She was ready, her case packed, the sense of wanting to fly and to return to normal competing with the pull of the place, the possibility of immersion in this other inheritance and this broken lineage. Daadi was already up, making her prayers in her pale nightdress, and Alia waited at her bedroom door, glimpsing her through the crack of light, an orange glow from the bedside lamp. When her grandmother was finished she removed the scarf from her head and climbed slowly onto her feet and Alia knocked gently.

'It's time for me to go.'

Daadi kissed her again and again, and, as if she was a little girl, blew softly on her face, protecting her from evil.

'I'll come back soon,' Alia said. She knew she probably wouldn't. The visit had hung by a thread of unreality, the suspension of belief, and if they actually lived alongside each other there would be many more demands. She wouldn't be given such a free pass, she'd have to marry, to guard her reputation, and live Nadima's life. She loved them for the fact that they understood this too, and that they could let her come and let her go.

PART TWO

1987

PART TWO

1957

10

AFTER A QUICK CUP OF TEA, MARK DENBY SAT DOWN IN HIS office chair and stretched out his hands, clicking his knuckles. There was a shallow basket stacked with letters on his right-hand side, about a dozen, a paperknife alongside it.

A Member of Parliament has to learn how to read things quickly. Literally, to scan documents hundreds, even thousands of pages long, also faces, situations, handwriting. People write the most shocking drivel, syntax and spelling just a rough gesture in the right direction. And the paper they used, did they even want their letters to be read? Within weeks of the election he could pretty much guess something about the writer from the envelope – the shaky little letters of the elderly (though mostly well spelled) worried about winter fuel bills, the looped biro of the wronged woman, often in bright colours. Only the rich did it properly, typed on headed paper. For everyone else it was a creative free for all.

Most of his postbag was about local matters back in Oxford, or generic petitions sweeping the whole country, or occasionally and sweetly, a little bit of fan mail tucked in among the rest, telling him to carry on, that he had done a good turn on the radio, that they'd have the Tories over a barrel next time.

Such a simple thing, public service, once you actually get elected: you've just got to work hard, stay clean, do what's required of you. Nobody thinks you can work miracles, your constituents just want to know that you exist and that you're human and trying your best to speak up for them whenever you get a chance to mention the biscuit factory or the location of a new outpatients unit. Such a simple thing and yet they all seemed to balls it up, and the more time that he spent in Westminster, the more he knew it might be his special job in life to point out when that happened.

'How's Penelope?' Linda started every day with the same enquiry. She appeared at the door with the teapot in hand, ready to refill. Linda had worked around the House for about a decade, long enough to know about wives.

'She's fine,' he lied. He didn't know, though he presumed she was fine. He never called last night in the end, after speaking to Peter. He missed the right moment to call and – in his defence – she could have called him too. Somehow, he knows that he has been avoiding having a proper conversation with Penny, because he might not be able to be honest, or, to put it another way, because he hadn't worked out what to say about last Saturday's visit to his mother.

He hadn't left her unkindly. He had regained his equilibrium, and handled it well, like an adult son should. He could see that she was upset, that it all ran deeper than he could know, and he embraced her at the door and told her not to worry. He patted the top of her hand and reassured her, and she stood at the front door and tried to explain. 'It must have been all the news about Solidarity in the newspapers which set me off.'

That was his mother. Her own emotions and other people's

all knotted together. The individual never more important than the collective.

She had gone back inside for the basket of Bramleys, which she insisted Penelope could make into crumble or stew up with cloves. They were lime green and hard as snooker balls. He didn't have the heart to tell her that Penny would never cook them, she was far too caught up with her clinic at the moment, and she wasn't much of a cook at the best of times. They would probably end up on the compost heap, like the last ones. Guilty about them, every time he saw them, decomposing, mulching into the brown.

The deep chimes of Big Ben resounded from the northern side of the building. Ten o'clock, radios being switched on around the country for the news bulletin. The combination of that funny little tune and the depth of the profound toll that followed. The place was full of bells, deep notes and high. Little division bells tinkling in the bar and in the corridors. It gave him the reassurance that he was lacking last night, the sense of rootedness in a place and a system.

He worked through the post, methodically. Linda had already intercepted some of it, removed some of the envelopes, sifted out the nutters. Elements of battiness were easy to spot – too many capitals, underlining – but she had left other things easily dealt with, requests for donations and invitations to events. He liked to see most things for himself. As a new MP it was important to spot things. He didn't receive much post as yet, and he had made it a routine to spend the first ten minutes of every day looking through. Some of it was for the former tenant – his Tory rival, dispatched in the summer, a 2,163 majority. The look on his blanched face, as they stood in that gym hall.

It had been bitter-sweet coming to Parliament. The electoral map of England was a blue sea, just some red swirls on it, like spilt blood. There was absolutely no chance of getting anything done; the prospect of winning was a fantasy, a myth in some quarters. They looked stark and isolated on the opposition benches in the face of the blue juggernaut, telling a story nobody in the country wanted to hear.

'Mark Denby, a flare in a dark night.' That's what the *Guardian* editorial had said the next day. Or words to that effect. He'd do his best for Oxford East in the face of it all, that's what he'd promised them and himself.

Something on white paper, a typed letter, caught his eye. Quite respectable-looking, an address on The Bishops Avenue.

Dear Mr Mark Denby MP,

The Bank of Credit and Commerce International. I bring it to your attention. You are an Economist and you may understand. As you must already know this is a very big bank. It has balance sheet assets of $22 billion. Are they worth the paper they are written on? It is in seventy-three countries and London is the Headquarters.

Who cares what this bank is funding? Who cares what they are doing? Look closely and you will see.

I am sorry to trouble you, you must be a busy man, and I do not mean to impinge on your time. I would like to say, sincerely, sir, that an investigation needs to happen to prevent possible disaster affecting the bank and its shareholders, of whom there are many in this country and abroad.

At the very least I would look for compensation for my own position. My husband and I are estranged and he is refusing any payment to me. This is why I write to you, and tell you the business that he has been involved in, and the company he has been keeping.

Mrs Zahra Asfour

Mrs Asfour was an angry wife, seeking revenge. Not exactly a neutral informant. He handled the letter a moment; where to send it on, if anywhere? He scribbled a note for Linda to send a copy to the Department of Employment which might be able to help with her maintenance case, which was pretty hopeless, in his experience. He hesitated before picking up the next letter in the pile.

It was interesting, this Bank of Credit and Commerce International. He didn't know much about it, but it wasn't hard to miss it. It was everywhere, springing up in all sorts of places – a new branch had just opened on the corner near Green Park station.

Perhaps a forwarding note to the Treasury was in order, too, just to cover all the bases. He would consult with Linda later.

He was lucky with his secretary. He'd been warned, not in a gentle way, by Peter, and he knew that it was such a cliché. 'There'll be legs everywhere and women in too tight blouses who should know better, and the awful thing is that they're bright, they'll argue with you and win, and then bring you a cuppa.'

And the MPs were the ones with the power wafting off them, and if they were known for squeezing a little bit too hard, they got called an old devil or quite a boy, and nobody minded in the slightest, as long as it wasn't a very young lad in a football strip, or hard drugs snorted in a den somewhere. Even then, you could get away with it if you were on good terms with the editors. And the new ones, like Denby, they had something fiery rushing inside them because they'd just fought and won. Like boxers coming out of the ring, they were giddy with winning. Nobody cared that much back in the constituency and their wives had had quite enough of the campaign, and wanted a return to normality. Here, in Westminster, it was a different story. They were little powerhouses, each one a victor.

So when Denby saw the woman who was going to work as his secretary he was relieved. She had described herself as unflappable in her interview.

Linda was the same age as him, born in exactly the same year, and she had worked for the Wilson government, the first one. She was married to a doctor and lived in Southwark, near where she grew up. She'd been a grammar school girl and studied politics at King's College, and she believed in the Labour Party and worked for it with all the zeal of a church helper, her mouth set with determination. A stout pair of legs.

She wasn't as serious as he had first presumed, and she had become a friend of sorts, able to minister advice and ideas at precisely the right moments.

AT LUNCHTIME HIS FEET JUST TOOK HIM THERE, STRIDING, DOWN to Victoria and onwards across Green Park and then onto Piccadilly. He had gone past Victoria coach station and a group of young backpackers, from Australia, unseasonally suntanned shoulders and massive backpacks, their walking boots and canisters dangling from their sides. Then around the perimeter wall of Buckingham Palace, topped with barbed wire and cameras. The traffic roared on and on. London was wearing on him. Nothing was more than twenty minutes on an old bike in Oxford, and people, if they didn't exactly look you in the eye and smile, acknowledged your presence, made room for you on the pavement, let you go before them in the queue at the cheesemongers or the bakers in the Covered Market. There might have been money in Oxford too, but it was underplayed. He found London people unsettling, their bossiness and cleverness. The city had got brasher since he was a student.

It was a longer walk than he'd expected and he returned well after two o'clock. Linda looked up but didn't stop typing and her fingers hopped across the keys. She was able to talk and type, which he always found impressive.

'Long lunch?'

'I stopped off on the way back. I wanted to have a look inside a bank branch – BCCI – I went to the one near Green Park. Ever been in there?'

'No.'

'It is incredible. From another planet.' Without thinking about it, the words came right out.

It wasn't hard to sense corruption. Denby had a nose for it. He liked to think his asset was that he didn't care for money. He liked to be comfortable, and he had been comfortable, since his UCL days. He didn't have to worry about how much things cost, and he bought in moderation, never to excess. It was just his good fortune in life: one small, good glass of wine, a single serving of pudding, one well-ironed shirt. His possessions told a story of modesty.

One of his favourite words was propriety, not because he

was pious but just because, if everyone lived like him, the world would be a better place and there'd probably be enough to go around. 'It's the Baptist blood,' Penelope teased him once, and there was a branch of non-conformist clergy, with clean aprons and well-read bibles, somewhere on his father's side. It pained him to see things go to waste, when people over-ordered in a restaurant, or when a page of paper was ripped from a notebook just for a scribbled phone number. Maybe it was something about wartime; the stories of making-do, the darning of socks. God, he was going to drive Zoe round the bend if he started talking like that.

The branch that he went into was excessive. Way too much money had been spent kitting out the place. The walls were white and preposterously high, there was floor to ceiling glass, an escalator leading to an upper floor, stainless steel fittings and the brightest lights. A fountain in the lobby played an annoying little tune while it spurted out water. Empty of customers, apart from one elderly Arab in a floor-length gown, carrying a leather moneybag, and a cocky young guy, Asian-looking, in suit and tie, his black hair slicked back, who was just leaving through the revolving doors.

Something from the future, a galactic bank branch.

Denby hardly went to the bank anymore, Penelope or Linda usually did it for him, but he knew the beige countertops and the feel of synthetic carpet in their local Natwest underfoot as he queued behind others to pay in a cheque.

This was a different kind of bank, somebody's dream of the future.

'May I help you?' A manager in a black suit had stepped forward from behind a glass screen, and welcomed him.

'I just want to take a look at this place.'

The man had hidden a frown, as if looking around was not the sort of business he entertained. 'Do you have an account with us, sir?'

'No.'

Denby had turned his back on the man and walked round the branch, proprietorially, running his fingers over the white leather chairs. The logo of the bank was prominently located on the wall, in large pieces of aluminium, cut to look like interlocking letters, angular and geometric. The manager had hovered too close to him.

'It must cost a lot to keep this place.'

'We are very fortunate to work here. BCCI is not like other banks, sir.'

Denby had not bothered to explain himself as he headed for the revolving doors. The exit led out to a dingy side-street on the corner of Piccadilly, where restaurant extractor fans whirred. As he headed towards Green Park station, he noticed a young couple kissing inside the doorway of a bookshop, and as he got closer, he saw that they were both men. They looked young, very tender. They pulled away from each other shyly as he approached, as if surprised by their own act.

Some other things he didn't say to Linda. Like how he'd never paid attention to fashion in his life, but there was something about London now, in his forties, which made him feel old and crumpled and like he might not be able to keep up. And a tiny voice, far quieter, which he ignored but which was there, which made him want to compete, which made him feel, when he compared the life he lived with Penny in Cowley, just a little poor himself, a little provincial, next to the wealthy bankers striding across Green Park, wearing wax jackets. As if they inhabited the real world, perhaps as if they really understood the world of the future.

Linda stopped typing and looked at him curiously as if he had said things that he shouldn't be saying, as if he was going off-script, moving away from the moorings of the things that he understood so well, the NHS, the car workers. Crossing an ocean.

'I'm a building society person myself.'

'Linda, do you think you could do me a favour, and dig up some research, anything on BCCI?' he said.

'About the whole bank? I should think there's rather a lot. Anything in particular?'

'Any mentions in Parliament, committee work, newspaper clippings. Whatever you can get your hands on.'

'No goal in mind?'

'Just a little look-see.'

'There's a lot of local councils putting in money, I heard, Lambeth for one.'

'Yes, that too, whatever you can find. The whole world's putting money in.'

'Just the British part of the operation? It's all over the world, isn't it?'

'Start with us, and see what you turn up.'

'I'll get to it then.'

The truth was, she had been at a bit of a loose end since the election. Denby was a good MP – the new ones usually were – dutiful and at his desk during office hours, so she hadn't had to clean up his mess like the last one. Just triage so far. She'd done much harder stuff in the past – for a Committee

Chair and once, temporarily, for someone in the shadow cabinet. A backbencher was small fry by comparison; the phone calls, and letters she could do in her sleep, and truth be told, it wasn't very exciting. She needed a project. Her friends were all talking about their children leaving home and it was another conversation she couldn't contribute to. This would be as interesting as anything else.

The next day Denby found she wasn't in the office at all. She'd left a note saying that she would spend the morning at the British Museum reading room. And the morning after that he made his own tea, and her desk stayed empty, as neat as a pin. Notes in a line down one edge, her pencils lined up like soldiers, waiting for orders. Her empty chair. It helped sometimes just to have someone there. She was, he realized with a slight sense of unease, his audience.

She popped back after lunchtime and raced through some dictation. A letter to a council leader, and a scientist at the University upset about the ozone layer.

'You seem distracted.'

'I am, yes.'

'Got anything to share?'

'Not yet.' She smiled and her eyes sparked with mischief.

What have I started? he thought.

'Research suits me. I'll be off again to the Commons Library. I've got some files on reserve. And then I'm going over to the City to speak to a couple of people. Unless there's anything you want?' she said, grabbing her red coat as if she was late for an appointment.

He hadn't meant to lose his secretary to the puzzle of BCCI and he found he was rather irritated at having to walk down the corridor that afternoon to the photocopier. It had just been a suggestion. She'd taken it very literally.

Now she might understand it all better than him.

He placed his letter face down on the glass plate but when he tried to make a copy, the paper jammed. The problem originated with the loading drawers which were low, placed parallel to the ground – he opened the drawer for A3 paper, which looked fine, and then he knelt down on the carpet to cajole open the bottom compartment which held two reams of A4, and was wedged tight.

He trapped his finger in the drawer as it sprung backwards unexpectedly.

'Shit!'

Piers Fletcher-Reid stuck his head out of the neighbouring office. 'Everything tickety boo?'

His girth and blotchy nose gave him a jolly look, as if he was cheered daily by the state of the nation. 'The longest-serving PM this century!' his presence seemed to announce. He was savouring each day like pudding. 'That damn machine buggered again?'

Denby bristled. There was something so viscerally rich about the Tory MP. And so stolid and immoveable – Piers pretty much filled the corridor. He wasn't daft, of course. Denby suspected he was more critical of some of the manifesto's most lurid plans than he let on, certainly more sympathetic to the EEC than most. But enchanted by the Lady.

'Tried turning it on and off again?'

Piers had a large signed photograph on his desk, in a silver frame, which Denby could see from his angle, crouched on the floor, while the door was propped open: the PM and Piers shaking hands, the man beaming as if he'd been the unexpected winner at a school prize-giving. The party was like some naval fleet ploughing on through the waters, never looking back, barely conscious of anything that might float in their way. Next to the picture were framed family photographs of Piers's two youngish daughters, in strapless ball gowns, showing, as Piers had once pointed out himself, too much décolletage.

'Just fine, thank you, Piers.' Denby got off his knees, and banged at the top of the photocopier, ineffectually, lifting open one heavy flap for no good reason and slamming it back down again.

'Well, I'm blowed if I can help in any case. You ought to get one of the typing pool onto it. Rather below your grade if you don't mind me saying.'

ON THURSDAY EVENING DENBY PICKED UP HIS SPORTS BAG from the corner of the office, to leave London and take the train from Paddington back to Oxford for the long weekend. Linda was still there, flicking through a large book and taking notes with the air of a scholar.

'No plans for the weekend?'

'Ah, you know, Adrian's on emergency call-out.'

'You should get home.'

'I'll just spend a couple more hours on this tonight.'

'I bet you were a good student.'

'I worked hard.'

'Life's not all about hard work, you know.' He didn't believe it for a second.

'It's always worked for me.'

HE ALLOWED HIMSELF ONE WARM SINGLE MALT ON THE
InterCity, as there was no ice available, and spread out his
papers and diary but couldn't bring himself to look at them, and
as they sped out of London his eyes turned to the sun coming
down fast and vertical over the flat black fields, ploughed ready
for something – God knew what. He was an urban man, and this
was how he liked to see the country, rushing through it between
one city and another.

Denby had been born into the Labour Party in all its post-
war beauty and hope.

He'd had a false start in life. Knew what real work was.
Swotted hard for his 11-plus but just missed the grammar
school. The pain of opening that envelope; he'd passed maths
and verbal reasoning, but for some reason the English paper
was a disappointment that day. He knew it as soon as he put
down his pencil. And that meant that, at first, there was a chasm
between his ambitions and what he had been able to do. His
father had asked him, as he approached sixteen, 'So what about
a job at the plant then, Mark?' and his reply, which they'd teased
him about afterwards, for many years, 'No, not really… I think
I am probably better than that.' In any case, it was inescapable:
he didn't have the contacts or the qualifications for university,
and so the factory tided him over for a few years between school
and whatever was going to come next.

The South Plant and the North Plant, strung out across the
Eastern Bypass, turning out the last of the Morris Minors and
the Morris Oxford – nowadays it was all about the Maestro – he
knew it like the back of his hand. The chimneys long and thin
as church tapers, on the edges of the ring road. Hundreds of
men in navy boiler suits arriving for their shifts on bicycles, or

in shared cars, with their dads and uncles, stubbing out their
fags, spirited inside the gates, with their thermos flasks and
sandwiches, for the factory day, making up the thirty-nine hours
per week, not one minute more or less.

The press shop and the body shop, the trim shop and the
paint shop. The beauty of that line as it kept moving, the
sparkling cars, unaffordable to the men, which they conjured
from nothing, moulded from sheets of plain steel, the way a
windscreen could be lowered down and glued in by hand, the
turning of a window handle, the metal pieces transformed into
a car, alive with an engine.

As it turned out, those years were a real asset when the politics
started to take off. And he learned a lot on the floor, entry level
stuff, a lot of hanging around with the union. How to heckle.

Through evening classes, and the Workers' Educational
Association, he'd decided to put in for a degree. Hours of real
work, after work, numbers suddenly taking on magic shapes
and possibilities. Still youthful enough to join the general entry
stream, to avoid becoming a mature student – two words which
terrified him at twenty-two – one enthusiastic tutor at the WEA
said Oxford was a real possibility. He'd seen it all already from
a distance – the daft bow-ties on acned boys, and the raven
gowns, and the posturing, the gentility inside the colleges, the
way that everyone pretended to know everything, and the way
that politics was held at arm's length, and examined politely as
if it was in a bell-jar.

He chose economics at UCL. He wrote a postcard to one
of the younger Oxford Fellows, saying, basically, thanks for
inviting me to look around your college but I would like to
study something more relevant to the world. Quite fearless.

And he went for broke. Hung up his overalls. A train to London. Denby's life blazed fiercely those years. He marched against Vietnam frequently, for CND once or maybe twice, idolised Bertrand Russell. He spent a lot of time in bed with a loud, single-minded girl, who preoccupied him for a summer. By his graduate years, though, he was more often in a smoky corner of the Marlborough Arms, debating welfare policy with his professors. He scored points, and he did it with humour. Old men in their corduroy and their horn-rimmed glasses, their values, their questions. They were honourable men and they knew their history, and they got hot under the collar about exactly how much you should tax or how far the cradle-to-grave net might stretch, but they saw things from the same place. It was about being human and bringing up humanity with you and raising the level, making progress and spreading it around, and seeing the graphs go upward. They were all working every day with the war graves at their back, all the ghosts of Europe around them. Britain had been on the side of right. They had won the war, and, eventually, he believed – fervently, almost religiously – they would win the peace.

So stupid for never guessing, though. He berated himself. Even the simple arithmetic didn't add up.

PART THREE

11

'So if you're sure, you can sign here please, Khalid.' Mr Lambert lent him his fountain pen for effect – it was a thoughtful gesture – it was an expensive pen, like an heirloom. Black ink. Bunny-headed paper, lots of small print, which he didn't read.

Khalid signed neatly, keeping carefully between the line and the allotted space.

'It's all subject to the usual checks, you understand – you'll have to be vetted for the work permit.' Lambert hadn't jumped at Nassau. 'Blighty is the place for me.' He was dealing with the contracts for the ones who were, and his office was the only place still functioning in the whole building. There were box files open, a neat pile of papers to be distributed and signed. Lambert was business-like about what needed to be done. They all trusted him, a diamond geezer, he used to pay out their wages and deal with the timesheets, with never an error. His plan was to sort out the staff, sign off the contracts and then that would be it, he said, he wasn't going to kiss Hefner's arse any longer. He was moving to Sussex, looking forward to the garden, and Sunday lunches in rural pubs. He might run a pub himself.

Khalid was going, though, he had their word. The Invitation To Apply had arrived, to his home address, and they had gone as far as issuing contracts. Khalid's concern was grabbing life today, doing something brave and being rewarded from above for the boldness. He couldn't think of what to say.

'Good luck, my darling,' Mr Lambert said. He ripped off a green carbon copy at the back and folded it in half, placed it in an envelope made of thick paper, the type with the flap that always bobbed up, and that would never seal.

Khalid placed it carefully inside his jacket pocket.

FUNNY BEING THERE IN THE DAYTIME, SEEING EVERYTHING IN A different light. A lot of people were milling around; he recognized them although they were alternate versions of themselves, bunnies in their jeans and T-shirts. One of the girls wore glasses with her hair scraped back, and was transformed into a college student, misplaced in the club. Gaggles of young folks, standing around with each other, hugging each other, saying goodbye, some of them were crying. Khalid had dressed in his usual work clothes that morning – black suit, jacket, bow-tie, cufflinks and pressed shirt. It just wasn't right, he felt, to step over the threshold in anything else. Disrespectful. These young kids, they didn't care, in their training shoes and tracksuits.

The removal men were hard at it, dismantling the dancefloor, unscrewing the legs on tables and taking apart the bar. There was a constant sound of drilling and hammering. Two removal men were wrangling the immense velvet curtain over the stage, trying to unhook it. Hefner wanted to ensure he kept what he could, that he didn't lose too many assets. The bar had gone first and everything else had quickly disappeared

– gin and vodka went out with the morning light. They had started stripping out the mahogany. It was going to look a wreck by the end of the day.

There wasn't much chance of proper loot, but anyone could pilfer the little stuff – cutlery, napkins, shot glasses. Khalid had an ashtray weighing in his pocket. Don't bite the hand that feeds you, he heard Suzie speak, and he took it out and put it back on a table, gently.

He went upstairs to see his gaming floor. The lifts weren't working, someone must have closed off the mains, so he walked up the back fire escape, shoes tapping hard on the concrete. It was cold on the staircase and the air smelled of Dettol, and when he reached the fourth floor, he was completely alone. He tried the lights.

The place was something that he had once dreamed. It wasn't exactly shabby but faded and worn. It was as if the days were always numbered. His footsteps still echoed despite the carpet in the room. It never could have gone on forever. It had had its time. It was like a great big party had come to an end. Twenty million dollars a year dropped at that old knees-up.

He sat on one of the punters' stools, spun the roulette wheel with his hand, and the heavy wood accelerated, and he heard the familiar clackety-clack of the ball, hopping madly across. Red-black-red-black. London-the Bahamas. It hadn't been a bad run of fate, he wasn't sorry to say goodbye to this place, although it was time for something new. The exhilaration of a new start was calling him.

Downstairs a new crowd had arrived; most of them he knew, one way or the other, even if they had been day shifters or working different floors. Handsome faces that he'd seen carrying trays, putting ice into glasses, flexing their knees at just the right angle as they served the tables.

Goodbye, good luck, he heard it a thousand times that day, everyone as raw as they were the day they first entered the club. A bunch of people scattering apart, coming unstuck from each other. People had collected their things from the lockers, and satin ears were folded into shopping bags. Most of them hadn't been offered Nassau – they were too new or not experienced enough.

And the judges. Dragging it through the courts like that, back and forth since September. Hefner had lost the appeal. That's it – the law said, close down the whole place, bring the whole thing to its knees. The Met and the Gaming Board working hand in hand.

They all rehearsed the same phrase for it. Hammer to crack a nut.

Habitual offences. That's what had enraged Hefner the most. The court judgment deemed that there had been habitual offences and the club was 'not fit and proper'. It tarnished them all, as if they were all not fit and proper individuals. There was no way it was about technical offences, everyone said so, it had been a full scale clamp-down on all the casinos by the Met. They were just looking for a pretext.

It had been everywhere, all over the papers. It wasn't as if they didn't know it was coming – it had dragged on for months, and the smart ones had seen which way the wind was blowing. They had put plans in place, and got out early, like Imran, following his dreams with those cameras and those plates. The press was savage; 'Nothing like a fallen hero,' Suzie said. They ripped Victor Lownes to shreds; some people said it was because there had been too much funny business going on between the bunnies and the punters – it had been raised in court during the appeal – and some of the girls felt bad about that. It was about more than screwing – there was never much of that, as far as Khalid knew.

It was about power, something slippery, way beyond brightly coloured chips. Scotland Yard had objected. Not enough cheques signed, too much credit given to the wrong people. Millions of it; he had to admit he was astonished to read about the way the cheques had been bouncing. Two or three million dollars of credit given just like that. On Sunday Suzie and Khalid read the papers with a hint of pride. But as she had pointed out, all those punters, the politicians and film stars and sheikhs – they didn't get the sack. Nassau would be better, Khalid thought, smaller, more sophisticated, just the cream of society – less trouble.

The place was buzzing with all the nervous energy of people making decisions about the future, deciding where the best jobs in London would be now. Gossip passed on like Chinese whispers.

Khalid needed to get out, his fondness for the club had evaporated – it was like seeing how a magic trick was done. He wanted to speak to Suzie and to imagine their future, to say something aloud so that it would be real. He ran out to one of the phone boxes on Hyde Park Corner. It was a blustery day, the wind whipping up the autumn leaves into tiny tornadoes, a man with a black umbrella wrestling it down, trying to turn it the right way out.

'It's done. I've signed. We're going, Suze, we'll be there in the new year.'

'The Bahamas. It sounds so unlikely on a day like today.' She was mashing potato or something, he could hear the clattering of pans. He imagined her with the saucepan in front of her, the receiver propped between her shoulder and her pretty ear, with a silver stud or a hoop threaded in the lobe.

She didn't sound as pleased as he'd hoped.

'The end of the Playboy Club in London, I cannot believe it.' Khalid tried to express something of the bewildered scene inside.

'It's their karma.' She had a habit of throwing in words that she had picked up on the King's Road in the 1960s when she didn't know what else to say. It went against his grain, but he let it pass.

'Just think, Hefner's bad luck can be the making of us.'

He tried to get her to enthuse, or to anticipate, where they might be in the next year, perhaps less, if everything went according to plan. He heard more clattering, a cutlery drawer.

'Don't get your hopes up, Kal. And we have to think about how to live until the new salary starts. We've probably only got six weeks covered.'

Three, he thought, with the ice shard of guilt, if you included a couple of disappointing results in the bookies the previous week.

'We'll manage.'

This was the first new day, he'd just signed the contract – couldn't she be pleased for him, for what it meant for them? He heard the sharp acid pips on the BT line, warning of a few seconds of speaking time remaining, and fumbled in a panic to find another ten-pence coin in his wallet.

'And... well, I was thinking...' her voice had become soft and inviting, 'it might be nice for you to get a job with regular hours, then we could see each other in the evening, go to bed at the same time... Maybe it's time to draw a line under this nightlife stuff.'

It was true. He would like to go to bed with her, but the time of day didn't matter. Not in the least. 'Suze, this is a big day for me, don't spoil it. This is the start of something.'

'OK. I'm just thinking about the practicalities.'

'Just trust me, Suzie, trust the future,' he said, as he tried to push the coin through, to prevent them being cut off.

'Khalid, did you just call me to tell me to trust Hugh Hefner? I mean, seriously?' she said, laughing.

You used to be fun, Suzie, he thought, but he said, 'I don't want to fight today,' just as the line beeped with finality, and cut out.

TONY KING WAS WAITING OUTSIDE THE MAIN ENTRANCE TO THE building; he had also come to sign his contract, and he slapped Khalid on the back. Tony had the look of a man who travelled light, and who didn't mind moving from place to place. His flared jeans were a decade out of date but he wore them like they were from a fashion catalogue, and he had tucked his Ray-Bans into his shirt pocket, so the gold rims glimmered promisingly. 'Flying out next week. I am well out of this place, man.'

Tony was going to stay with his mum in Kingston while he waited for the Nassau contract to come through.

'Khalid.' He placed his large hands on his shoulders, as if he might swoop him into an embrace. 'We are actually going! We are going to have such a blast!'

145

Khalid felt like he did when he gambled, which was a good thing – sharply attentive and fizzing with possibilities, holding his breath until the line was crossed.

'I don't know about you, Tony, but I need a drink.'

'Rose and Crown, my friend? See you there in ten?'

THE IRONY OF IT WAS THAT HE DIDN'T GAMBLE THAT DAY. AND he wasn't rat-arsed either. He must have walked past half a dozen betting shops, and he stayed away from all the machines in the pub. His body was alive enough with the prospect of changing clubs, and the fresh start ahead, the vision of starting up life in the West Indies. And Tony was the sort of friend who gave him life too, who steered him away from the machines without even knowing it. The patter about turtles and fishing boats, and the times they had ahead of them.

They drank about three pints of lager – maybe it was four. Two at the Rose and Crown, he remembered that well, one or two at the King's Arms which was busier and louder, with music blaring. Tony told someone they'd been sacked from Playboy, which got them a lot of attention, and the barman handed them whisky chasers, on the house, in commiseration. Khalid ate dry roasted peanuts, flicking them up with his thumb, and watched Tony showing off playing darts, like always, hitting the trebles without even looking as if he was trying. Some woman, a drunk tourist in knee-high white leather boots, kissed Tony on the cheek, and he squeezed her arse. That was when Khalid thought it was best to go.

He remembered the Datsun, still on a parking meter, and offered to give Tony a lift.

That was all it was. A good night. Just a plain old good night, nothing too crazy. No boogie, no Babycham.

They got in the car. It was parked in a side-street at the back of an apartment block, at the rear of Park Lane.

Was he drunk? Of course he was, but wasn't everyone coming out of the pub that night? They all drank, they all drove. And Khalid could handle his drink, he just got more talkative, nothing daft, nothing too out of control.

He had offered to drop Tony home to his place in Notting Hill, and his plan had been to loop round onto the Crowell Road, out west onto the Hammersmith flyover. Tony's long legs, his crisp jeans, folded into the passenger seat, his afro skimming the interior roof.

As they had pulled out of Park Lane, the traffic lights were all green and they raced through Cumberland Gate. The place looked so good now that Khalid was leaving London for another country. He loved London like this, with its statues floodlit, in all its pompous glory, the black cabs dancing round under the street lamps, and the lights from the hotels and the cars blurring like stars. 'Best city in the world,' he said to Tony, and he accelerated and decided to do another round of Park Lane, past Hyde Park and the Wellington Arch. A victory lap.

His route was a figure of eight, around the great loops of road encircling the corner of Hyde Park. They raced past Apsley House and turned, like ice-skaters, flew past butch Achilles on his plinth, with his shield raised high.

He should have seen him coming and nobody could have said whose fault it was. They'd both moved into the middle lane at exactly the same time. Khalid accelerated too quickly, but the van did too. He'd been trying to cut him up, Khalid was sure of it. The Ford Transit was coming from the right, some tradesman trying to get home. He didn't see it clearly enough, it was dark and it all happened very quickly. A Datsun and a Ford, coming together for a few seconds, like drunken dancers. Khalid heard the horn just as the van swerved round in front of him. He braked hard and they rammed into it. Khalid and Tony flew forward in their seats. There was shocked silence.

The other driver opened his door, and came over, before they'd even spoken.

'Ah shit, this is bad. You've got to turn the engine off, Khalid, stop the car.' Tony put his hand on his arm.

The man was rapping on the windscreen, shouting, 'What the hell was that? Look at my van.'

Khalid got out and inspected the damage.

The Ford's rear did look bad, undeniably dented, but the Datsun looked worse, the corner of the bonnet had concertinaed.

'Hey, keep it simple, man,' Tony said, leaning out of the passenger window.

'And you can bloody well stay out of it.'

Tony went silent, stayed in the car, drumming his hands on the dashboard.

'I'm calling the police. Could have killed me. Do you think it's OK to drive like that? Might be OK in Bangladesh, not here, mate. Shouldn't fucking be allowed to drive in this country.'

The traffic was building behind them, people swerving dangerously around the car, to get in a free lane. Khalid needed to say something – urgently – but he couldn't think what would help.

'Truly sorry, mate, I am truly. It was just an accident, I think we were both at fault.' He turned penitent, put his hands together in a gesture of supplication. 'Look, let me write you a cheque.' He groped around as if he had a cheque book in his inside jacket pocket. His fingers brushed the thick envelope with the Bahamas contract tucked inside it. He would have put his arms around that man at that moment and stood him a pint, if he could have eased the whole thing, and siphoned away his anger.

But this man was pure oxygen, waiting to find a spark, and now they had set him off.

'Let's settle this without police, hey?' said Khalid, and he wanted him to understand that it didn't need to be like that, all anger and accusation, that they were both free men, that they could move on, that there was an island waiting for him — that he was just about to leave this city anyway — the man just wasn't listening to him. The van driver was spinning in his own little world of pain, and he was dragging Khalid into that with him.

'I ain't got no reason to fear the coppers. You do, though.' And he gave him a smile, as if he'd been sent from Satan himself to ruin him.

'WHAT'S A CLEAN LICENCE?' ALIA ASKED FROM THE FLOOR, THE next afternoon, where she was dividing up the pieces of her jigsaw puzzle, putting the pieces with straight edges on one side, the jagged ones on the other. Khalid looked down at her. To her, a clean licence sounded like something wiped with a sponge, or put in the bath with bubbles. Clean licences, dirty licences. If only it was that simple.

'Clean licence?' Suzie repeated in a numb voice.

He was standing in the doorway, dishevelled, the bow-tie hanging lifelessly around his neck, like a defeated snooker player. For the first time it occurred to him that it was ridiculous to be talking about a new life in the Caribbean in the gathering dark of Hammersmith. On the television some blond queers were dancing about in cricket whites. One of them was carrying a teddy bear like Alia's, and looked as if he was about to cry. Behind the men were towers and spires and long green lawns, a make-believe England. Suzie had turned the volume down but she hadn't turned it off. She wasn't listening properly.

Tony had been decent. They had bailed Khalid about eleven in the morning. He had stayed with him, stood surety, and all the rest of it. Khalid would have done the same for him. He'd made his call to Suzie from the phone on the Custody Sergeant's desk, penitent and sad, about midnight, and she hadn't said much – he'd woken her up – and there was little use her coming out to the station, with Alia tucked up in her little bed and everything. They had kept him in overnight and Tony had come back in the morning with an egg roll and a newspaper, and tried to crack jokes.

All the time he wasn't thinking about the shame of it all, the embarrassment of losing his licence and not being able to drive, the pity of that dent in the Datsun's bonnet, which couldn't be easily righted, and the car that would never be the same – all these things were painful, but that wasn't what troubled him. He wasn't even thinking of himself, or the concrete bunk, cold against his spine through the blankets, or how the man in the Ford had sauntered off without so much as a parking ticket. No, what hurt him, and stopped him sleeping in that ugly cell all through the night, was his detailed knowledge of the process of getting to the Bahamas. Tony had known it too. That's why he'd been so nice, trying to sweeten the pill.

'You need a clean licence.'

'What?' Suzie said.

'A clean driving licence.'

'What do you mean?' Suzie switched off the television at last and pulled her cardigan around her bony shoulders.

'To make the application for the work permit. There's no way Playboy will take me now. It's over.'

'There must be something they can do, some strings they can pull?'

God, she was getting thin – he hadn't noticed. When did she last eat? He wasn't sure. They hadn't eaten a meal together at home for a while.

'They're strict, one of the strictest places in the world. And croupiers – you've got to be clean. No record, no black marks against you.'

'That's barmy – you've worked for them for years, Khalid.'

'It's just the way of the world.' He reached out and shook out the last one of her Bensons from the packet lying on the coffee table. He wasn't much of a smoker, not the way she was, drawing on the filter as if it was air itself, thirstily. Tonight he would try anything to steady himself.

'So we can't go?' She tried to look concerned, and she was concerned for him, for the bust-up and the crash and the magistrate's court. She would be doing all the driving from now on. But he could recognize when she cared about something – and this wasn't it. She was worried about him losing his licence but she wasn't disturbed by their new fortunes, and the fate of the move. She'd given up on their dream already; Suzie had already left their beach fantasy behind.

'Do you care?'

She didn't answer.

Playboy would be the sponsor of his work visa – that was the understanding, that was the agreement he had signed. The expectation had been that it would turn into citizenship or residency over time – eventually maybe even a green card – there might have been work in other clubs, like Miami or New York. They'd drop him like a hot potato now. There was nothing that any of them would be able to do – it was well out of their hands. And frankly, who would care? They were laying off staff all over the world, all those people in London just yesterday. He was just one more now, another lost soul they couldn't save.

'What are you going to do?' She didn't say we.

He'd rather she raged at him about the crash. Not this. As cold as the early morning air.

'We need to plan something, Khalid' – she waved her hand round the flat – 'there's mortgage payments on this place.'

God, he needed something, he couldn't say what. What time was it? William Hill was open for another half hour, that was a physical comfort, his body eased a notch. There was the possibility of Coral too. And if they were closed, then there were always the fruit machines in the pub. His brain was like a big calculator, computing times, odds and distances. How much money was left in his wallet – he found he wasn't listening to Suzie.

Alia tugged at his trouser leg, insisted on showing him the puzzle; she'd put it together quickly, a tree filled with parrots, in neon colours assembled in the middle of the floor. He glanced at it and summoned an approving sound, and then his brain was like the puzzle, and he stood on it, without meaning to, breaking up the shapes as he tried to get to the fridge for a tin of beer. He got a grip on himself.

'I can solve it, Suzie, I can fix this.'

He could win his way out of this. This was a near-miss. Wins came after near-misses. Every punter knew that. All he needed was a thousand, or twenty thousand. Who cares if you can't drive if you have a chauffeur? Who cares about a lousy night shift at a casino if you have thousands in the bank? He'd look back on this in a month, maybe a year, and it would all be bad memories, like a film he once watched, or as if it all happened to a younger, more foolish man.

She moved her hands nervously, rotating her fingers as if she was expecting to find a ring there, which had been mislaid. She reached for the cigarette packet.

'That was your last one.'

'Oh.' Her face fell with disappointment. She had her own calculations too. She had cash in her purse, at least twenty pounds. Today was the day she had picked up the child benefit from the post office.

'No duty free left?'

'It's all gone.'

There was usually a stash in the kitchen cupboard, brought by relatives and friends making stopovers, a lot of PIA people, a few from Air India. Sometimes they came at odd hours, bearing gifts, big cartons of Bensons and Silk Cut, bricks wrapped in cellophane. He sold two hundred last month. Sometimes they smuggled miniatures off the aircraft too, Jack Daniel's,

Gordon's, produced magically from cabin bags. Today it had all run out.

'Pass me your purse and I'll go for you.'

She almost handed him her purse, and considered, grasped it for a moment longer, and took out a ten. Enough for a little flutter, nothing serious, just to take the edge away.

'Don't be too long,' she frowned, and reached for the empty packet as if there might have been a cigarette in there, hidden in the corner of the foil, one that they had overlooked.

LITTLE PLASTIC FRAGMENTS SCATTERED ON THE TABLE, SHARDS of plastic, slashed signatures across the back. They could be assembled again like tiny jigsaws, and Alia started to play with the sharp pieces, putting her father's name back together.

'There's been no salary for at least four months,' Suzie was saying. Loan sharks circling on every side. 'Yes, well, he used to be a reliable family man. Married, employed, home-owning, fixed abode. All the boxes were ticked.'

Credit cards, at least seven of them. Access, American Express (at least two of those), Visa in rainbow colours, some of them had his name in different spellings and combinations. Each one had been as good as a new promise. Some had a different name on altogether.

Suzie had taken her kitchen scissors to them and scattered the pieces. She hung up the phone just as Khalid walked in.

He'd been out looking for work again. That was what he had said.

He hadn't got anywhere.

The bailiffs. The first time they came he was out. Suzie said she had hidden behind the sofa with Alia while they banged on the door and called through the letterbox. 'Mr Quraishi, we are from the credit agency, we need to talk to you.' The shadow of the man against the window, standing in the rose bushes, trying to look in.

The next time they were cleverer, they came early in the morning in a pack, and swooped like stormtroopers. Suzie had opened the door to take Alia to school and they were waiting round the side by the bins. The man wedged his foot in the door.

They filled up the living room and started fiddling with the plug sockets, disentangling the cables from the radio cassette player and the television. The television was on hire-purchase, and that was what they had come for. Only a few instalments left to pay, that was the cheek of it. Khalid didn't watch much, but minded for Suzie, who said she'd never find out what happened in *Dallas* now.

And he still hadn't quit. He still hadn't got away from the bookies. He'd just come from there, in fact. The search for work was fruitless, pointless, he was buggered if he was going to step into that Job Centre with all those riff-raff with snotty tissues and sob stories. No way he would take DSS. Like petitioners in a feudal village, wanting handouts. A punt was taking action, manly at least, a better use of time, he reasoned.

'Do you know what happened today at school? What happened to Alia?'

'No.' His communications with Suzie had shrunk to binary answers, yes and no.

She had a new variety of fury in her eyes, which was making him regret coming back home.

'A boy in her class said you worked at William Hill. Worked

there, Khalid, like a nine to five, as if it was your job.' Her laugh was bitter; it didn't suit her, detracted from her prettiness.

He was going to make it better, because a win was the quickest way to sort the whole mess, and it was so frustrating that Suzie just couldn't see that.

'I've spoken to Imran and Hasina,' she said, sweeping the shards of plastic from the tabletop into her cupped hand. 'They'll take you in, for a few weeks. Just while we clear our heads. I need to get things back on track here, Khalid, I can't do this anymore.'

He hadn't the foggiest what she was talking about, until she showed him his suitcase, which she had already packed.

12

On Thursday evening Penny collected him from Oxford station. She was waiting with the engine turning over, on a double yellow line. She had been listening to something on Radio 4 and was irritated to be disturbed when he got in the car.

'It's nearly over... do you mind if I just catch the end?' Like he'd never been away and not in a reassuring way. No kiss, no smile. She patted him on the hand before shifting into reverse.

It was often like this, her obvious readjustment to his presence. She didn't hide her self-sufficiency in the house: she'd been making tea with teabags in a cup instead of loose-leaf in a pot, eating at odd times and she'd started watching some dreadful crap on TV that they never would have watched together. It's like this now, on Thursdays, they rub against each other's habits, finding their way back to being a couple. He could commute – some of the other Oxfordshire MPs managed it – and once or twice he's thought about getting on the coach that trundles up and down the M40, he sees it sometimes turning into Victoria station. He could come home, impromptu, and surprise her by turning up mid-week with a bottle in hand. He hasn't managed it yet, and perhaps also, he doesn't quite admit to himself, his arrival would not be that much of a pleasant surprise. Disturbing the peace.

They drove in silence, away from the station and towards the centre of the city. Oxford was black and wet. Too late for the day-trippers, too early for the drunks.

'Are you going to see your mother this weekend?' she asked.

'I don't think I will, this weekend, no.'

She slowed at the traffic lights outside the Ashmolean Museum, and in the streetlights he could see the great classical pillars upholding a pediment on one side, the oversized flags of the Randolph Hotel on the other, bored doormen in top hats at the entrance.

'How's Zoe?'

'Pink hair this week. Don't say anything.'

'I thought the point was to be shocked.'

'It suits her, actually.'

His clever, infuriating Zoe, probably screaming her head off in a club somewhere with her androgynous friends. Ink around her fingernails from the lino printing. Denby never saw the process, just the end results. She was a good artist, his daughter, he could appreciate that, although he didn't know anything about art. She had a way of making black lines run across the page so that they invoked spirits, captured the movement of a flag waved. Political stuff, anti-fascist, being copied onto T-shirts and reproduced in small magazines.

'We can't even call them punks anymore – they are post-punk, apparently.'

He could see the argument for guilt. This man would be Zoe's real grandfather, maybe she had a right to know? She'd probably enjoy it, to have a story like that to latch on to. Nowadays with genetics and so on, what if this man – this Pole – was carrying a hereditary disease or something like that? Or was a murderer – or indeed, murdered?

How would it sound? Should he talk about it – on the record? He could tell his friends, let it leak out gently. It would make a nice little piece on the inside of the *Guardian* or the *Mirror*, maybe even Radio 4? He could show his human side and the discovery of these roots, they'd even print the black and white photograph of his father. Politician discovers real father was a wartime hero, or something like that. His fantasy goes further; a genealogist, bored and sympathetic, might pick up on it and dig the archives for him, and pinpoint the town, the village, excavate the birth certificates of his grandparents, unfurl the whole damn tree, a family bible inscribed with Catholic baptisms. There'd be sympathy – it was wartime after all – no one would think less of his mother, she might even be glad to see it come out in the open.

These were wild thoughts. Polish. It was an odd association. It just didn't fit with his public image. He heard the question: so you're not really English then? His campaign pamphlets even mentioned his father and his grandfather – rooted in the Cowley motor industry for several generations – his constituents knew him as a local man. This might change things, twist their perceptions of him. He could hear Peter's voice, which was, he would allow, often well tuned to the right frequency on these matters. They thought of Denby as one of their own. There were rumblings about politicians being placed in safe seats and jetted in from London, it's not a popular policy. One of his strong suits was that he belonged. He didn't want to complicate people's idea of himself. Anyway, it was private – a personal matter, best kept under wraps.

What was a little bit of DNA helix, a fluke, a twist of nature? He isn't going to start eating cabbage rolls or traipsing round Polish villages like a nostalgist. He isn't linked to this man who had no hand in his upbringing. It was Dad who sat round a tea table with him night after night talking about Oxford United's struggles and came to his wedding wearing a new suit; he has had nothing to do with this stranger at all.

It's not as if he looked exactly like him. The uniform was generic, and the haircuts, even the smiles from wartime. There was an essence, though, something in the eyes which made him recognize his genetic past, that there was a line which reached back to this man.

And Penelope too. Whichever way he looks at it, Penny would expect him to share that conversation with her, and expect him to recognize its import. He swallowed. There would be a right time.

'Sometimes you shouldn't speak your mind, Mark,' Penny reprimanded, turning right. He wasn't sure if she was still talking about Zoe's hair.

They drove past some college glories in the dark – the spires of St Mary's and All Souls, the medieval towers of Magdalen on the bridge, gargoyles gurning and laughing all the way, and towards the roundabout which marked the centre of his constituency, and the start of the real city. He wasn't sentimental about the university. It was a seasonal affair, students were transient, they made fickle constituents. His real people lived to the east, across the Isis, in the scruffy brick suburbs of Cowley, on the bus routes, and in the plant that would be pressing and joining even now, as a fresh set of workers came in for their night shift.

They parked on a side-street, and as they turned the corner and walked back to their place on the Iffley Road, Penny looped her arm through his, as if they were coming back from the cinema or after a bottle of Chianti in the local Italian.

That morning she'd done a second round of plastic surgery. A nine-year-old boy. Penny was assembling one side of his face, restoring it, as she liked to say, as if it was furniture.

'I think we'll do well by him,' Penny said.

'Rather you than me,' Denby said. He wouldn't have the stomach, couldn't have dealt with the blood, the tiny, crucial stitching, the risk, the parents, any of it.

He was glad he hadn't said anything. He should pick his moment.

He dug out his keys from his jacket pocket, the pleasure of his own key-ring in his hand, the anticipation of his real life, the fakery of London dissolving in the warmth of Penny, next to him on their doorstep.

'Is something up with you, Mark?'

'It's funny, all this coming and going, up and down from London. Sometimes I lose track of where I am.'

'Well, you're home. Forget politics for a night.'

The house. Considerably bigger than the house he grew up in. A piano, classics and atlases, a dresser stacked with nicely matching porcelain plates, and all sorts of furniture they'd bought in moments of debated enthusiasm.

On the mantelpiece Penny had arranged a few cards that had arrived during the week. A couple of invitations to local events, a flyer for Zoe's end of year show.

Penny had left a spiral-bound pad on the table. He flicked through the familiar names, while she gathered supper from the fridge.

Penelope was a second-year medical student at UCL when they met. He was in the Marlborough Arms and she was holding court at a table covered with tacky beer mats and dregs of beer. She was wearing a turquoise sweater pulled in around her waist, and large hoop earrings, and had everyone listening, as she spoke in between quick inhalations of cigarette. She was talking about *The Female Eunuch*, expanding the arguments, making gentle critiques, relating it to her own experiences, the men assembled around her agog, as they drank their pints and none of them dared to argue.

He found out much later there was a tradition of women going to university in her family, which went back to the 1920s. Being brainy didn't mean being frumpy anymore.

She left the pub that night with a bespectacled mathematician, who looked several years younger, and Denby felt spurned. He hadn't said a word to her.

It was pure chance that he saw her in a café off Russell Square a few weeks later, and now he knew his moment, and asked if there was space at her table. She was less outrageous than when he'd seen her first, less tipsy, a little more open to other people's ideas. She said she had exams to study for although she put away her textbook and made room for his pot of tea. The same earrings. He felt emboldened.

It turned out she came from a big, ramshackle pile near Bristol, with a Tudor fireplace in the kitchen. All sorts of things in the attic, she said, bits of armour and a rocking horse that Gladstone's children had ridden on. She didn't take him back there to meet her parents for a long time. When she did, the house was five times as big as he could have imagined, the type of thing his own parents paid entry to. She was shaking off the dust of the house, she didn't want to be smeared with it. She told him she wanted to live in an ordinary house.

If he'd met her a few years earlier she would have been too frightening, too assured about her place in the fashionable sets, au fait with the names of Scottish country houses. He would have run. University for him had been a steep curve, the scrabble to find a footing with people who knew how to open wine or had already been on aeroplanes, and didn't even think anything of it. But he'd been a student for five years in London by the time he met Penny, he had a master's degree in macroeconomics, he'd eased into the wide world, and although he still got a familiar anxiety when he pulled up in his classmates' sweeping driveways, he had sat around in enough dinner parties not to be daunted by the sheer prospect.

She wasn't steeped in the party like him, though her instincts were against her family traditions. He wanted to keep gazing at her, to see if she was honest, if there was something dirtier, less palatable under the surface. He'd never found it.

Over the years she hadn't taken a penny from her family, and the estate would all pass to her elder brother in any case. She looked on from the sidelines, when she needed to be photographed for the leaflets, or brought out on the big days, like the election count. Otherwise they had given each other their freedom, found a way of running on parallel tracks, of having lives that sometimes touched.

She returned bringing in a plate of leftovers covered in cling film. Some cold roast chicken and potato salad. In her other hand she had half a bottle of red with the cork pushed into it.

She found two tumblers in the dresser, and pulled up a chair to the table.

He was turning through the pad with the usual list of their neighbours and friends. Their Advent party had become an annual tradition, ever since Zoe was a baby, and the thing had grown so that for many of their friends it was an annual fixture, one of the few times they got to see each other every year.

'Having a look at the names? It's a few more than usual this year. Do you think we should invite George again?'

'Well, he never comes.'

'We've never struck him off.'

George had been in the year above Denby at UCL. He was the son of a butcher from Kent. As students they had recognized each other, sons of working class men from the provinces, quicker than the rest of their cohort and competing to get the best marks in their exams.

They had drifted apart over the years.

'Let's leave him on the list,' Denby said, pouring himself a glass of wine. 'It can't do any harm.'

That night, Penelope slipped into bed beside him, and tucked herself under his arm, while he lay flat on his back staring at the ceiling. She rolled his pyjama buttons between thumb and finger, as if she was making playdough cherries with children. He found her attractive, he always had done, in the way that he found eating a roast lunch appealing or sitting in a sun-lounger with a long drink and the last of the summer sun on his face. It was comforting and predictable and that didn't stop his enjoyment. In fact, it might have even increased it. He didn't think much about it, one way or the other. The idea of not having sex with Penelope panicked him, it would be like becoming homeless, or losing his mind. She was there, and he was there, and their world spun as it always had done, and he liked it that way.

13

THE NEXT MORNING THE HOUSE WAS EMPTY WHEN HE ROSE AT eight. He showered and fixed a puncture on his rear bike tyre, before heading out again.

There was a group hanging around outside the Job Centre, smoking, and one of them waved at him as he passed on his bike.

Denby found his prematurely and completely bald head an asset these days. Alongside his natural slenderness, he had the aura of a racing cyclist, a look of aerodynamism, someone energetic who moved quickly from A to B. What had seemed an annoyance had turned into an advantage, making him instantly recognizable, and the incongruity of his baldness and his quite youthful chiselled features, he was told by Zoe, worked surprisingly well.

The constituency office was a tatty place rented above a video shop, with two rooms, his office at the back and a waiting room at the front separated by a glass door. Amazing how many people viewed Oxford through a haze and saw what they wanted to see, a kind of wonderland. Not the teenager, not much older than Zoe, in a sleeping bag near the doorway of Ratner's, always reading the same book, or the man trying to wrangle his tot in a buggy through the door of the pub. Not the Oxford of puddles and pigeon shit.

A small crowd had already arrived for his surgery – some of them regulars who came every week, sitting on the row of orange chairs, underneath public health posters pinned on noticeboards on every available space, in several languages, warning about AIDS and how to claim DSS. Boxes of handouts and leftovers from the election were still stacked under the desks. Penelope had come in once and brought a pot plant, and never returned.

Denby liked the way the stairs shook a little as he ascended.

Peter was already there, with a mug in his hand. He closed the door so that he could speak to him privately in the office the second he arrived. Peter had been a terrific asset during the election, propelling him into this Labour seat against all the odds. The way he lifted him clean off the ground at the count, and how they stood in the car park of the Town Hall, exhausted and pissed, watching the sun come up over the city. But the man hadn't calmed down. His mind was one great printer churning out press copy. He was a bundle of fury, raging against the government, as if he was never going to stop campaigning.

'Go on.'

'Word is there was a tour laid on, after hours, for some hotshot from British Aerospace. You've not got wind of anything you're not sharing?'

'No, not at all. Not a sniff of it.'

'Well then, Mark, if you're sure, we need you as our eyes and ears. Tories will flog off anything when they get the chance. The lads are going back to the buses rather than live in the shadow of it. We know what's coming – only got to look at the pits to see.'

The rumour mills never stopped and Denby couldn't help but take them with a dose of scepticism. The government was going to close the South Plant one day, no, it was going to be the North one the next, jobs were going to fly to Longbridge, no, it would be Swindon. These words spread about, without substance, doing more harm than good. But there was an underlying truth – something was going to give.

'And the big squeeze is on. Breaks back down from fifteen to ten, no washing-up time anymore. And union right in the pocket of management. What are the men to do?'

Denby remembered a man he'd met recently, a worker from the press shop:

Nearly thirty years they've had me – I'm not hanging around for candles and cake – going to take the payout and get out. Got myself a part-timer up at one of the colleges, sitting in the lodge, doffing my cap to profs – how hard's that going to be?

What could anyone do? That old factory Denby was raised to respect, and yet, when he saw it now, there was an old-fashioned look about it, the funny little brick entrance with the clock for the workers. It belonged to the 1930s, not the new century that was approaching. And those cars, could they honestly say they could compete with what Honda was making? What about R & D? The life was going out of it, and they all knew it. They were digging their heels in and saying it must never change, pretending they could keep the Germans and the Japs away.

Denby wanted to stick up for their jobs, but the lads themselves were in disarray, the AEU and the TGWU and the Labour Council all at odds, and no one sure how to steer things forward, how to keep these workers' lives on track. Soldered to the place. How to swim against the tide, the way the world was pitching on its axis, shaking them off like ants?

Denby would never admit it to Peter, barely to himself, but there was a part of him that knew they had lost the battle. They could only pick up some scraps from the table. There hadn't been a single victory over layoffs for years. They wouldn't be able to buy back the council houses, tarted up and sold on within months of sale. And a secret part of himself, barely articulated, wondered if there was a middle ground, a way of squaring the circle. A third way. Getting investment from outside, to keep the show on the road. If the Japanese turned up with sacks of yen, would that be such a bad thing? Kinnock and the shadow cabinet, digging their heels in, bloody Tories this, bloody Tories that, Denby couldn't help believing that they were going to have to change, to adapt, to modernise. They needed to be able to win.

'Look, Peter, I've got something to show you.' The leisure centre was their dream. Their joint fantasy. And Denby was making it happen day by day. Bringing together council players, local charities, donors. The site was vast – leisure centre didn't do it justice – Olympic-size swimming pool, state-of-the art adventure playground. A skate park for the teens, the architect had even thought of so-called rough areas, where the hotters could spray graffiti, and smoke, but all in a way that would contain them, and keep them safely hemmed in.

The blueprints unrolled on the desk, too large for the surface area. Intricate details – electricity connections, water mains – rectangles of floor space, and changing rooms and carefully planted parks.

'Imagine the flow of people through the automatic doors, Peter. Skinny-legged old men with their towels in the early morning, the excited kids coming in for the wave machine on Sunday afternoons...'

The cranes were hard at work in Temple Cowley; he could just see the tops of the heavy machinery moving, a stately dance, above the treeline. Occasionally he saw flashes of neon yellow, the jackets of workmen, in hard hats.

Peter welled up a little, and patted Denby on the flank, like a winning racehorse.

'This is what it is all about, Pete. This is what we're making happen. Focus on this.'

Back in London. The porter in uniform acknowledged Mark Denby as he entered the mansion block, with an absent-minded gesture, like a royal wave, though he never looked up from his newspaper.

He'd rented this studio after the election, as a place to stay on weekdays, when Parliament was sitting. The carpet in the hallway had thick pile, like a hotel, so you couldn't hear people walking down the corridors. Denby couldn't name any of his fellow residents.

Jarringly different to Cowley; faceless and alienating.

Denby made a cup of tea in the kitchenette; below the window he heard the sound of a taxi as an anonymous neighbour came or went. The heavy doors of a black cab slamming and reversing.

The milk in the fridge smelled bad, it had started to separate, a creamy layer floating on the top. He sighed, a short inner struggle – he couldn't survive on black tea until the morning

— reached for his keys and took his jacket from the peg near the door.

The winter night had come down quickly, and there was a streak of violet left in the sky.

A double-decker roared past and puddle water overspilled the gutter onto his shoes. Everyone else was moving in the other direction, away from the Tube and along the broad pavements, towards their flats and the tall stucco townhouses on the other. All of them alone, blank-faced, unencumbered by heavy shopping or small children.

At the corner shop the man who ran it, fat and jowly, sat with the telephone tucked under his ear as he always did, his palm resting upwards on the surface of the counter so that he could take money without moving an inch or without acknowledging his customer in any way. He needed a shave and his shirt was open at the top, showing thick black curls of chest hair that pushed between the buttons and spread right up to his neck, speaking rapidly in a language that Denby didn't recognize. Denby reached inside the small fridge and took out a pint; he checked the best-before date and there were barely twenty-four hours before this milk would be yellowing too. The whole place smelled sweaty, of stale spices. He sighed and took it to the till.

As he took the money for the milk, the man continued to talk without turning his head. With the briefest of glances, as if he could tell the value of the money by its weight alone, the man flipped his hand into the till and turned the change onto the desk, palm-down. 'Thanks,' said Denby. No response, no nod of the head, more jabbering in Arabic or whatever it was. As he left the shop, Denby glanced at the porn mags stacked on the other side of the counter, brazenly on sale, women staring like petulant children, legs spread defiantly.

For some reason, for the first time since the weekend, Denby thought again of that peculiar Pakistani bank, BCCI, and wondered what, if anything, Linda had managed to turn up.

14

OXFORD WAS DRAB AND MONOTONOUS AFTER KARACHI. EVERYONE wearing morbid coats of black and grey. She waited for the new term to begin, browsing the rows of stationery in Ryman's, checking her reading lists in case they needed refreshing. She cooked simple cheap food for herself, making enough for Stefan in case he was there: baked potatoes, tacos. He tended not to come back until later, so she ate in front of the TV by herself. She banked a small cheque, money earned for the additional work involved in marking some exam papers, and spent it on a haircut.

The week before term started, Stefan went to Stockholm for a few days to visit his parents, and she tried to clean up some more. One day she forced herself to dig a flowerbed and plant bulbs that might come up in the summer. She wanted to feel a connection with the earth. There was nothing, just irritation at the dirt wedged under her fingernails.

'How was Pakistan?' a few friends asked. Most people hadn't even noticed her absence. And all the time, she looked away from the memories, and turned her mind away from the water. She didn't think about Portsmouth, and she told herself not to dwell on any of it. The sea is a long way from here, she thought. I am landlocked.

ON THURSDAY NIGHT SHE HAD DINNER AT COLLEGE. SHE KNEW the drill of lukewarm fish and austere portraits.

Thick candlesticks and cruets were dotted along the long tables, and she clambered unsteadily over the edge of the bench. The High Table was perpendicular to them, where the most senior Fellows and their guests looked down on them from on high, like judges. Waiters shuffled nervously behind them, young people earning extra money, filling up glasses with wine, bringing and taking soup.

At the High Table she noticed the Provost talking with a few guests, and a sight that made her look twice. A recognizable face from the TV. Lord Denby of Littlemore, a well-known politician. That unmistakable profile, Denby's famous domed head. The tabloids had made much of his ability to make baldness attractive; he was one of the early adopters of something which had become fashionable, like a certain type of action hero, the eyes and brows had a commanding presence. He had been a senior cabinet minister for a short time, was pushed up to the Lords, a Labour peer. Thinner than on the television, and more lined, another version of himself.

Her table was made from a polished plank of oak so wide that she could barely hear her colleague who was sitting opposite her, and they soon gave up trying to speak loudly across the benches.

Marooned on the end of the bench with two other people that she didn't know, Alia attempted conversation with a very shy medievalist on her left, a Fellow at the college, stilted talk, with questions and answers volleyed once, like bad tennis. She soon had the impression that the woman would prefer silence.

On her other side was a man in designer glasses and cufflinks and slicked-back hair.

It turned out that he was an accountant, working for KPMG, one of the big four. He was an alumnus returning for an event the following evening when he expected that the college would try and squeeze him to make a donation. He was quite endearing. He audited multinationals and was falsely modest about his unjustified wealth, and his life in Docklands, and how boring his job had become.

'Have you ever heard of BCCI?' she asked.

He spluttered, and had to raise his napkin to his mouth.

'Of course. It was our rivals who messed it up.'

'Who?'

'Price Waterhouse. They made a pig's ear of it.'

'What went wrong?'

'The bank was rotten to the core – not a leg to stand on. No real assets, being bailed out from the personal account of an Abu Dhabi prince. It should have been shut down in the 1980s but it went on and on. And Price Waterhouse were the auditors, they filed reports saying everything was dandy, and the Bank of England signed them off.'

'So they cooked the books?'

'Accountants don't use that kind of language.' He made a mock frown and sipped some wine. 'Although let's just say that the Bank had its own part to play. The blind Old Lady.'

'I don't understand, how can you miss fraud as an auditor?'

'Ah, you know, not checking where the loans are actually going, where the money is coming from, letting trails go cold. It was the Americans who busted it and called them out – I remember it because it was my first year in the job and overnight everyone was clamping down, talking about regulation, the old boys didn't like it.' He was warming to his theme. 'Why are you interested?'

His name was Nathan. His self-deprecation was endearing. She almost told him about her father and then didn't, because what would she say? That he had vanished and he was doing something, God knows what, for BCCI?

A dead-end to the conversation, maybe even souring the mood, to make it personal, to make it about herself.

'I read about it and I just got interested,' she said blandly. He wasn't so stupid and probably guessed that she was linked somehow; perhaps he assumed her parents were grocery shop owners, with a small savings account, planning for her wedding, bemoaning the loss of their lifetime savings.

She could look all of these other things up. There were trials and accounts and reports that had been presented in Parliament and on Capitol Hill. 'Just Google them,' he said.

The Provost and Lord Denby swept past them, along the line of portraits and under the large doorway which led out of the dining hall.

'If you ever want to know more about it, about accounting...' They both smiled, it was the worst chat-up line ever. Nathan handed her his card. 'Come and have a day out in the City, it's not all bad, you know.'

SHE CALLED HIM ON THE SUNDAY NIGHT.

She left a message on his answerphone, a central London number, imagining the room she was calling – probably a low bed, and manly gadgets, a Rubik's Cube, Newton's cradles.

Angular and clean, she thought, looking around her kitchen, where Stefan's cooking pot and dishes still stood decaying in the sink. He called straight back and they arranged to meet at his office in Canary Wharf on the following Tuesday afternoon, towards the end of the day. It wasn't quite clear if they were meeting to talk about Price Waterhouse or to go out for dinner.

The woman at the reception was aloof and polished in a way that Alia didn't see often in Oxford, layers of dusky make-up, hair razor sharp, shimmering above the marble block that she manned. Alia wondered for a moment if she shouldn't have made more of an effort, as she untangled her lanyard and rearranged it over her scarf.

Nathan met her at the front desk under the atrium.

He had the brisk confidence of being on his own turf. The building had only been opened the previous year, and he made a joke about how they hadn't found a window cleaner yet.

Miles of glass, it wasn't possible to imagine this much glass. The glassy sky above them, competing with other colossal buildings she'd never seen, on other continents. It was oddly silent, for such a vast place, with only a cleaner in corporate overalls buffing the floor with a humming, rotating machine.

'Come on, I've got stuff for you,' Nathan said, as if she was an old friend, and he did a sort of jazz slide on the marble towards the lift, and led her briskly through the security barrier and then up all the way to a boxy room on the fifteenth floor. Strips of hot pink over the Thames, perhaps he was trying to impress her? But he settled her away from the best view and placed a cardboard box file on the table.

'Haven't you got too much to do, to be fussing over this?'

'Ah, auditing is easier than it looks.'

He pulled out two black ring binders, one for each report, and showed her some newspaper clippings he'd also printed off and assembled in a clear wallet.

'Presents for you. Two reports into the BCCI affair, one American and the other British, the Kerry and the Bingham. So you can see that I wasn't just telling tales out of school.'

She flicked through the Kerry one first, presented to the Senate Committee on Foreign Relations in 1992.

'It doesn't muck about,' he said.

She skimmed over the earnest sentences.

'The murky realms of underhand dealing and illegality,' she scowled, in a faux shocked voice, trying to match Nathan's tone. 'This is too cartoonish to be real, surely?' she said as she flicked through, scanning at speed.

The litany was vulgar, and it was clichéd. Billions of dollars; money laundering, bribery, support of terrorism, arms trafficking, the sale of nuclear technologies; prostitution; income tax evasion, smuggling and people smuggling, 'a panoply of crimes limited only by the imagination of its officers and customers,' she read out loud to him. It all conjured images of dastardly masterminds.

Then a line on the first page startled her so much that she went silent, her smile fell away, stopping on the page.

'BCCI's conception, growth, collapse, and criminality are inextricably linked with the personality of its founder, Agha Hasan Abedi, who in turn was a product of the unique conditions of Muslim India in the final period of British rule prior to partition, and the first years after partition.'

Her heart lurched. These were her father's people. Which part of that catalogue had entangled him?

Nathan looked at her. 'You OK? Want a coffee?'

There was a stainless steel espresso machine in one corner and he started clinking cups and spoons, as if to give her a breathing space, leaving to find cold water with a metallic jug in his hand.

The facts of the BCCI case were easy to see on the surface, the way they were presented by the newspapers when it tumbled in 1991. It was a newspaper editor's dream: dodgy bank, oriental wheeler-dealers, deception by crooks, phony loans, shady customers, red ink, spilt ink. 'The culture of the bank was criminal,' pronounced one banker in stripes, standing on the steps of the Bank of England.

It was a place left to run free, not checking what was coming in, what was going out, not securing its collateral in banking parlance, or basically not giving a shit if it got caught out or not, if things could be repaid or not. It was a deep web of honour and prestige, propped up by Sheikh Zayed of Abu Dhabi and his wives and retainers and cousins and friends who kept the money swirling around so fast, across so many accounts, nobody could untangle the twisted knots of the thing when it finally came to light.

The facts were all there to be seen, plainly. A number of investigators had spent months and years, digging up the dirt, chasing the leads from Abu Dhabi to Geneva.

'You can keep all this stuff, no need to read it all now. But it was messy, wasn't it?' Nathan sat down with the coffees and started leafing through the files too.

'You see, the auditors should have said, "whoa, hold on a

minute, boys, what's going on here?" But they didn't. And that's where it all went wrong, because it ran on for so damn long. Someone should have called time.'

'And KPMG wouldn't get up to those tricks?'

'Might if we were allowed to, if there weren't rules. But there are, and we stick to them.'

'Can I just read this for a bit longer? Then we can go and get some food?'

They ended up having noodles at a place that was as new and corporate as the building that Nathan worked in, sitting side by side on bar stools at the window.

They discussed the current war, and where they stood on the demonstrations. Nathan had been resigned to the inevitability of invasion, and said some dark things about the last one, between Iran and Iraq. 'Those two neighbours trying to extinguish each other, and the rest of the world pouring in weapons, and fanning the flames. No one remembers that one.' She was embarrassed not knowing more about that, and he said that he would send her a book.

He had got back into Christianity at Oxford; his parents were teachers and Sunday church-goers, and he'd lost touch with his faith as a student, until he had tipped up at the church on St Aldate's in his final year. 'Hungover, not sure why I even went in,' and now he was setting up the Alpha course in East London, 'helping people get into it.' He didn't preach and she thought he was scrupulously honest and very good-looking, and wished she could find him attractive.

It would have been like trying to light damp wood. Poor kindling. They both recognized it.

On the way back, she took the Docklands Light Railway,

gliding over the starry skyscrapers of West India Quay, London's new East, watched the disco ball towers recede, as enticing as another planet, until the train levelled out towards Bank.

The next day, she went back through the files. She laid out her things carefully in her usual library ritual. Sharpened pencils, library card, laptop, and a book she should have been reading spread out before her.

Lord Bingham was precise, but a man constrained, saying the most he could, censuring at the limits of what was advisable, of what was permissible for a man of his station. A judge put in a position, the terms of the report so narrowly defined. Boxed in by his remit, trying his best. Given his little balls to play with. The things he must have known.

There was something she couldn't find, though. She kept searching for it, an appendix to Bingham.

Appendices 1 to 8 recount this history in greater detail, much of it subject to statutory restrictions on disclosure, some of it sensitive for other reasons and some of it subject to a high security classification.

The next day she read it over again. She checked library catalogues, got nowhere, and asked a specialist librarian to help.

Appendix 8 was still unpublished, blocked from public view, sealed. 'It might be released in the year 2042,' said the librarian, looking up from his terminal with a sceptical look at Alia.

What did all this have to do with Khalid? It was unclear. She took out the passport from her bag, opened it up and scrutinized his face again. What did she have to go on? Some business dealings on the Edgware Road, BCCI, the passport, the lighter – she looked at the documents in front of her, trying to find some pattern in it all, and some sense that this connected to her own life, asking how a man's life could be ensnared in all this, and how her father could have been dragged under the water.

Nathan was as good as his word. A book with scuffed fly leaves arrived in a jiffy bag the following morning. Postage paid by the firm. Nathan had underlined some parts of it in pencil. The subject was the war of the 1980s.

A big crack across the Middle East. The world had poured in its weapons and the earth soaked up men and money: artillery radar guidance systems, rapier surface to air missiles, MiGs and Tomcats and Gazelles and Cobras and Chinooks. She read of men shaking inside craters, the earth pocked from bombs, planes seeking them at low altitude.

She read of an abandoned town, a stray cat wandering the empty rooms, its ribs protruding, its tail a stump. A boy who threw himself across barbed wire, to make a bridge so his friend could cross. The promise of victories plucked like ripe plums, the sweet taste of martyrdom on the tongue. Trenches dug in lines, with turrets and barbed wire, men lying sleepless waiting to gun down or be gunned down. Verdun in the desert.

The sounds of it washed over her: the ambulance sirens, the azan, the motorbikes weaving through the marketplace, the piff-puff of cluster bombs. She found more books. For the rest of the week she read without taking notes, haphazardly, from earnest memoirs to dense articles in specialist journals. Men in fatigues in the dust, running with bazookas on their shoulders. A war in which the endgame was blowing your opponent to smithereens, in which no holds were barred, and chemicals hung over villages like dense clouds on a rainy day. The kind of war you thanked God you never saw.

Child-soldiers, in green bandanas, given the plastic keys to the gates of paradise. A teenager riding his bicycle with one hand on the handle bars and the other gripping a grenade, waving goodbye, showing off to his girlfriend. Sky and earth the colour of sandbags. The maimed, the mothers crushed and their uncontrollable weeping. Scorpion tanks gritted with dust. An interminable war, men pitted against each other, wave upon wave of death, thousands dead in each grasp, trying to get a grip on pieces of the desert. The sand trailing through stiff fingers.

15

HE HAD BEEN STAYING WITH IMRAN ON THE PUT-YOU-UP FOR seven months. It was just a temporary arrangement. Imran's twin boys liked having him there, and he hardly ever came back empty-handed in the evenings – sweets, yo-yos, little things – he enjoyed choosing them at the newsagents. Hasina was tolerant, and said repeatedly that she liked having someone with a proper appetite to feed, and he was very respectful, careful not to return smelling of alcohol, keeping gum in his pocket. The food was good – big pots of homemade dal, roti and meat stews – and he ate heartily, felt healthier, was sleeping a little better during the past fortnight. They insisted it was no big deal to feed him because they bought in bulk at Makro cash-and-carry.

Still, it wasn't a big house, just a terrace with one bathroom, and he didn't want to get in their way, and sometimes he felt that he needed to stay out a bit longer. Lately he had found himself on the Edgware Road several times after work, walking without a destination, making a small coffee last in a café, slowing his steps a little to delay his arrival. He preferred to take his things to the launderette and this had the added advantage of acting as an excuse for his absences – Hasina offered, of course – but he couldn't bring himself to hand over his soiled underwear. So, often he waited for the tumbledryer to end its churning, and read the newspaper and it was warm in there.

He had been staying away from the fruit machines, and walking straight past the bookies. Partly that had become necessity. It had all got very bad, he knew that. Rock bottom, Suzie called it, though that was exaggeration. The bank manager wouldn't look him in the eye anymore, his credit all dried up like an old river, credit cards all useless – he had kept one American Express, printed with an alternative version of his name, but even that was confiscated last month at Marks & Spencer by a zealous cashier who did her utmost to embarrass him in front of the other customers in the queue.

Suzie had sliced his cheque books in half with big pinking shears with jagged edges, the sort used by tailors for cutting cloth. All his streams had been cut off. Imran wouldn't lend him a penny, under clear instructions from Suze. 'Sorry, mate,' he said and shrugged. A clean slate, that's what he had said. There was no point crying over it, over spilt milk – over her. He knew he should start giving her some money for Alia soon. Maintenance, that's what they called it. That's what he should do. Maybe it was all for the best. Still, he missed the horses. Badly. Even when he was losing it was better than this. Without the peaks and troughs – life as a flat line – what use was that?

He had started working as a croupier at the Grosvenor Victoria on the Edgware Road a few weeks after the break-up. Imran had helped broker that through a friend, no minor thing, considering how awkward jobs had become for everyone and what a state he'd been in.

His salary had to be handed over to his creditors, after tax; the rest was hand to mouth.

The Vic was like a gaming supermarket, in a totally different league to Playboy, and not in a good way. Khalid resented the disco pop which blared out in the lobby and the tacky red chairs, which reminded him of a Beefeater restaurant that Suzie's parents had insisted on the one time they had gone to visit them in Doncaster. Much scruffier than Playboy with a different clientele – the punters serious as sin, even though the stakes were lower. There was no real pride in the club, and the customers – nearly all men – coming in for the tables, and not much else. Quite a salary cut. Not that he was complaining. The best thing to be said about the place was that it was dull enough to avoid attention, which meant it was in no danger of closing.

One Sunday in October he was flicking through a days-old copy of the *Standard*, sitting on a ledge in the launderette, the big drums rumbling behind him. On the third page, in black and white, taken with a tele lens. Adnan Khashoggi sitting at a café table lit from every angle with the white light of the Mediterranean, in some beachfront café in Monaco. His yacht was one of the specks in the harbour behind him, and the café chairs were covered with linen and tied with big floppy bows. Opposite him sat a haughty woman, in ruffles and a choker. Adnan had his little hand on top of the woman's hand, clutching the fingers, as if pinning a butterfly into position. At the side, just at the edge of the picture, Lucky, at another table, his bright dark eyes fixed on his master.

Something boiled inside him, something he used to feel at the bookies or watching the ball jump around the wheel, the feeling of being alive, and of a game about to start.

'Know anything about Adnan Khashoggi?' he asked casually.

'Adnan Khashoggi?' Imran gave him a sharp look. They

were sitting in Imran's kitchen that evening, their dirty plates still lying on the table, while Hasina put the boys to bed.

'He came into Playboy once, some time last year.'

'Stay well clear if I was you.'

'I've got a phone number, for one of his people.'

'Ah, shit, Khalid.'

'He's got class. Elegance.'

'Not the hanger-on?'

'No, not him. Mr K.'

'He's a camel driver that behenchod.' Imran didn't usually swear.

'There's a lot of talk – who knows the truth?'

'I've seen enough of this world to know where the stuff comes from, where the stuff goes.' Imran was on his high horse.

'He's not a goon. Just clever. Playing to win.'

'Selling the big stuff, your man.'

'Since when did you become the imam? And he's not my man.'

'He's doing the devil's work.' Imran had got up and turned his back, clattering at the kitchen worktop. He started to clear the table, screwing the lids onto the pickle jars and pouring the leftover gravy into a Tupperware tub.

'Ah Imran, come on, import-export, no harm in that.'

'So where's his money coming from? Lots of swimming pools coming out of the desert.'

'And don't you want to make money?'

'Not like that. And not that sort of money.'

'Well, I don't want a house in St John's Wood either.'

And as he had said it, Khalid thought, I do want just that. I want to be a lord of my manor, with the girls off to department stores for shopping, Suzie stepping out of the car with a Cartier diamond like the north star weighing her hand down, and the doormen bending down to help her out of the car. Alia in bows and petticoats behind her, racing horses in a paddock somewhere and Roedean, and a little bell that brings people running to me with a tray of cold mango lassi or a cold beer. Good schools, private schools, my girl should be around the best kind of people.

It's the closest to a personal creed he had ever had. And for no apparent reason, he heard the tinkle of the bell on his father's desk. The tea brought out to his study in porcelain cups, the tray lined with French lace.

They all had it, these players: Hefner, Khashoggi. It was just a spin away. Why should he not have it too? To be the paymaster. Nothing else in the world could give you authority, and respect. When you spoke people would not only listen, they would do what you asked. And the best thing of all was how you could give to others, please others, and bring them up with you to a place of delight and mastery.

It was actually his right. His ancestors had stomped all over North India in the eighteenth century, they had the Mughals quaking in their boots for a few years. And his grandmother's cousin was a Nawab, introduced to him at a family gathering in India when he was a child. The sunlight, slanting onto the man and his pinstripe suit, the best-looking man he'd ever set eyes on, as if he'd walked off a film set. He'd stuffed a foreign chocolate into Khalid's little mouth and patted him on the cheek, dismissively, while he turned to someone else.

So he hadn't lied to Suzie – everyone in his extended family in Karachi was related to some Nawabi household or other, that's just how it was; it wasn't an achievement, when everyone intermarried and had so many kids. Nonetheless, there was a pride in him, in the blood, and Suze had liked it, and understood it. Better than her own grey hometown. 'Married to royalty, put that in your pipe and smoke it,' she'd said to some imaginary teacher who'd slighted her at her comprehensive.

Deep within him was the desire to be a princeling, a little lord, but that was where his logic failed him, because those sorts of people didn't ever have to think about making it, they just had to keep it and look the part. And Khalid was an expert in looking the part. Making it, though – well, that was a challenge. And he still believed that he could rely on his old-world charm, that something about his entitlement would shine through, and that's exactly what he expected K would see too.

That evening he dialled the operator and reversed the charges. That was a good solution, he told himself. This way the phone call wouldn't show on Imran's BT statement. He waited for thirty seconds that stretched and wheeled into another time zone, and then he heard the operator confirm that the number had been accepted.

'We met, a while ago, at Playboy, before it got closed down.'

'I wondered to myself would that bastard ever dare pick up the phone.' Lucky's distinctive voice made him smile, like he had met him yesterday, like all the time in between and all that had happened since was immaterial.

'Well, here I am.'

THREE NIGHTS LATER, LUCKY CAME INTO THE VIC BY HIMSELF, and waited for Khalid's break. A dead-ringer for a novice punter, in a leather jacket, starting out, bound to lose to the house, the sort who got taken for a ride. Khalid was dealing blackjack and wasn't surprised to see him sitting there on a bar stool, after the jolt of recognition, the old lingering flavour of that first encounter, the thrill of the kid. Lucky sat looking over the shoulders of the players at his table.

The punters were casual walk-ins, one in a bright red sweater who fancied himself as a card sharp, but Khalid knew he had them licked as soon as he saw their faces. They were playing for peanuts. He shuffled two decks simultaneously, then flicked through the packs with his thumbs, held symmetrically, so that the cards beat as fast as a bird's wings. 'No more bets.' He dealt. Two of them went bust immediately. Just the other fellow in red was left, thinking he knew what he was doing. Khalid's own hand wasn't great, a queen of clubs and a three of diamonds, but he knew he could get closer to twenty-one if the sharpie didn't stick. The punter in red hesitated, twisted, drew a five. He stood at nineteen now and looked smug. But Khalid calculated in a flash that with that many aces and queens out on the table, he still stood a chance. Twist, he said, and pulled a seven.

All the time, Khalid pretended not to notice Lucky standing there, and he didn't show a flicker of emotion at his win — he would never have lasted in the business without a blank face. 'Meet you at the staff exit when you can get away,' Lucky murmured as he moved past him.

His break came twenty minutes later. Khalid took out a lighter and a packet of Bensons from his locker, ran a small plastic comb through his hair, grabbed his jacket, and allowed himself to be patted down at the stage door by the security guard.

It was one of those deceptive autumn evenings when the sky was still surprisingly light at six or seven in the evening, but the air had turned wintry. A few people had sat outside the pub across the road, without winter coats, as if everyone was pretending it was warmer than it really was.

Lucky was leaning against a wall, in the shadows of the street corner, with a dark woollen hat pulled down over his ears. The little runaway from Lucknow, his parents probably still harvesting sugar cane. He slapped Khalid on the back, as if he was congratulating him. He started talking too fast, firmly steering him round the corner by his elbow, along the road, and Khalid could only digest some of the things he said, as they moved past the Beirut café and Argos, then onto the private squares and quiet elegance behind the shopfronts, along Norfolk Crescent and Cambridge Square, Lucky still gabbling and never pausing or noticing anything around him.

'We used to buy chips in the house – accha? – walk away with the clean money. Let's just call it doing the laundry. I'd buy a load of chips, they'd get sold on for cash, they'd get played by another roller. You see? Easy peasy, no risk for the house, no need for croupiers to bat an eyelid.'

Khalid nodded. This was one of those things he knew about but had never regarded as part of his concern or his domain.

'But the amounts are getting bigger, I can't just rock up at the Vic with ten suitcases full of fifties. What do you do with tens of thousands, hundreds of thousands? I literally can't get it washed out fast enough.'

'What a problem to have,' muttered Khalid.

'Yeah!' said Lucky. 'But K's cracked it, he's got access to the management and they are going to sink some for him directly, but they need some help – basically, our people have to lose. We want you to help us lose.'

Stopping at Talbot Square Gardens, Lucky hesitated before they made through the archway into the garden demarcated by black spiked iron railings. The square was tucked discreetly behind the main road, no shops, and no people rushing to get from one place to another. A woman in black, wearing a maid's apron, slowly walked a small lapdog, which was sniffing around the base of a tree, and a faint siren came from the direction of Paddington. On every side of the square, the tall Georgian mansions loomed over them. They reared up faceless and monumental, anonymously white, casting shadow over most of the garden. So much wealth was compressed into those bricks, so visible and solid, that what Lucky was asking seemed to Khalid like nothing in comparison.

'I thought to myself, that is a fortunate thing, to meet a man like you, with the same roots as me, in a place like a casino. You're the class of man we like. And you're the one who can help us. You can steer the ball, right? Avoid a section of the wheel?'

Khalid shrugged. Everyone had a signature spin. No one talked about it, a way of placing the ball, night after night. After you'd released it ten thousand times, you knew which way it might slow and land. The way your muscles and your fingers worked. The way the white ball might tend towards a pocket. Stuttering, clinking down, like a marble in a pot. Not infallible, but useful. No help for winning – no one could guarantee that – but losing, well, that could be controlled.

Khalid was the floor manager, so he was entirely responsible for the croupiers in his part of the casino. The only man who could inspect him was the house manager. Very little risk. They would just have to stack the tables at the club so that Khashoggi's associates would keep throwing their money away.

'What's in it for me?'

'Nothing. Nothing yet. K likes to see some loyalty in the first place, he values that.' Khashoggi has a nose for people, Lucky explained – for their trustworthiness, for their desires – bringing them in when they're useful, dropping them like hot potatoes when they're not. Khashoggi spends his life going in and out of skyscrapers, hotel suites, yachts, like a monarch touring his fiefdom. Lavished with gifts by company presidents and heads of state – a Stradivarius violin, a Greek statue, or an illuminated manuscript – there's a warehouse bulging with all this stuff somewhere. 'He couldn't care less about most of it. There's absolutely nothing you can give him. Devotion, well, that is worth something to him.'

That is what Khalid had been banking on.

Lucky said that Khashoggi was in Morocco with the Emir of Qatar hunting, with falcons. The Emir had violet leather interiors in his plane. He's thinking of copying it for himself. He likes hunting, not with foxes, not the crazy English way. He'll be back in London again soon.

'You'll get to meet him, I promise, you'll get to meet him one day.'

THEY STARTED IMMEDIATELY, THE NEXT EVENING.

They were good at pulling disappointed faces. One or two of the more theatrical ones even slammed their fists down on the table. They cursed and gathered up their girlfriends and left looking moody. Lots of black money being sunk into the deep pits of the casino that could resurface as shiny discs. The management must have taken their cut, once the money was on their books. Khalid never asked how it was washed out, through the back office. Did they really need this performance? Perhaps Khalid might have thought, if he'd thought about it at all, it was a test of nerves. An initiation ritual.

There still wasn't much risk, he told himself.

THE THIRD NIGHT, THE HOUSE MANAGER WALKED THROUGH, arms behind his back, patrolling.

One of Khashoggi's men, in a black suit, surrounded by more Khashoggi men, slightly different suits and slightly different ties — different enough to blend in — were gathered around his table. Khalid placed the dolly on a red. The main contact gently placed thirty thousand down. It was swept away. He sighed and placed the same chips again. He had to lose them. They needed to deposit at least one hundred thousand that evening.

Khalid continued to sweep the chips across the felt with his rake. Losers, losers, losers. If it went red or black, it didn't matter. He had confidence in his actions, avoided the winning section again and again.

Khalid's breathing stayed regular; he sensed the house manager was there but he didn't look across. Khalid kept his body square to the table, and his eyes on the ball. He needed to change direction.

A win. A small pile of blue and yellow chips were returned to the customer; he forced a smile, and Khalid continued to spin the wheel. He knew how calm he was, there was no sweat on his collar, no increase in his heartbeat. He had complete control of the situation and this sensation surged through him, a cold shot of undiluted adrenalin. Awake and sharp, as if he could dance.

There was a slight shadow on the table. The manager beckoned Khalid with his crooked finger. 'A word. Those hotshots aren't doing very well tonight. Is everything OK?'

'Bad streak for them,' Khalid said, looking him directly in the eye.

'Are they taking it badly?' The manager had been at the Vic a long time.

'No, seem fine.'

'And who are they?' This was another way of asking which country they were from.

'I've never seen them before.'

'Several limousines out the back.'

'Hmm.' Khalid kept his gaze steady.

'Well, keep an eye on them for me, will you? I don't want any trouble if they lose too much.'

And this is where Khalid's instincts were so beautiful, and so ideally suited to this kind of game. Because anyone else would have gone back to the table and had them start winning at that point. It would have told such a simple story, and the manager would have smelt it like a dog. Khalid just plunged in deeper; they lost more. He let them sink in another twenty thousand, another thirty thousand. Their night was so bad, such a wash-out, that it couldn't have possibly been plotted like that. That was the kind of imagination that Khashoggi prized.

Lucky said that K was in Monte Carlo, then he was in Geneva. He would be returning to London around the end of the month. He was away from his wife, seeing some people, mixing business with pleasure.

Khalid tried to learn from Lucky everything that he could about the man. He asked him about his preferences, and his tastes, and Lucky told him — the time he ate puffer fish sushi in Japan and how it was more dangerous than cyanide, but tasted like nothing, like the most tasteless chicken. Worse. K wasn't so keen on the best restaurants. You could eat better on the Edgware Road, he said. Khashoggi said paintings were an asset but a bitch to sell on. Rubens, El Greco, Picasso and Degas — Lucky listed the names as if he was reciting a religious text. And it was all true. It wasn't even the half of it.

Khalid didn't tell Imran and Hasina. Nothing had changed. He was still going to work in the Vic, still sleeping on their lumpy put-you-up. Perhaps Imran guessed something was going on. Over dinner the next Friday, he asked him, pointedly, how Suzie was, in front of Hasina, trying to shame him. What he was really asking was had Khalid given her any money yet.

Khalid shrugged. 'I'm going to see them soon. I'll sort everything, Imran, don't worry. By the end of the month things will be on track.'

It felt sometimes like they were on some sort of mission to save him. The way Hasina fussed around him, trying to get him to eat, and the way Imran prayed in front of him in the living room, rolling out his little worn-out mat in the mornings while Khalid was folding away his blankets. They were starting to irritate him and he couldn't even say why. He ended up spending longer out of the house, walking the Edgware Road; sometimes he went to the takeaway for fried chicken and ate it in the shop window, even though Hasina's cooking was so much better.

He still had time for the twins. They woke him up sometimes by jumping on him and he offered to practise their reading with them, when they came home after school, or tested them on their knowledge of capital cities. Soon the books got dropped on the floor and they found a game to play. It started with draughts and soon he was teaching them chess. Although they looked similar, the boys weren't identical and Khalid knew how to deal with their quarrels, how to keep them focused on the game. The bigger boy was stronger, more confident, and competitive. He always wanted to race across the board, and convert his pieces to queens. The younger one was less certain, and called the pieces prawns, and reminded Khalid of Alia.

16

THE NEXT WEEK, LUCKY MET HIM AGAIN OUTSIDE THE STAFF EXIT. They crossed the road and went inside the pub opposite, the Red Lion, which was packed, and Lucky waited for Khalid to offer to get drinks, which he did, bringing back a pint in each hand, with a packet of salted peanuts tucked in his jacket pocket. Lucky had found a little corner and pulled up two low stools.

'He's back from Geneva but he's proper grumpy,' he said, sipping the froth off the top.

'What happened?'

'He can't get his credit flowing, he needs capital.'

Khalid was genuinely shocked; men like Khashoggi had so much money. Why would they need more, why wouldn't anyone advance it to them?

Lucky explained that it wasn't that easy. 'The sums he needs on account are not, what do they say, typical for a lender.' His usual bank had pulled the leash. 'Can't understand it, why they are letting him down. Mr K always repays, he repays with interest.' All the usual sources in Switzerland had got sniffy with Khashoggi, he'd been in the news too much recently for his own good. 'Bastards,' said Lucky, looking around as if someone treacherous could be listening. The bank managers had smiled at his representatives apologetically, walked them to the door.

'I've got a cousin, quite involved with this bank, in Pakistan,' Khalid said, shuffling some peanuts into his palm, trying to think of something to contribute to the conversation.

'BCCI? We know all about it. We've made contact. How high does your cousin reach?' Lucky said. Lucky had hardly drunk a third of his pint although Khalid himself felt ready for another one, and he couldn't quite stretch to a second round.

'He knows the chief, I knew him once a bit too. We used to see each other as kids, at family events.'

'Abedi?' Lucky had looked up, listening more intently.

'Agha Sahib we called him.'

'That is interesting, brother.'

'He's done well for himself, my cousin speaks to him quite regularly.' Khalid was showing off, and he couldn't help himself, carrying on, once he could see that Lucky was impressed.

'Could you make the connection, Khalid-bhai?' Lucky asked.

WASIM WAS STAYING IN THE SHERATON NEAR TERMINAL 4 where he had a stopover between flights and he suggested that Khalid come down and meet him at the hotel room. Khalid had to find his way to the hotel from Hatton Cross station, which proved unexpectedly complex, on a small red bus in the dark, and he ended up standing on the wrong side of a three-lane road, on an anonymous traffic island, with a vast 747 swooping low and aggressively overhead towards the runway. Around him there was nothing but coiled barbed wire on one side and the piercing lights of the runway, and then the big blue S of the hotel's name on the other side, some ten minutes' walk along the verge. He was quite shaken by the time he found his way into the lobby, which was like a spacious oasis, with piped classical music and thick double glazing blocking out the industrial park outside.

He found Wasim lying on the bed when he got to his room, his large feet in socks, hanging off the edge of the duvet. He lumbered off the bed, where his body had left a deep imprint on the soft mattress, and embraced his cousin.

'So you finally did it, you old rascal. Mubarak!' Khalid said, groping for the form of words he used to exchange with his cousin, embracing him. Khalid had brought a wedding gift with him, which he started to extricate from the gift bag, elaborately decorated with horseshoes and small scissor-made twirls. 'I'm sorry I didn't make it to the wedding. You know I was going to...'

'You were missed.' Wasim found he was not quite ready to let him off the hook for not coming, although he held onto his hand. It was, everyone agreed in Karachi, really inexplicable.

'So that's it for you then,' Khalid said, looking around the room, noticing the numerous pillows stacked on the bed, the glare of the airport lights through the venetian blinds. 'Settled down?' Khalid hadn't meant it to sound like a question.

'Well, time will tell.' Wasim smiled, as if to indicate that his commitment was provisional. 'Anyway,' he added hastily, 'it's better to do it the traditional way, don't you think?'

Khalid ignored the question, as if it didn't matter that Wasim had just said that. His cousin only had a stopover for one night on his way from Karachi back to Newark and he didn't want anything to mar the occasion.

'OK, gifts... lots of gifts!' Wasim said heartily. Folks from home had sent things, and he went over to his two enormous suitcases, stacked on top of each other on the floor. The sight of the suitcases, their brown leather, and the way the clasps had to be unlocked, Khalid found incredibly touching as if they were old familiar friends – silly being moved by the sight of battered old luggage and he turned his face away from Wasim. Wasim hauled one of the cases up onto the king-size bed and unbuckled the straps, unzipped the long central zip with one pleasing run.

He unpacked a bundle. Two jars of homemade achaar, lime and mango, precariously packaged in many layers of newspaper taken from old copies of the *Friday Times*, the lids bound on with thick rubber bands, and Wasim had been lucky that they hadn't leaked their orange oil over everything else.

Wasim also took out a shalwar suit, wrapped in polythene, that had clearly been made for Khalid for the wedding, midnight blue with immaculate gold thread, seams ironed into the silk. Carefully folded so as not to crease on the journey and exactly the right length, although they probably thought he was a little thinner than he was these days. He didn't imagine that there was an occasion in London when he would be able to wear it.

'Your mother misses you,' said Wasim. It was a statement of fact for which Khalid had no reply.

They called room service and ordered up some chow mein. Khalid suggested a couple of alcohol-free beers.

'So I had a word with Abedi Sahib,' Wasim said.

'Good, what did he say?'

'He's interested in this Khashoggi, he thinks he's a man he could do business with. I think it will work out.'

'Khashoggi needs new accounts, his old sources have dried up. Loans, big sums – millions – a little stopgap – only for a few days – it's a cash-flow problem,' Khalid explained, realizing as he spoke that he was parroting Lucky, and had little grasp of the detail.

'Abedi can help. Can you broker the introduction?'

'Khashoggi's not the sort of person you can make an appointment with.'

'Just give the word. Abedi is keen to make the contact, he'll contemplate. That's all that needs to be said. I think the rest will take care of itself.' Wasim lay back on the bed, his hands on his belly.

'I don't know, Wasim, sometimes I feel like I'm getting in deeper into this, I don't know where it all leads.' Khalid was attracted and repelled by the proposition of coming between these two giants – it was all too big, too glaringly obvious to ever work out right.

'You were always the brightest at school, Khalid – remember how I used to try and keep pace with you, and how you would do my homework for me sometimes?'

'We all helped each other.'

'Exactly. And I would hide you when your father came out with that cane – or was it a broom handle?'

'Yes, I remember.' Khalid inspected the pictures on the walls of the hotel room. He didn't understand art, but these were very dreary. Sketches of carthorses and ploughs, as if purchased from some old pub sell-off. These rural scenes, an odd way to welcome people to London.

'There's someone you should meet, who will do the needful. His name is Sammy. Sammy Wadia. He's an acquaintance of Abedi Sahib and he will act as his agent in the matter.'

'Wadia?' Khalid asked. There was a question, ages old. Names – a shorthand for collective belonging, a code for trust, or at least the starting place for trust.

'Yes, Sammy, he's from London. Good Bombay family, originally. You have nothing to fear.' Wasim rearranged the pillow behind his head.

'OK,' said Khalid, with a doubtful inflection and all the adrenalin of a derby surging in his veins.

There was a knock at the door, startling them. A young Punjabi boy delivered the food on a vast platter with a stainless steel cloche, which promised more than it delivered. He placed the tray on the end of the bed. When they removed the domed cover they found wilting vegetables and noodles, curled up in soy sauce.

THE NEXT EVENING, IMRAN WAS TETCHY. HE CAME IN WITH HIS cases of equipment and left them in the hallway, changed his shoes, and told the kids to go upstairs and wash their hands.

Khalid was sitting on one of the squashy brown sofas in the living room when he heard him come in. On the wall there were portrait photographs of Imran's sons and relatives, printed in technicolour, professionally framed in Imran's company style, and above them, on a high shelf, the Quran, the only book in the house, bound in an embroidered cloth.

'A man wants a bit of peace and quiet when he's been

working all day,' Imran said as he sat down. The noise of the boys thundering about upstairs was reverberating through the ceiling.

Khalid wondered if it was a reproach. Did he want him to leave the room? Not to stay there with them at all? He didn't dare ask, or even think about it – the truth was he had nowhere to go. Where would he sleep? He still had the Datsun parked outside, dented and bashed. It had reclining seats. Imran sank into the armchair and Hasina brought him tea on a tray with biscuits.

Business wasn't as good as Imran would have liked. He was wondering if he had quit the chemist too quickly. Self-made people don't get any holiday time, he said; he'd like to go back to Faisalabad, visit his parents – they've only seen the boys once. He can't afford not to earn.

Was he asking for money? Khalid had known him all those years, considered him his best friend, and now he couldn't fathom the meaning of his words. He found he was looking for hidden insults and demands.

Imran slid his feet out of his slippers and felt the floor with his toes.

'So how is Suzie? When are you going round?'

Imran believed in the fundamental basics of marriage. Getting on with it, accommodating each other, not wanting too much, and keeping your blinkers on. It had served him pretty well. Hasina was introduced to him by his parents. They had known her grandparents before Independence – they'd supplied bolts of cloth to their shop in Amritsar – and the two of them could be brother and sister, with their moon-shaped faces and glossy hair. She was an expert in seeing what he needed; he chatted away to her about every little thing he felt, telling her everything he had done all day. And she sang away in the kitchen.

Khalid's bust-up, blow-out, whatever you wanted to call it, was incomprehensible to Imran. 'It's not that I haven't got your passion,' he had said once with a bashful grin. And Khalid saw him once grab Hasina by the waist in the kitchen when he thought no one was there. Things were pretty good between them. He didn't understand a thing about Khalid's life.

'Just go and say sorry. Tell her you've changed your ways. Bring Alia over here, the boys want to see her.'

'It's not that simple.'

'Ah, humbug, Khalid. You're both just bloody stubborn donkeys.'

Khalid's shutters came down. It was almost too difficult to think about, his brain started to hurt. He couldn't even give voice to the sounds that would make the words to express how he felt about any of it, the mess. You've left me high and dry, Khalid, up shit creek without a paddle. Suzie had tried to find some way of explaining it, some form of words. He was lost. There were words which came into his mind – bankruptcy, bailiffs, credit, eviction – they swirled around disconnected, as if they couldn't be attached to him.

All he knew was that he had made her promises, about the life that she deserved, the life she should have, both of them deserved, and the future was still unwritten, and he intended to keep his promises.

'I'm going to get away, Imran. It's time for me to try something new. My cousin, Wasim, you've met him once, he's got some business ideas, he's invited me to stay with him in the States, he's got a place in New Jersey.' In the back of his mind was an idea of something pukka, about making a fresh start. Wasim had several ideas on the boil and he needed a hand – someone who could deal with the numbers, make a smart impression – his main business plan was starting these international calling cards. He was completely convinced that there were fortunes to be made out of long distance telephoning, untapped millions in scratch-cards, and he had brought Khalid round to his way of thinking. Maybe getting further away from Lucky was a good idea; perhaps he had been getting drawn into something that he didn't really want or need.

Buoyed up with the idea, he called to tell her.

'Suzie, I've got an opportunity. I'm going to quit the Vic, I'm going to work with Wasim. New Jersey. You remember my cousin, Wasim? I've got a break with him. It's a real chance.'

'But New Jersey is in the United States of America.' She spelled it out as if he didn't know where it was located.

'Wasim has mastered the phone cards, the long distance dialling. He's hired a computer engineer. Everyone on the planet will want one of these phone cards. The end of long distance charges.' Wasim's plan was exhilarating and practically foolproof. He couldn't believe she didn't understand the genius of it.

'And what about Alia? Will you be calling her long distance?'

'It will just be for a few months, Suzie. Until we get the office established. Until we can sell on the company. Honestly, this is the big one. I'm doing it for you, for both of you.' He didn't say, but also felt, that he'd had a near-miss with Khashoggi's people. It was better to get to safer ground, to America – all its lovely virgin newness.

She said she couldn't stop him going. He would call, of

course, and try to remember the time difference, and send impressive dollar postal orders. Suzie would explain all of this to Alia but with the firm understanding that he would be returning in the spring.

'Khalid. By the way, the papers are ready to sign.' She was speaking slowly and enunciating each word again. 'My solicitor is posting them out tomorrow.'

All this talk of papers. Parroting the way that women spoke in those television serials. He felt it was better just to ignore it.

THE NEXT DAY HE HAD AN AFTERNOON SHIFT AT THE Grosvenor. It was a quiet few hours, nothing special. When his shift ended he stepped out from the gaming floor into the neon-lit corridor at the back of the casino. Khalid hated the moment of walking out, squinting in the garish light after the dim. Everything lit with too much detail. He could see the cigarette burns in the tables and a slight shabbiness to the women talking by the lockers, and peeling off their false eyelashes. The end of the illusion. There were a few tables and chairs with ashtrays on them and lockers where you could place your things if you didn't want to take them home or if your next shift was coming up again soon.

Lucky was waiting for him, sitting at one of the little staff tables, looking fidgety and bored. He shouldn't have been allowed access to that part of the club – you needed a security pass to enter the area. Khalid didn't know how he got in, and he didn't ask.

'Sorry to hear you're going to the States.' Lucky was a little stand-offish, as if he was personally disappointed. 'We are

210

here for you whenever you want to come back. Mr Khashoggi is very pleased with you. Sincerely. He wanted to convey his thanks.' And Lucky handed Khalid a gift in a small cardboard box, wrapped so tightly in cellophane that he couldn't open it. Eventually Lucky offered his penknife to help him prise the lid open. Inside was a solid gold Ronson lighter, twenty-two carat, which had been engraved with his name.

17

WHEN MARK DENBY RETURNED ON MONDAY MORNING THERE was a new side table arranged next to Linda's desk in their office, under the window, with foolscap files stacked on it, ordered by alphabet, some of them bulging. There were several books, marked with fluorescent sticky notes, and he could see press clippings, biographical notes about men he'd vaguely heard of: Agha Hasan Abedi, the Sheikh of Dubai. Linda had marked a map with little spots to show where the bank was located in the UK and compiled background notes under themes such as acquisitions and shareholders.

It stank to high heaven. No one understood where the money came from, or how the bank did so well year after year. The bank appeared to be running a parallel system, funnelling things off wherever they liked.

'So our friend was right. Unrecorded deposits, lump sums palmed off?' Denby leafed through the files, while Linda answered his questions.

'Everyone in the City agrees it's shaky. It's an open secret. It just goes on year after year.'

'What about evidence, though?' Denby respected her work but he couldn't quite see anything incriminating.

'That's the thing. It's so hard to pin them down. They've got accounts signed off.' Linda sighed as if she was running out of patience.

It turned out that there had been one exposé – two anonymous short articles in the *New Statesman* years earlier – which mapped it all out – the dictators and crooks on the payroll, the arms twisted and profits stashed. It was the only time a journalist ever went near it, and the magazine ended up paying out damages; the whole affair brought it to its knees. 'God knows who they have in their pockets,' Linda said; did she think they were better off leaving it alone?

Abedi had started the bank in 1973. It radiated out from Pakistan, wrapping its tentacles around hundreds, then thousands, then millions of deposit accounts. It had gobbled up crappy American banks like the National Bank of Georgia and First American. Easy prey. Then it had split like an amoeba, set up two heads, two sets of auditors. Its internal operations incorporated in Luxembourg and the Cayman Islands. The headquarters in London on Leadenhall Street. There were plenty of whispers about insolvency. It was hardly as if it hadn't been talked about.

'People in the City, they don't want to go on the record, they say it's overtrading, trading at a loss, lending to too many businesses, doing too little business with other banks. The BCCI bankers probably move accounts around to cover up losses, and because it's based in more than one place, it's got more than one set of auditors, and nobody gets the full picture.' Linda made another effort at explaining it to him.

'That's what people say? But where's the evidence?'

The ruler of the UAE had been pouring money in, like crude oil into a tanker: Sheikh Zayed bin Sultan al Nahyan. Denby looked at a picture of the man, which Linda had clipped out of *The Times*. 'Twenty sons and nobody knows how many daughters.' A family with the wealth of several countries. They needed a bank in every place that they wanted to shop, ski and hunt, the right currencies to hand. These people didn't check their change.

'And this Abedi fellow?'

'He's a smooth-talking financier – from Karachi – quite dapper, silvery tongued, has everyone who works for him in his thrall. He's conjured this massive confection. The Sheikh has opened the biggest sweetshop in the world for him.'

It was jobs for the boys. Wages for young Asian men in every major capital city, and they looked up to Abedi with his gabardine suit and his Windsor knot like a rich uncle. They were the audience for his philosophizing.

'It's just too convenient,' Denby said later after reading through the files all morning.

'What do you mean?' Linda looked quizzical.

She had been wonderfully thorough but she hadn't grasped the seriousness of what she had uncovered. 'This bank has been allowed to grow and grow, with so much unknown about it, so much allowed to go unnoticed.'

'Go on.'

'Abedi is hiding in plain sight. No one is hitting the panic button.'

'Who should do that?'

'The Bank of England must know. They are the regulator.'

'Well, you're an economist, aren't you?'

Her faith in him was touching.

'I taught students for a few years. I don't think that means I'm equipped to do battle with the Governor of the Bank of England.'

He looked through the papers again, carefully turning them over and piecing it together in his mind. He knew enough about banking to understand the abstractions, the statistics running like water through his fingers. Banking happens on paper, along wires, in telephone calls, in numbers tapped into calculators by eager fingers. By its nature it's hard to get a grip on. It was nothing like the Cowley factory with its metal parts hammered into something you could see, the lads clocking in each day and looking forward to the Friday payslip. And yet he also saw a collision course with reality, as hard and brutal as a smash on the M40, with real bodies and broken bones. A bank as big and rotten as this was going to reap, like a scythe, when it fell, slashing down little men as it went.

He had a minicab driver recently on the way back home from Oxford railway station, who was working the cars by night and waiting at the curry house by day to get a deposit down on a house in Temple Cowley. Royal Cars. He was a worrier, a little fellow with a close-cut beard, never stopped complaining about the cost of his daughter's wedding, and the way the in-laws kept upping their demands – *they're saying we should have another set of suits made for all the relatives. We got them made up in yellow and now they're saying they want red*. Denby had barely listened, and hardly understood what he was talking about. He was tired from the journey and had a whole day of constituents ahead of him. That driver could have been saving up with a BCCI account. His life could turn on this coin.

'You could put up a question, an Early Day Motion or something?' Linda said.

'I have got a friend I need to talk to first,' Denby said, pulling out his address book.

HE DIDN'T KNOW WHY THEY DECIDED TO GO TO WIMPY'S OR whose idea it was, like something studenty. They used to go to football matches together sometimes at White Hart Lane, although they never ate this E-number rubbish. It was quick, the fast food crap, and it left more time to talk. They had their polystyrene boxes and coffee in paper cups in minutes and took them down to St James's Park.

George led him towards the pond and decided where to sit. Their bench overlooked the reeds, where hungry swans circled and occasionally reared up with their wings open. Denby glimpsed the grey heights of Buckingham Palace behind the trees. It was cold and he was under-dressed compared to George, who had a thick overcoat over his suit, and sturdy boots instead of brogues. It put Denby at a disadvantage, and sucking on the straw of a milkshake, he felt childish, reduced to a less confident version of himself, the bookish student that George knew at university.

George still looked like a butcher's boy – his hands, his face, like he was reared on pastry and cold meat. Ever since he was eighteen he'd had that look about him, the spectre of middle age. He wasn't a party friend, and his views were always a bit opaque. But they'd seen each other age, and they shared those years, when all they owned could be packed into a cardboard box, and that counted for something.

'So you got here in the end, Denby.'

'Well, I only tried twice.'

'Wasn't a safe seat, though, was it? Bucking the trend.'

'You know me.'

'I always knew you'd make it to the House. How you finding it?'

'Well, there's a lot of people willing to do things for you. That's a change. Is it any harder over the bridge?'

He won't be drawn. It is an open secret where George works. He bit down on the cheeseburger.

'If my dad could see me eating this burger, he'd be rolling in his grave. Got to admit it's tasty, though. And how's Penny? That voice. Gorgeous woman.'

'We're alright. She sends her best.'

Somewhere in the back of Mark's mind he knew that Penelope had kissed George when they were students. It was a drunken thing, at the bar of a dancefloor in some sweaty, blacked-out club, what they would have called a snog, and Denby wasn't even together with her at the time, in a serious way, in a way that either of them recognized enough as a claim. There was no tie strong enough between them at that stage that would have prevented her from stumbling across to George at two in the morning. It was as innocent as that, and he doesn't have any reason to believe they ever slept together. The whole episode was relayed back to him by an earnest housemate who had witnessed the scene, and he's never mentioned it to Penny. Somehow, however, the thought rankled.

The right moment to say anything passed decades ago.

Still, occasionally, when he looks at George, he thinks of their tongues, entangled like snakes. There was something sensuous about him, even in his girth, the way he ate ravenously, without disguising his appetite. George had an effect on women. There's a civil servant, for instance, Denby would have thought too busy, too principled. He spotted her walking once with George, laughing. Mark had seen them again at a discreet table at a Westminster bistro and walked out again before he was noticed.

'Haven't seen you since the election.'

'If I hear the word landslide one more time.'

'Got to look on the bright side. Enoch's out. And you're here.'

'She's got the hat-trick – three in a row – it's unbearable.' Denby feared deep down that the woman was unshakeable, that she could never be shifted, she was bending the country in her own image. 'There are names for whole new types of people who will vote for her – she's coined an -ism, for Christ's sake.' He rolled his eyes to hide his anxiety. It was as bad as George's flippancy. That was the trouble with George, Denby realized: I end up concealing, just like him.

'Your time will come. Anyway, what's niggling?'

'BCCI.'

George paused. It was just a couple of seconds, but a definite pause. He prodded at his sesame bun.

'I can't stand these gherkin things, some folks love them.' He was pulling them out with his fingers, dark green slivers. 'Tell me more.'

'It's rotten, everyone knows it's rotten, and it could be heading for a fall. And it's all plain as daylight yet no one will talk about it.'

'And how rotten do apples have to be before they fall from the tree?'

'It's the tree, the root, branch, the whole pissing lot,' Denby said.

'Abu Dhabi, isn't it?'

'Oh George, I've known you too long. Pull the other one.'

'OK, OK.'

'So you know?'

George hesitated, and, perhaps cornered, took the option of candid disclosure. 'Of course we do.'

'So why let it go on and on?'

'Let's just say, it's better to keep the ones you want to watch close. See where they stuff their petro-dollars, what they do with it, watch the whole merry-go-round. It's the wildcards like the Paddies, squirrelling away their cash, who come out of nowhere, give us a great big bejesus shock. We like to see things coming, even if we can't do much about it. And BCCI is one of the ways we can have a little look-see at all the mental ragheads.'

'Drugs?'

'Christ, you are green.'

'They are a big bank. There's a lot of investment here, in the UK.'

'Ah, don't worry about little Mohammad's giro from the cash-and-carry. That's safe as houses.' George bit down so hard on his burger that the enamel on his teeth connected. 'How's your mother, by the way?'

'She's fine.'

The ludicrous idea that George might already know his parentage knocked Mark into silence.

Two swans reared up again, one dangerously close, the

power of its broad grey-white wings as surprising as if he had never seen a swan before.

'Perhaps we should move from here?' George said, gathering up their boxes and sachets as they stood and moved to the next bench, some six feet away, while the swan turned and eased back out regally onto the water.

'So I should just stay away from it, is that what you're saying? There's nothing more to say?' George had said nothing of the sort. That's what he wanted to be told and so he was opening the door for him.

'Yeah, I'd say it's not your forte.' He was squeezing the very end of a little sachet of ketchup onto his French fries, pushing out every last bit. 'You'll do the home stuff seriously well, you'll be a real constituency man. Look,' he carried on, 'it isn't as exciting as it appears. It sounds all big-game – but really it's just number-crunching, watching who owns what, who buys what, who sells what. Useful, but pretty damn boring. Not helping anyone, the way you can on the benches, making policy.'

'George, we've been out of power since 1979. Do you think I'm making policy?'

'Ah well, things never stay the same.'

THERE WAS A DELIVERY FOR HIM THE NEXT DAY. A BOTTLE OF Scotch and a box of chicken nuggets left on his desk. The office smelled of the grease. On top was a scribbled note in familiar handwriting.

'Oxford East comes first! Yours, George.'

The exclamation mark was uncharacteristic. It hit the wrong note.

IT WAS A MISH-MASH OF A STREET. SO MANY SIGNS AND hoardings and window displays written in Arabic, so many unfamiliar brands and things in shop windows: different types of coffee pots, cans of strange fruit drinks, buckets with mops and packets of round flatbreads. Sign boards offering residency and translation, Hajj and Umrah, gold for cash. The traffic was relentless and Denby walked as briskly as he could. He was interested in the place, as if he was on holiday. He'd also have liked to get away and be somewhere more comfortable. For a second he stepped inside the cold clean lines of Marks & Spencer just to breathe, just to be away from the people on the pavement, to see something familiar.

Back outside, the air smelled of apple smoke and charred meat.

A man with a shisha pipe sat alone with a chess game; he held the pipe in his hand, and looked at Denby, eyeing his suit, sensing he was a man in the wrong place.

A few of the cafés had set out woven carpets with pot plants on them as if they were oases in the desert, as if the owners couldn't see the puddles forming in the places where the wide pavements needed repairing, and where the pigeons circled, hoping for scraps of bread. Everywhere there were watermelons and peaches, long out of season.

As he walked up towards Marble Arch from the station the street grew smarter. Soon he was leaving behind the rough-looking men with dull eyes and oiled hair, the shopfronts with spider web cracks in their glass. The shops looked better, and more prosperous. More English people at this end of the road, and fancy apartment complexes overlooking the street.

He'd like to buy Zoe something from here, but he would feel

at a disadvantage shopping – he wouldn't know the names for things, he might embarrass himself by confusing ingredients or by giving the wrong amount of money. He'd cause offence by saying the wrong word or handling cash in the wrong way.

He knew the community leaders in his constituency pretty well. He was relaxed with the Pakistani guys, had a lot of support from the Cowley majlis in the election, but this was another kettle of fish. A blacked-out Mercedes purred majestically along, prayer beads strung at the rear-view mirror. Some big players here, people you didn't want to mess with.

The counter held salad and chopped onions and a man in a white apron was twisting meat onto skewers. The place smelled of grease and dough.

Perhaps she was the woman in a headscarf at the window of the café, with a baby on her lap. She held the baby outwards, bouncing him gently, so that the boy – he guessed it was a boy, in a blue hat – could look out at the world, at the buses and passers-by through the window, even though he could barely hold his head up, and his eyes were wrinkled up, averted, as if he'd rather block out the light.

It turned out that it wasn't her.

Zahra Asfour was sitting adjacent to them, at a separate table, further away from the window, and alone. The frame of a teenager, narrow shoulders in skin-tight black clothes, although when he looked closer he reckoned she must be in her thirties. Very straight black hair, hanging down as if it had been ironed. Her coat had a fur trim, even though it was warm in the café. She reminded him of a woman he had seen once outside Harrods for a few seconds between the shop door and the chauffeured car. She was tapping a glass of mint tea with a sharp nail.

'I wanted to tell you – to ask you—' he began clumsily.

'Have a coffee first,' she commanded. There was a mismatch between the letter and this closed, serious person.

He ordered a coffee from the bar, and when he returned to the table she looked at him, as if she might work out from his raincoat, from his walk, if he could be trusted.

'You live near here?' she asked.

'Pimlico, well, Oxford. It's complicated.'

The place was quite empty and she kept her voice low. 'I was angry, OK?'

Her English was technically perfect and slightly accented, hinting at a childhood in the Middle East, a private school in England perhaps, unaccompanied journeys with kind stewardesses.

'I'm glad you wrote.'

'And what have you done about it?'

'Well, I'm just considering it. Perhaps we should involve the relevant authorities.'

How easy it was to slip into ways of speaking, to draw on official terms, and to obscure meaning when you needed to.

'Yes. It's a mess, something needs to be done.' She wasn't asking him for anything, just stating a fact. 'But I'm not going to be drawn into it.'

She looked away again, glanced at the waiter who brought a glass of coffee with a plate. Then she pushed the baklava away with a gesture of disgust.

Denby was still distracted by the woman at the other table, who held her baby, shifting the weight of the child slightly from side to side, bouncing him towards the light.

Mrs Asfour was, it turned out, regretful – the letter was

written in a fury. She had just fought with her husband – there had been a terrible row in a hotel room – a television broken, smashed by a glass bottle. She still had several bank accounts, though she was worried about where the money would come from in the future. She let him know that she spoke four languages, Arabic, English, French and Farsi.

'He's got himself a wonderful place in Abu Dhabi, everyone's raving about his Range Rovers and his quad bikes. And I won't see a penny. And I have a lot of questions to answer. My family... are not pleased. So you see, this bank has cost me a lot.'

'And what's next for you?'

'It's not easy. I'm alone.' She was wearing jewellery, but no wedding ring. 'Look. I sent you a letter because the bank has destroyed my family, my husband – once he got involved – he changed. He should not have been involved.'

'I'm a Member of Parliament, Mrs Asfour. We can do some things but we can't work miracles.'

There was a silence, just the shrill whine of coffee beans grinding in the background, and the woman near the window rocked her baby with one hand. His little head bobbed, his eyes relaxed into sleep, and she rested him in his pram, pulling a blanket up over his legs. He lay there with his arms outstretched upwards alongside his head, vulnerable and trusting.

Denby sipped his coffee. It was very bitter.

'Why did he leave you?'

'He didn't leave me – I left him, Mr Denby. A lot of women put up with it, blue bruises in hidden places. You can find a scarf, use make-up. You go and cheer yourself up in Selfridges. I am a proud woman, my sisters taught me well. I know my worth. And I was angry. When I wrote the letter, I knew a lot and I wanted him to understand my pain. I had rather you had destroyed it, though. Forget I sent it. It was a mistake.'

ON THE WAY BACK TO THE OFFICE, HE WAS UNSETTLED. THE Tube was crowded and stuffy, and he was caught in the middle of the carriage; a woman next to him in a beige trench coat shuffled to create millimetres of distance between them, and he tried not to look at the row of passengers sitting below him, his crotch at their eyeline. They all stared into the middle distance, expert at averting contact, so many strange faces, intent on their newspapers, so many different types of humans. He stood holding onto a strap above his head, trying to work out why there was a dissonance, between Zahra Asfour and what she wrote in her letter and what she said today. She was civil, cordial, and she appeared to speak frankly. She had written a letter to him in a rage, and now regretted it. It was justified that she didn't want to take the matter further. And yet... there was something else. As the train shuddered to a halt at Victoria, the light in the carriage flickered off then came back on, the carriage emptied and refilled, people changed lines, and Denby saw it clearly.

Zahra Asfour had pride. She knew how to hide her feelings. She was making a fine show of not being scared.

18

ALIA WALKED OUT OF THE STATION, AWAY FROM THE FLYOVER, and towards the tower blocks at the grubbier end of the road. She passed betting shops, and shopfronts advertising Cash for Gold, Currency Exchange and Money Transfer. Some of the shops had their metal shutters drawn down, others displayed small flashing signs, blinking day or night: *casino-massage-casino-massage*. People looked noticeably different to Oxford – more cautious.

Turning into Church Street, the last dregs of the market were strewn around, the remnants of the stalls from earlier in the day, trampled cabbage leaves and empty crates. A man packed away boxes of fake gold rings and earrings, all inlaid with the same turquoise stone, and a woman in a headscarf with a shopping trolley trundled by, stacked full of cardboard. Alia wondered if she was homeless or just collecting discarded things.

Number 323 was set on the right-hand of the side-street, above a grocery shop which was piled high with Pampers and imported canned drinks. Looking up she saw net curtains, sash windows on the second storey, the peeling remnants of an Edwardian façade. And then a side door made of plywood, and a plastic buzzer. A boy with an L plate on his moped, with

Domino's pizza boxes stacked on the back, sat watching her from the yellow lines.

Alia couldn't bear to look at herself, or to examine too closely what she was doing here. She winced with her own stupidity. Why wasn't she safely in her study in Oxford, making sparky conversation with a young student? She berated herself for wasting her own time.

She rang the buzzer.

There was a long silence, but then the resonance of loud footsteps coming downwards. A woman opened the door wearing a vinyl apron and a purple hairnet.

She seemed neither surprised nor worried to see Alia on her doorstep, as if answering the door to strangers happened to her often, and she didn't mind questions. Alia was young enough and scruffy enough not to be someone on official business.

She leaned against the door in a way that suggested a memory of leaning against garden fences to talk to neighbours. She liked a bit of gossip, wasn't in a hurry to send Alia away.

'Yes, I do remember him. Quiet bloke, kept to himself.'

Alia didn't want to push her luck but this was the closest to information that she had so far, and so she asked a little more.

'He was the tenant, used to rent it from my mother, then he cleared out, to India, wasn't it? It must have been fifteen years ago now. She had others in after that, Poles. They kept it spick and span. And after that my old mum moved back in. She just died last month – stroke in the night, they think – otherwise she could have told you more about him. Shame, you've come too late, pet.'

Alia's hope plummeted.

'The thing is, I think my father lived here too. With Sammy.

I think he might know about it. He died you see, my father, and
I want to know more about it. About him.'

She had never said these things so clearly out loud, and
found it easier to say on a stranger's doorstep; the woman
didn't mind, she was open to talking about death, and there was
a solidarity of grief between them. 'Seen it all on this street.'
She was certifiably unshockable, proofed against rough justice
and against street girls and the black market and all the other
things that she had seen there. She prided herself on her ability
to absorb information without much impact.

'Ah pet, so it's about your dad, is it?'

She invited her upstairs to see the flat. She was sorry she
hadn't got any milk so the tea wouldn't be any good. They
were cleaning the place out, and she was just scrubbing the
bathroom.

The place was being packed up. Cardboard boxes waited for
their removal van and there were black binbags overspilling
with pastel-coloured cardigans and bric-a-brac waiting for the
jumble. The smell of old fragrances – violets, rose – eked from
glass bottles that could no longer be bought anywhere. Alia
turned around in the small space. A soulless little room, with
beige walls and a glass table too big for the room. Nothing
here reminded her of her father and yet she also had a sense, a
bodily sensation, a memory stored in her actual cells and fibre,
so that without recognizing anything she knew that she had
been here before.

'It's coming back to me now, that fellow Sammy went to
Goa,' says the woman. 'He sent some money from there, nice
stamps he used, to settle his debts. Mum was pleased, she'd
always liked him and she couldn't understand why he'd upped

and left like that. Then he made it up to her, wrote her a note. Anjuna Beach, I think it was.'

She talked for a long time about the way her mother died, the shock of finding her in the morning, though it must have been a good way for her to go. Her eyes were closed and everything, and how she missed cooking her lunch and running her down to the shops, even though she complained about caring for her all the time when she was alive and never understood why she needed to go to the hairdresser so often. What was the point in perming it?

Alia looked around, waiting for more, and all she knew was that she had been here before, and nothing else. And once she started listening to the woman again, she was amazed that some people could talk this way about their lost ones, so plainly, opening their hearts to strangers.

STEFAN WAS AT HOME WHEN SHE GOT BACK, SPRAWLED ON THE sofa, with a can of beer precariously leaning on a pile of books. He was watching something sporty on the television, and when he saw her he turned it off in a respectful way and sat up straight. It was like coming back to a puppy. She could see that he'd made an effort: the place had been straightened out, the curtains had been opened and the ashtrays emptied.

She flopped down on the armchair, unzipped her boots and eased her feet out. 'Give me a sip of that.' She took a glug from his tin.

'How are you?' He eyed her curiously. 'Have you found out anything more?'

Bus tickets, train tickets, Pakistan–London and back again,

jet lag, question marks. As if she was circling around a big sky like a hawk while the crops below had been razed, there wasn't a speck underneath that would yield anything. Only one lead, a village in Goa where she might meet someone who might know something, if he was actually there at all, and not mad, or murdered, or imprisoned.

'You know what? I'm going to leave it alone. I don't think I should be away from college any more days – the students will start to complain if I miss any more tutorials. I've got to get on with work, with my real life. And I've got about a thousand and one things to do for the English Faculty, I haven't done any marking for days.' She started to dig around in her backpack, an old reflex.

'You know your problem?' he said.

'Don't start sentences like that, it sounds like you've watched too many American films.'

'You're too nice. You don't know your own worth. You don't know your own value, you let the faculty trample all over you, you let your mother take what she needs from you. You need to be, what's that word? Assertive. You think all these things, and you never say them, and you just let the whole world boss you around.'

'You're sounding kind of bossy yourself, Stefan.' The words had stung her to the core, winded her in fact, because she knew he was right.

It had always been like that. Times when she should have spoken up, being pushed in front of in a queue when she was a teenager, the way that shopkeepers didn't seem to see her, or hear her, or gave her back the wrong change: love, pet, darling.

And now Stefan, of all people. There was a man, underneath

all the scruffy T-shirts. He was just playing at all this student stuff. This is all a prelude to his real adult life, and he'll probably have a farmhouse and a hemmafru and make jokes to his kids about the dump where he used to live in Oxford. This is my actual adult life, though, she thought. This is it for me.

'I met a nice man at a college dinner the other night. An *accountant*, no less.' She said it with a mock drawl, like it was a funny word.

Stefan pushed up his vest a little bit and rubbed his hands on his smooth belly, yawning, completely lacking in self-consciousness. His skin looked like an athlete's. If she had a ball in her hand she would have hurled it at him. Hard.

'Great.' He held the remote as if he was about to flick the TV on again, and lay back down.

Don't do it, she told herself. It will end in tears. You need a housemate to pay the rent next month, it's such a pain finding someone for that room, and he probably just wants to try it on with anyone, or try anything, it's nothing personal.

The room had gone quiet.

'Want to?' he said quietly.

'Is that a Swedish saying?'

'Don't you want to?' He sounded annoyed, and reached up and ran his fingers into the ends of her hair. He had never touched her before. The potential for disaster. A memory came to her from childhood of an accident at a tube station, when the train driver had failed to stop at the end of the District Line, and went crashing past the buffers onto the concourse.

'I've got a tickets for a play at seven.'

She kissed his mouth, very chastely at first, as if to end

the matter, but then something took over, and they stumbled towards his room, clumsily.

It started off with her laughing, because of his *Star Wars* poster and the single bed. He took off his jeans and she lay back on his bed, looking at the engineering books on his shelf and the incomprehensible titles.

But then, without warning, and unfairly – she thought afterwards – it ramped up and turned into something else, more earthy, less explicable. As if there were other Stefans that she hadn't contemplated, more sensitive and complicated Stefans, stacked inside him, so that he became intensely, peculiarly desirable. A multitude of Stefans, and all of them shameless mind readers.

Afterwards, they were lying on the bed the wrong way up, and she couldn't have said how they got there. He dangled his hand down and pulled out a faded little tin from under his bed and drew out the papers, rolling a joint with his thumb and fore-finger, and she couldn't quite look at him, and he didn't say anything at all. She wondered for a moment if they had de-stroyed something between themselves, but then he smiled and pulled up the duvet tightly around them so she was swaddled, and began talking about some of his ecological ideas, about the planting at the allotment he was planning, and she went into a deep sleep until the alarm went off on his digital watch at half past six and she awoke in the disorienting, darkening afternoon. 'I didn't want you to miss the theatre,' he whispered.

PART FOUR

1987 & 2003

19

SUZIE OPENED THE DOOR IN A COLOURFUL WOOLLEN JUMPER which he had never seen before. Yak wool or something mountainous, and itchy. He was taken aback. Also by her hair, which had a similar fluffiness about it now that she had cut it shorter, so that the edges stuck out in a way that he found both endearing and disconcerting. Her face was rounder, less taut. Healthier, he would have said, like a country cousin of the Suzie he had once been married to.

'Oh, hello you.' She wasn't unfriendly, there was residual affection in her voice, and they both saw the natural humour of the situation, the fact that he was knocking on a front door that used to belong to him, like a cold caller.

It was a stand-off; neither of them moved across the step which seemed to hold a magic power, the line between her space and his own.

'Well, come on in then,' she said at last.

Inside nothing had changed at all, which he found both astonishing and reassuring. The furniture was all the same stuff they'd bought together, the beige and mustard stripe running through the armchairs and settee which had then been so fashionable. Even the spider plant hanging down from a raffia basket suspended from the ceiling didn't seem to have grown, or changed. It made Suzie's own face seem so much more unlikely, and out of place.

He needed to piss, and it would have been the most natural thing in the world to go to the bathroom – no doubt also looking the same; he could picture its pale green tiles and the bottle of Head & Shoulders on the side of the bath tub – he knew every inch of this place. But there were also invisible lines and barriers all over this flat now, all sorts of new ways that he should move and conduct himself, and he appreciated that he couldn't ask Suzie to go to the toilet, so he held on and ignored the feeling of pressure building in his bladder. He stood there in the middle of the room, in his overcoat like a door-to-door salesman, who could be ushered out at any minute.

'All OK?' she asked.

'Not so bad,' he said.

'Is that all you have to offer?' There was a note of weary frustration in her voice.

The gap – he hadn't counted it, but he knew it was long – hung there threatening to sour everything.

'It's been a while,' he said.

'Four years and eight months, Khalid!' Her voice rose but it was more exasperated than angry, as if she had realized she was dealing with someone with an illness or an injury, someone who needed to be carefully stewarded for their own sake.

'I did call,' he said, refusing to believe that it had been really that many months. She might have miscounted. He glanced around at the front room again, it couldn't have been that long. He had been doing it all for them in any case.

'It was a long time for a kid.'

'Well, it's been busy.' He thought about trying to explain the way that the room at Imran's had been needed eventually, and how he had understood that he should leave, without being asked directly to by Hasina, and that he had made the right decision to move on. And he also thought he might tell her about Wasim's place in Newark, the square footage of his condo, and how he'd stayed for longer than he'd expected because Wasim had put him up and he had no other place to go. It was only an hour and forty from Manhattan on the New Jersey Transit, and he had seen the Statue of Liberty at last, and rode in a yellow cab driven by a guy from Peshawar, and Suzie might have been interested in how far they'd got with developing the telephone card business, despite a few setbacks. He had other things he wanted to say – about how he'd gone away because he knew he shouldn't get too involved with Khashoggi after all, and that he had tried to dodge getting cut in on a bigger deal. But he didn't voice any of it, because her face was a warning, and it hadn't all quite come to fruition yet. The phone cards hadn't clicked. He didn't have a lot to show, truth be told, for all that time away, on the other side of the Atlantic.

'I sent some postal orders. I called.' It sounded plaintive and he knew he shouldn't have said it. A pink money order in dollars which may or may not have bounced, but was so expensive to convert into pounds that Suzie had decided not to cash it. Phone calls that came too late at night, long after Alia's bedtime, when he had forgotten to calculate the international time difference.

'It was always temporary.'

'Hmm,' said Suzie and she looked a little bewildered, as if she was cycling through too many emotions at high speed. 'I'll go and get her then.'

Once Suzie had gone, he looked around more deliberately, with open curiosity. Suzie had laid a paperback she was reading, *The Women's Room*, face down on the coffee table, so that its pages had splayed on either side of the spine. The front cover was plain white apart from a picture of a large glossy apple, with a bite taken out of it.

On the mantelpiece above the gas fire was a card printed with sunflowers on the front. He picked it up, and turned it over thoughtlessly, knowing it might be something he shouldn't touch. The gas fire blasted his knees with unexpected warmth, unpleasant through his suit and overcoat. The writing wasn't a child's and it wasn't familiar to him.

Darling, thank you so much. Come again soon, M. xxx

He put it down again.

And then Alia stood there, but she didn't greet him enthusiastically. She was the same but taller, more stretched out in places – her hands looked like an adult's – and squashed in others, and some elements of her body were out of proportion, as if she was a bundle of kinetic energy ready to explode into maturity and life. But she didn't refuse to come with him and there weren't any of the scenarios that had crossed his mind and she took her coat down from the peg in the hallway.

KHALID TOOK ALIA TO BURGER KING ON KING STREET. HE had 2-for-1 vouchers on the meal deals. The rain was coming down in sheets, weighing down the shop awnings with monsoon heft. One shopkeeper outside the pound shop brushed away the rain with a broom, as if he was in Punjab, as if he could stop the dirty monsoon water creeping into his shop, and keep it away from his door. His fellow shopkeeper, in a grey woollen pullover, carried out a stand with cheap umbrellas on it, knowing how to turn a profit on the weather. God, those folks worked hard, and all for what? Driving themselves into the ground, never leaving their little hutches and living above the shop all the time, with the threat of the till being raided, selling bottles of cider to teens. Khalid felt better about his own life just looking at them.

'Look at it this way,' he wanted to say to Alia, 'I could have just vanished, never bothered at all, but I'm not that person. I am making an effort.'

Instead he asked, 'What flavour do you like?'

She selected a bean-burger and a chocolate milkshake; he didn't comment, and the voucher still worked for a non-meat dish, to his relief. They sat up on high bar stools at a counter, running parallel up against the window, looking out onto the street.

She unwrapped the funny little parcel of bean-burger – it looked dry and unappetizing to him and he tried to persuade her to have the sachet of mayo.

'So you're living with a man, Mum says,' she said between bites.

'It's what's called a flat-share. We're starting a business together.'

She said very little in return and to be honest Khalid didn't really listen to what she did say, because he was noticing parts of her face that looked like bits of his face when it was younger, and also wondering what he should buy her and wishing that he had more cash so that he could take her to buy something right now, from anywhere. He wasn't fully listening to her because he was considering the right sort of jewellery for her, probably a locket or a little pair of earrings.

'I sat the 11-plus!' she looked up proudly, as if this had particular importance to her.

'That's good, very good,' he said enthusiastically, although they both realized he didn't understand anything about the school system, or what this meant.

'Do you like my boots? They're new. I customized them, some of my friends said I can do theirs.' She swung out her feet to show him the swirls running up the back seams of the Doc Martens, the multi-coloured laces.

'They're not my cup of tea,' he apologized, unable to lie about it.

'OK, sure.' She didn't look offended, as if she knew that already. 'I'm growing out my fringe,' she offered, and he appreciated these attempts to strike conversation, even if they faltered and he didn't know how to take them forward. She kicked her legs against the bar stool in a restless way, as though she wanted to move on and was forced to sit there.

'Let's walk a bit,' he said, and gathered up the paper and cardboard waste to take over to the bins.

The rain was easing, although he didn't like being out in it, and would rather have been inside, but then, they had no actual place to go to in Hammersmith, so really it was a choice of Burger King or the street, and it seemed better to keep moving. They went down and looked at the suspension bridge, which rumbled with heavy traffic, and walked across halfway to peer at the Thames through the hatched metal, down at the water from the gaps in the railings. The bridge was elegant, with its long curves and exotic swirls, painted in Persian green when you saw it up close, topped with gold twirls and coats of arms; he had never paid it any attention at all when he'd lived there, usually driving across it in the dark. Alia said it reminded her of a Chinese dragon, which made him laugh, and he could see what she meant. They were both soaked by then, and he decided it was time to take her back home.

The Queen Caroline was older, properly bedded in, smarter, even in the grey drizzle. Saplings had grown into thickened trunks. Some people had customized their front doors, added small porches and extended rooms on the ground floor, by building outwards onto the front lawns.

When Suzie came to the door, she left him standing on the step, and told Alia to go and find a hairdryer. She offered Khalid a towel but he declined. 'I was thinking... I could send her over to you,' she said, 'when you drop her off... you could just put Alia on the Tube and I can meet her at the other end. It's only about eight stops, isn't it? You can ring me when you're leaving. Save you the trouble,' she said.

'Sure,' said Khalid and that was how they picked it up again.

'HOW WAS IT?' SAMMY LOOKED UP FROM A STACK OF PAPERS arranged on the glass tabletop when Khalid arrived back at the flat.

'She hasn't changed much,' Khalid said, taking off his coat. 'Any news?'

'Nothing – dead. Got any pictures of your girl?'

'It's a bit out of date.' Khalid drew out his wallet.

'Cute – smart-looking.'

'She's doing well. She's just done the 11-plus,' Khalid said, and couldn't find any other words for this picture, taken in a school hall of Alia in a red school jumper with a posed grimace.

'And you? Any kids?'

'Probably. No one ever came looking for me, though. What happened with the mother?'

'She threw me out,' said Khalid in a way that suggested there was nothing else to say. He took back the photo and slipped it back carefully into the clear section at the front of his wallet.

'Play the field, no better advice. Keep it simple. Jiggy-jiggy, that's all it's ever been about – don't need to buy up Hatton Garden for that,' said Sammy.

'I'm seeing her again soon actually. She'll come over here, on the Tube. Her mother has agreed.' That wasn't strictly true. She had said, 'Let's see how Alia feels about it.'

'Should be OK. As long as this doesn't all kick off. It's as quiet as the grave right now. Once it gets moving I'll need you right here, come rain or shine.'

SAMMY HAD SHOWED KHALID ROUND THE FLAT WHEN HE'D arrived back in London. Khalid had come straight from the airport, leaving one cold city for another. 'Wasim said you needed somewhere to live – well, here it is,' Sammy had said at the front door, and shown him up the stairs. Rackety and cramped, especially after Wasim's place, but Khalid couldn't complain.

Church Street was a short-term rental, a one-bedroom flat for two men. Sammy had the bedroom, and Khalid had the living room. Few signs of homeliness in the place, clean toilet but stinking of bleach and there was a rough flannel to dry their hands on. The rooms were functional and plain, with nylon carpets and beige walls.

Sammy had gone out the first morning after his arrival, while Khalid had a shower and shave, and returned with fresh rolls and black coffee.

'So, partner. You and I are in the motor trade together. Import-export,' Sammy had said as they sat together at the table. He wore a fashionable black bomber jacket, made from parachute material, and didn't smile readily.

'Motors.' Khalid repeated; it had been made quite plain to him by Lucky.

'You're being cut in, my friend, it's your lucky day, lucky year, actually. How about it?'

'OK,' Khalid had nodded.

'We're going to export some things which are badly needed in Saudi Arabia. What shall we call our little company? You're the director, what do you think? Can you think of a boring little name?'

Khalid was ready. 'First Arabco? Or Arabia Motors? Or Kingdom... Kingdom AK.'

'Khalid, you are a man after my own heart. I prefer something without the first letters of the alphabet. We don't want to be first on anyone's list. So First Arabco it is.'

'And what are we exporting?'

'Engines. Cars,' he said it as if it was a loaded word, 'need engines. We have an envelope here with some magic numbers in it. This should get us started...'

Khalid had been immediately registered as the Company Director. They had an envelope with an account number and cash on account waiting for them at BCCI. To be honest, it promised to be the easiest money Khalid had ever been in a position to make. They would be paid a percentage of the sale price, for their attention to detail, for their watchfulness and for the tension that it would wreak on their sleep and their nerves.

Khalid had been restless that first night. Jet lag had been propelling him forward in time, making him jumpy. He lay in bed more awake than asleep and drummed his feet against the bed board. The bed was short, he thought, and he wasn't a tall man. It wasn't a bed, but a sofa. His feet were pushed up hard against the arms of the sofa, and he was in the front room.

IT WAS MOSTLY A WAITING GAME, ONCE THEY HAD SET UP THE front company. They tried to make sure someone was in the flat, so they didn't miss any phone calls.

A few nights after he had seen Alia in Hammersmith, Khalid offered to go out and get food for Sammy. 'Pizza or burger?' It was the usual question. The kitchen was stacked with yellow polystyrene cartons, and there were sachets of ketchup and mayonnaise scattered on the work surface.

Downstairs on the street it was busy with traffic peeling off from the Marylebone flyover, and an ambulance screeched round the corner from St Mary's Hospital. Khalid opted for Chick-King and waited behind a gang in tracksuits and puffers. One fellow in a bomber jacket sat alone, eating fries, staring out of the window. Halal, it flashed on and off in orange letters above the counter. A lot of them were recent arrivals, he could tell by their accents, and their trainers. Fresh off the Boat. Chipping away at life, having a go at making it. Khalid knew the scene; he thought he'd left this street behind, and that he'd moved on to a house of his own and home-cooked dinners. It was only temporary in any case, Khalid told himself as he handed over the cash.

The man behind the counter wore a baseball cap with the Chick-King logo, and shovelled the fries into cardboard sleeves and handed him a blue carrier bag. 'Alright, boss,' he said, with a grin, with the look of someone who wanted to move into his shoes. Khalid's brogues were glassy and he still got his shirts done at the dry cleaners. It was an old habit and expensive, but it was an investment, he would have told anyone, in himself and in his future.

As he left the shop, his feet stuck to the lino a little and he heard the deep fat fryer flare as a new batch of chips was poured.

When he got back to the flat, he saw a pair of men's shoes left by the front door. Good quality but scuffed, unloved. Someone had kicked them off inside the doorway, on instinct, but without care.

'Lucky's here,' Sammy called down.

It was a warning.

Lucky was in the bathroom, and he took ages. No sound of taps running, and when he came out the bathroom was silent; the cistern usually groaned and clanked when it had been flushed. Lucky wore the same leather jacket as always, and he had grown a little black beard – it hid a scar across his cheek – and he paced around the room and slapped Khalid on the back and flicked through the papers on the glass desk, as if he was inspecting the place.

He wiped the back of his hand across his nose.

'Salaam, brother, so what's cooking? You got everything under control here, everyone know what's what?'

He had a key of his own to the flat and he let himself in from time to time. There was no knowing when. Khalid saw all this and he didn't say anything and Sammy must have known it too. Neither of them touched the stuff.

Lucky was jumpy, turning a razor blade in his fingers, spinning it over and over again, as if it was comforting.

'That's not a toy, Lucky,' Sammy said.

'And I'm not a kid.'

Khalid opened up the polystyrene cartons and went to get a roll of kitchen paper.

'So what's happening up at the big house?' Sammy asked.

Sometimes Lucky told them things, where Khashoggi was, who he had been visiting, but his eyes didn't twinkle like they used to with the stories of hidden ski resorts in the Appalachians reached only by helicopter, or Khashoggi's new fleet of Bentleys, lined with real zebra hide. He told them stuff, but the spice had gone out of his voice, like he was going through the motions.

And Khalid had worked out that Lucky wasn't involved in much high-level action anymore. Just eyes and ears on the old London patch, making sure everyone was getting protection when they needed it, and sending out the heavies when it was better to nail something down, or shut something up. Sammy had said something about a young woman who'd been found tied up at a mansion on The Bishops Avenue. Her throat had been slit. Her husband had been the real target, people said. But he had been in Abu Dhabi. It was news for a day, it was even in the *Standard*, but the case went cold. When he looked at Lucky, Khalid reckoned it must have been a rumour. There were plenty of people who would have liked to take his place, living on the Park, right in the inner circle. He was always going to have enemies. Khalid still saw the little boy from Uttar Pradesh, showing off to the adults.

It would be better if the kid got off the gear, though; he was looking rough, and his nose was running.

'K's got his eye on a girl. We've lost track of her, though.'

Lucky spun around as if there could be women behind any curtain, under any bed. Chance would be a fine thing, thought Khalid ruefully.

'And security?' Sammy took a handful of fries.

'It's tight. Very tight. This is serious shit, Sammy.'

Lucky shook his head, as if it was all too overwhelming, and darted into the bathroom again.

They ate in silence until Lucky came out again, jangling his keys on his hip. His body was alive, wired, although his face was prematurely lined.

'OK, brothers, I'm going back over to the house. Anything you want? Anything you need? No one bothering you?' he asked.

He asked it without wanting an answer and left a wad of notes on the table. A few hundred for their basics. Sammy was in charge of the petty cash and peeled off a ten, took the rest and patted it inside his jacket. 'I'll pay the landlady, Kal. We need cigarettes, whatever you want from the corner shop.'

They heard Lucky's steps on the stairs and the door slamming behind as he left, and the whine of his moped as he took off.

'Koskhol, he needs to get off that stuff. It's a mug's game,' sighed Sammy as soon as the sound of the moped had died away.

'K will never get rid of Lucky. He's like a father to him,' Khalid said, laughing, as he wiped his greasy hands on the paper towel.

'Wise up, Khalid. We are all disposable.' Sammy ripped the last shreds of spiced chicken from a bone with his fingers. 'Who would notice if Lucky went missing? Or me? Or you? I didn't think I had to spell it out to you.'

NEARLY MIDNIGHT AT THE BEGINNING OF DECEMBER, A FEW days after they had carefully completed preparing the invoices for Vickers, Khalid sat on the sofa, tapping into a calculator, with a can of beer at his side. Snooker was on the television, and the room filled with the soft clack of the cue ball as it broke, sending the reds reeling out against the cushions, followed by the low murmur of the crowd. A skinny player in a bow-tie inhaled as he walked around the table, finding his angle. Khalid didn't pay attention, and he just stared at the calculator as if it could divine something for him.

He tapped numbers in, different combinations and percentages.

'What are you up to?' Sammy said as he walked in.

'Just calculations.'

He was working out the odds on getting busted. Ten to one, twenty to one? If he was placing a bet on the game, he'd have said there was a fair chance of beating the house. He'd have said it was worth a punt.

'Khalid, excuse me for saying it, but you need to get off your arse. You don't move enough, and all this fried chicken. It's not doing you any good.'

'Yes, alright.'

'I'm serious, you need to go swimming, go for a run or something.'

Sammy liked jogging. He often got up very early and put on his Walkman, which he wore on an elasticated belt around his waist. He wore a sweatband in a matching colour – turquoise or lime green usually – around his forehead. Khalid thought that he looked ridiculous; it wasn't a way any grown man should be seen out in the street.

'I'm doing alright.'

He contemplated his belly, which had grown harder and rounder lately. At night sometimes he woke, and felt as if his heart might have jumped ahead in a staccato, as if not keeping rhythm properly, like an unreliable watch. In fact, he hadn't thought about his body much lately at all. He looked down at his arms, which were once taut but where the muscle was dropping tone, and becoming slack. He hadn't touched anyone for a long time, or been touched.

'You want to get laid again, don't you?'

Sammy was speaking as a friend, as if he was on his side, but Khalid found this an affront to his dignity. Sammy couldn't help flaunting his virility; Khalid has never seen him in action but he gave the impression that he could meld women to his will, like Uri Geller bending spoons. Just this week, there was some auburn air stewardess for American Airlines he'd met in a nightclub, with a flat-share in Ealing. Khalid had fielded a few calls when he hadn't wanted to pick up since.

When was the last time he'd had sex? It must have been at least five years now. It was a long time to be alone, but he had never thought of it as starkly as that and he resents the need to tot it up as if it were the odds, as if he had to bet against himself. He was not going to share that information with Sammy at any point.

20

'IT LOOKS TO ME LIKE IT'S SOMETHING TO DO WITH ARMS. THE bank being used to pay for illicit arms sales.'

'Arms sales?' Linda sounded sceptical. Despite everything she knew, she was precise and liked facts. She didn't want Denby to speculate without evidence. She held his version carefully to account.

It was an octopus. The tentacles reached into all sorts of industries and potential parts of government. They were trying to disentangle what they knew, and could prove, from what they suspected.

Linda swivelled her office chair away from her desk so that she was facing him, with a spiral-bound pad held in one hand, as if she was ready for dictation. He pulled the door closed so that people in the corridor couldn't hear them. As he relayed as much as he could about the meeting with Zahra Asfour, they both picked around the meanings and possibilities, the roads that could definitely be said to be open, and the paths that led to dead-ends and supposition.

'There is no way they'd let it roll on, unless they had a use for it,' Denby said.

'Surveillance?'

'That too, but it runs deeper. Someone is using the bank to buy and sell materials. Things they don't want the rest of us to see.'

'Aren't you jumping the gun?' Linda asked.

'Is that a joke?' He raised his eyebrows in an arch way.

'I mean... we would need much more evidence.'

'Look, everyone's acting like Iran–Contra is some aberration, a shock, Reagan the Cowboy – I think...' He paused. Just to articulate it aloud was to set something in motion. 'I think... we have our own little deals right here, right under our nose.'

'Has someone told you that?' Linda was suspicious of anything that didn't follow correct procedure and wasn't backed by solid paperwork.

'As good as told me.' The way George wiped the ketchup off his chin and how he could have hurled him into the river at that moment.

She paused. It added up. It was hardly surprising, but it was also fragile, a piece of information that could dissolve into nothing, like a bitter aspirin on the tongue. Or it could be explosive – setting off chain reactions, headline news stories, and haunting ministers in their beds.

She backed away a little, and took her hands off the papers stretched out in front of her. 'This is a bit bigger than the things I usually deal with.'

There have been stories recently in the papers; about the bodies on the roads out of Basra, the men burned inside their helmets and lining the trenches in piles. The numbers of dead in the war have just become zeros, different types of zeros, which she hears on the radio, sometimes in bed before she turns it off.

'You ought to consult someone in the party. Go to the front

bench.' She started reeling off all the options. He had thought about each one of them already. Considered each one quietly and methodically in the night.

'I've decided already, Linda. I'm not going to kick up a fuss. I'm going to follow parliamentary procedure. I will table a question. That gives the government a chance to respond. And I will send the question — and the answer — to the papers. To the right people who will know what to do with it. A very heavy hint. And they can take it from there. Then it's out of our hands.' There was a note of excitement in his voice. 'Look,' he went on, 'I'm not trying to make a career out of this, I didn't even go looking for it.'

'What would be the harm? You're a good man, you are trusted. It would put you on the front page.' Her glance was admiring, but not transgressive.

She honestly just thinks I'm a decent person, he thought.

His own vanity was stirred but he knew they needed to do things properly. It wasn't about him personally and he didn't want to use it as a way of scoring points.

'No, this isn't a story about me. It's about the bank, and what they are doing, about their links to the government. It looks like a time bomb to me. They'll probably want to wash their hands of it.'

'So why say anything at all? Is there any merit in just keeping quiet?' she asked.

He had been asking himself this. It was nothing about Iran or Iraq. He could barely tell you the difference between them, truth be told. It was a sense of moral outrage, the sense of a good system perverted, or perhaps the betrayal that comes with maturity, the child discovering the reality of the parents. His sense of the way the world worked had been skewed, pushed awry, his belief in duty.

He was angry at the arbitrary way their powers could be diverted. What was the House there for, a national pantomime every week? He may as well have been back in Cowley. That's what's pissed him off. He had a rising sense of outrage, which made him physically tense, like a dog on a leash about to run, and it worried him too, the part of him which still observed himself, because it might not be logical.

'So, this question?' she said, with her pen poised.

'Let's draft it.'

He pulled up a chair beside her. They worked on the wording together, deftly, in only a matter of minutes. Denby made frequent sharp lines through their drafts with a pencil, until they realized they wanted to ask two different things so in the end they drafted two parliamentary questions for written answers. One more specific and addressed to the MoD, the other a more general question about banking regulation to go to the Treasury.

He read over what they had written.

To ask the Secretary of State for Defence how many transactions for dual-use materials have been made using the Bank of Credit and Commerce International; what were the transactions for; and who were the purchasers.

The second question, for the Chancellor of the Exchequer.

To ask the Chancellor of the Exchequer about the auditing of the Bank of Credit and Commerce International, and his confidence in the auditors, and the bank's competence.

Linda typed them up on letterhead in seconds and he scribbled his signature at the bottom, twice. He examined the final copies as they came off the word processor, printed on creamy paper with the green portcullis at the top. Just another bit of parliamentary business, slips of paper in a sea of thousands.

Linda usually delivered questions to the Table Office, where the clerks processed the business and passed it on to the ministries, harrying them with deadlines for written replies. Today, Denby decided to walk across with her. She moved swiftly, and knew her way around the long corridors and turnings better than him.

They walked quickly, excitedly, and although they said nothing to each other as they did so, there was the silent understanding of doing something vital. An experiment with truth. For a moment they were missionaries, zealots, crusaders. Denby held the papers by the edges, as if they might be covered in a toxic substance.

The clerk in the Table Office gave the papers a dismissive look, and added them to a pile of documents. The questions seemed innocuous lying there, just a few typed lines. The clerks would check the wording for style, and for impropriety, to see whether the questions could stand. Then they would be submitted upwards, to the relevant departments of state.

'I'LL WALK WITH YOU,' HE SAID.

They slipped out of a side gate into Old Palace Yard together, and turned towards the river. Linda took the bus home from Lambeth Palace Road. It was only four o'clock although it was as dark as midnight. The exhausts smelled noxious and headlights shimmered in the rain. Denby carried his leather briefcase, and Linda levered up her umbrella.

He said he'd cross the bridge with her and walk her over to the south side of the river; unusually, he'd never done anything like that before, but they shared a secret, and it was too early to part company. He needed to work off the adrenalin, and walking alongside her would be good for him, and help him clear his head.

They skirted past a few political reporters, cameramen waiting around on College Green for the news hour, and along the path through Victoria Tower Gardens. The pavement was flat and anonymous here, much quieter as soon as they were out of the shadow of Westminster.

They walked in companionable silence, although it was also unfamiliar walking and being outdoors with Linda, when they were usually in the office together, confined between the same four walls.

Double-deckers edged across the bridge, bumper to bumper, and the wind pushed against them.

They reached Lambeth Palace, squat and rust red. Great hoardings from the election still up by the side of the road.

Britain is Great Again. Let's not wreck it.

'Someone should have taken those down,' Linda said.

They continued a little way along the road, heading north. The traffic was relentless, and they stopped and waited to cross.

'I was born there,' Linda said, pointing up to St Thomas's ahead of them, lit by rows of white lights behind identical curtains. 'That midwife made such an impression on my mother. She'd left her own children behind in Trinidad. My mother used to talk about it – she had been alone with that woman, all night, while my father waited at home.'

Zoe as a baby. A bundle of life-force. And his inability to do anything helpful, apart from driving extra slowly down the road from the John Radcliffe back to Cowley, to protect her from the speed-bumps. And then Penny's trip and fall into unconditional love. She said it was like that, like falling on a pavement. Smash.

'My father came here too. He came by ship, into Tilbury docks. He didn't stay.'

They waited at a pedestrian crossing for a gap in the stream of traffic.

'I thought he was from Oxford. Wasn't he a factory worker?' Part of her job was to know his biography.

'Yes, he was, I mean, the man who raised me was. But I found out recently – I talked to my mother, and would you believe' – he laughed and told it like a funny old anecdote, something for a dinner party – 'my real father was a Polish pilot. Mother kept it to herself all those years, sly old bird.'

She wasn't so easily fooled.

They hadn't crossed although the lights had now turned green.

'That must have been one hell of a shock.'

'I haven't given it a lot of thought.'

'And did you ever meet him?'

'No. Didn't know anything about him. Still don't.'

'Well, that's quite a turn-up for the books,' she said. It was enigmatic and final. She sensed that he didn't want to say more, the sharing of information was enough.

She crossed the road and was quite firm that she would go the rest of the way alone, and the 344 rolled up within seconds.

'Goodnight, Mark,' Linda said and waved, generously, as she boarded, and he turned to head back the way they had come.

The rain was falling in sheets now, with people taking shelter in doorways, and he spotted a bus heading the right way, back across the river, and he jumped on board on impulse. Inside the windows were steamed with people's breath and the smell of damp winter coats, and he found himself humming, a theme tune to one of the programmes Zoe used to like as a child. A programme with hand puppets, and moonscapes made from cardboard. A simple, repetitive tune, he couldn't get it out of his head. And when he reached Pimlico he hopped down from the back of the platform, lighter than he had been for days, with a new energy and purpose.

Was it wrong that he had told Linda about this thing, that conversation that he had with his mother? He doesn't even have a name for it. It's just a piece of knowledge that could vanish. He'd dislodged it like a lump of apple stuck in the throat, and now maybe he could forget about it and move on. It wasn't important enough, not worth making a fuss about with Penelope and Zoe. They would be too invested in it, they would see themselves as part of the plot, and want to write themselves into it, whereas Linda was objective, and at one remove. He was not prepared to start rewriting his life-history just because of something his mother had said, a few sentences uttered aloud, best forgotten.

'BUT HE NEVER COMES.'

'Well, he is this year.'

When Denby was back home at the weekend, slicing some bread at a wooden block on the kitchen table, for sandwiches, Penny told him that George had accepted their invitation to the Advent party. He had sent a postcard, an old master of the Virgin and Child. She'd propped it on the dresser. The virgin had an improbably round bosom.

'Alone?'

'Of course. When's that man going to settle down?' It was rhetorical, slightly teasing. She was grating cheese into a bowl.

'He's having his cake and eating it.'

'What does that mean?'

'He's not shying away from married women.'

'George? Honestly?' He can't believe he's never discussed it with her before or that she doesn't know this open secret. She must see it. So why would she pretend otherwise?

'Hasn't he tried it on you?' He said it in an offhand way, as if it didn't really matter, as he rooted around in the fridge for the butter.

'Oh, George is just a bit wicked,' she said.

'Well, it works on some of them.'

'Not on this one.' She wiped the crumbs from her hands and put an arm round him, in a friendly way. It was exactly the same gesture you would give a troubled colleague or neighbour whose pet had gone astray.

21

THE SUMMER TERM WAS DRAWING TO A CLOSE. STUDENTS WHO HAD finished their exams walked around dazed, attempting to celebrate, covered in shaving foam by their friends, garlands strung round their necks. The grass lawns were dotted with people. She walked out of the college quadrangle and passed a student she knew lying on the lawns, her hands behind her head, exhaling.

Alia had started working again, and something was driving her on. She couldn't wait to get to the library, grabbed hours in between marking and exam meetings.

Something had caught on her, snagged.

She had started reading about the very first years of the East India Company, the seventeenth-century voyages – a galleon called the *Red Dragon*. The ship had had a previous name, a better name, which was the *Scourge of Malice*.

This *Red Dragon* sailed back and forth, from Britain to the East Indies, right round the Cape of Good Hope, probing Asia; sometimes it was thrown back by storms, by Dutch cannon, or by Portuguese guns. It was hauled up onto beaches and docks, onto tiny spice islands, and stuffed full of cloves and sacks of pepper. The men on board had got scurvy, some had died of boredom or heartache, others had gone stark raving mad.

Still it kept sailing, it kept coming back. And finally, on its tenth mission, in 1612, it had made it to India, to Surat, on the Gujarati coast. A man called Thomas Best planted his flag on the ground and decided to secure trading rights. By the next year he was boasting about his trade in Agra.

What attracted Alia to this ship was the story of the plays acted out by the sailors on board. *Hamlet* was performed on the deck – one of the earliest recorded performances.

There was very little known about this. She was sure she could find out more about the history of the ship; the captain was fairly well documented, so perhaps she could dig up some unknown records about these performances and about the links between the explorers and the theatre. *Hamlet* in those conditions, the ship moored at Sierra Leone. What the sailors had seen. A quartermaster as Hamlet, a cabin boy as Ophelia. There had to be a book in it.

Nathan was in Oxford again that week, dispatched to recruit students, a milkround. She went to find him in a large sports hall, where he was manning a stand. Rows of neatly demarcated exhibition stalls, with a variety of colourful slogans and posters, designed to appeal to hungry, ambitious graduates. He looked awkward carrying a tote bag, with reams of handouts, corporate sweatshirt mismatched with his suit trousers. 'Could they get any more logos on you?' She smiled and gave him the takeaway coffee that she'd brought for him.

'I've got to win them to the cause of accountancy.' He shrugged, looked mildly defeated. Unpinned the name badge from his sweatshirt.

She glanced at a flyer with the starting salary for a graduate trainee. 'Nice work if you can get it.'

They left the stall unmanned and went out onto the street.

She told him what had happened the previous day.

She had run into the Head of the Faculty, as she was leaving the English Faculty Library. The woman looked harassed, with oversized brown paper envelopes under her arm stuffed with piles of exam scripts, needing to be urgently marked.

She didn't quite know what Alia was talking about when she broached it, but then she had blinked and comprehended, and remembered the backstory. They stood near the turnstiles where students were exiting, with a beep of the electronic mechanism.

'Ah yes. We tried to do it, but we haven't been able to renew your contract. A year is the most we could stretch out that sort of lectureship. I'm sorry. We did try. I know you've been such a help this year.'

So that was that. She was cast out. She didn't have a job from September.

'I'm thinking about going travelling for a year. I'd like to volunteer – I've been reading about this charity that does great work in Sierra Leone. They need teachers, I could go for six months. There's this drama school, they do plays, Shakespeare, touring. I could help, teach literature. I've got this idea about a book too...'

The problem is the expense. She'd be a volunteer. She would need at least a few thousand to keep going. How to break free of the hamster wheel of work.

'Can your family lend you some?'

She couldn't ask her mother – everything of significance came from Milton, and he was generous to a fault, but he wouldn't support her.

'He's tight. Generous with stuff that he can give. Meals,

holidays. But he's philosophically against handing over money. And I can't be indebted like that.'

'I can lend you something.'

'No, thank you, but it's not like that. I need freedom, independence. I can't see a way out of this system. I'm going to have to keep teaching, and producing papers like a printing machine, and if I'm lucky someone will pay me for a year or two, but a real job is so far off, and I've never had a moment just to think about what I'd do if I wasn't caught up in this mental game.'

'Alia, can I ask, what's it all about? What was all that BCCI stuff about for you?'

'It's about my father,' she said, releasing as much information as she could spare. 'I'm trying to discover what happened to him.'

He put a hand lightly on hers.

He'd accepted that he wouldn't bring her over to the church, that there was only so much that he might help with. His efforts were a sweet kind of conversion, nothing heavy handed or damning. No confessions.

'Anyway, we've got a treat next week, a guest speaker, coming into college to give a talk. Lord Denby. Remember him, from the cabinet? He's going to give a lecture. If I get the chance, I'm going to ask him a few questions, see what he says.'

IN THE EVENINGS, SHE'D STARTED PLAYING BOARD GAMES WITH Stefan and his friends. Sometimes a big bunch came over, and they had to squeeze into the sitting room, and that's when it was boisterous and silly, and sometimes it was just a few of them. They turned up with six-packs of beer and boxes full of coloured cards and complicated rules. She used to think they were juvenile, but one night she joined in and found herself laughing more than she had done for a long time.

Once Stefan said, 'We could play for money' – and she refused. Her voice was more vehement than she had meant it to be. They stuck to matchsticks. She sometimes found herself in the library towards the end of the day, working hard, and looking forward to returning to the flat. They haven't turned the television on for weeks. They haven't talked about what happened in April, either.

'Screw Oxford,' Stefan said. 'Go somewhere else. Do something else. You shouldn't get hung up on this place. The whole world is out there.'

'It's easy for you to say. You have backing too.' Mean bringing it up, and also self-righteous. He had an uncle who was one of the early computing pioneers, and who lived on a hillside in a glass house outside Stockholm, with a view across the archipelago.

'He's completely out of date,' said Stefan, trying to shake off the accusation of privilege.

'He's an expert, he's respected. That must be helpful.'

Stefan was slightly offended. 'It's not like I got into university because of my name, or anything like that.'

She knew he was being honest. It was so much more complicated, a mystical osmosis, a fusion of privilege and suggestion, of talent and encouragement, a charmed circle.

'Anyway, I'm not sure you want money in any case.'

'What's money got to do with anything? We're not even talking about money. We're talking about opportunities.'

'OK.'

'What did you mean?'

'The way you are with coins.'

'The way I am with coins?'

'Yeah, your change.'

And he gestured to the coins all over the kitchen table, in a plant pot, scattered everywhere – some rupees left from the trip to Pakistan, tiny little copper cents, the change from French bakeries.

She knew all about coins, the different colours and textures, the feel of them, whether they were newly minted or covered in the dirt of a hundred hands, the graininess that they acquired among the bits of tobacco and pencil sharpenings in her coat pockets. She knew everything about coins apart from how to keep them.

He had a point.

'These aren't going to change my fortune,' she said, but she started to scoop them up into the palm of her hand in any case.

22

By ten a cloud of smoke had already pooled in the house, and the ashtrays on every flat surface needed emptying. The study on the ground floor was full of coats and bags.

There was a slightly wilder edge to the Advent party than in previous years. Sometimes they'd only had about thirty people but this year the house was packed. Denby heard rock music coming from the living room, not to his taste.

He retreated into the kitchen and stirred a saucepan of mulled wine on the stove, and people came in and out, merrily, helping themselves to drinks. He had tried to mingle a bit. Some of the clusters were old friends, and they hugged him warmly, others – juniors from Penny's hospital, a group of women from her tennis club – he barely recognized and couldn't recall by name.

He had greeted George when he arrived on the doorstep and had been avoiding him since, although he clocked him clinched in an intense debate with Penny in the dining room, filling her glass with too much red wine.

Zoe had come in around nine and stayed for an hour or so, with a couple of friends in leather jackets. They had helped hand round olives and crisps, and Zoe had made an effort to chat to some of her parents' friends who she'd known since she was little. The kids had disappeared off to a gig at the Zodiac, and Mark had begun feeling a bit lost in the party in his own house. The last thing he wanted tonight was to be drawn into a conversation about the possibility of a poll tax, and he wondered, as he watched the dark wine swirl around his wooden spoon, if they should have held a party at all this year. This house was meant to be his private retreat.

Peter wandered into the kitchen, looking as if he wanted to corner him, to get him to sign something, or to introduce him to someone who would be useful to them.

'Who would have thought it, this time last year, that we'd have this seat, we'd be doing all this for the parliamentary party? Remember the count night?' He leaned against the fridge. Peter was drinking whisky neat on the rocks, and he looked a little teary.

Of late, Peter had been speaking about them both in the plural, as if they were a couple. As if they would sink or swim together.

Peter's children and wife had gone ice-skating at the municipal rink, for some kind of birthday party there, with other children. Peter didn't seem to care that he was missing it although he adored his family. He's a strange man, Denby thought, he believes that what I do matters. Peter tottered a little and righted himself, suggesting that he was incredibly drunk for the hour in the evening.

'Great story about us in the *Standard* this weekend. Rising star, they say. We're going to do it, aren't we? Cabinet, the works. Come on, what's on your mind? Talk to me.'

'Let me get you some water, Peter, alright?'

He rinsed out a stained tea mug a couple of times from the wire dish rack, and handed it to him.

'Cheers!'

'Another thing, though. You need to keep an eye on Penny. Keep it all happy families.'

'It is!' Mark was affronted. He knew he should ignore Peter but he was drawn to the conversation, attracted horribly to it — Peter's instincts were good whether drunk or sober.

'She was quite a girl in her youth, wasn't she?'

He didn't need to say more. Denby had never asked. How many? Probably double figures at least; she enjoyed it, it didn't mean anything, she told him when they were first married, like a confession, all the things their mothers never had, though sometimes there were men on night shifts who she'd just intended to walk home with and they ended up upstairs and she hadn't the skill or the heart or whatever to get them away, they couldn't be dissuaded. The grip on the elbow. She'd shrugged and he had never mentioned it again.

He hadn't played the same game. He'd had some kind of old-world honour about sex. Truth be told, he'd only ever completely relaxed with Penny. He'd seen it all around him, in parties and student digs, the men with a bit of cash buying the drinks with the strings. George was probably one of them and he saw it clearly, shining in front of him, a pristine piece of information.

'She was no different to anyone else.'

'We have to watch out for things in the past. They can upset the apple cart.'

'Let's talk about this another time, Peter, alright.'

He wasn't upset with Peter; he just had this way of making him look at things which he'd rather ignore, and that was what made him a tactician, and that was what was going to carry them both far. He understood and he was grateful for it. Denby needed him, and what he said came from the right place. They embraced, in the manner of footballers.

He moved into the living room.

In a quiet corner by the window, on dining seats pushed together, his mother was talking to the wife of a union boss, nodding and putting her arm on hers. They went quiet and reset their faces when he appeared.

At the last meeting one man had pushed another. No one was injured, and though they'd kept the police out of it, a lot of the workers have been talking about it. He hadn't been up to the plant for weeks.

As if she had read his mind his mother said, 'You'll sort it out, won't you, Mark?'

For a second — it might have been the wine — Denby saw his father sitting next to his mother, listening on silently while his mother talked to some third person for ages, without interrupting or hurrying her along. The way he would sit like that for hours, a tie tucked into his knitted pullover, next to the window at parties.

Denby patted the woman on the arm firmly, as if to communicate both reassurance and commiseration.

It was time to get some air.

He sat in the cold, damp back garden, on one of the patio chairs. A slug was leaving a thick gluey trail across the stone tiles.

He wasn't alone for long. George stepped out, pulling the

sliding patio doors shut, and the noise of the party inside faded to a distant hum. He pulled up a chair alongside Denby.

'You've found me. Good of you to come.'

'What do you mean? You invited me,' George said.

'We invite you every year. You never trek to the provinces.'

'Good for the lungs. I've been having a delightful row with your wife. You've turned her quite left wing, you know.'

George was agitated. It was false bonhomie; he was tapping his foot violently against the path as if listening to music when there wasn't anything to hear, only the distant chatter of the party.

'George, is something up?'

'No, well, sort of.'

George lit up a cigarette, looked up at the dark, clouded sky as if he would find some stars there if he squinted hard enough.

Denby was already irritated enough by the party and his patience was wearing thin. George's pauses were too long, too considered. It just wasn't like him.

'George, if you came here to say something to me, just come out with it.'

'You've been talking about BCCI – too much. I heard about the letter from a disgruntled wife.'

'Well, somebody's got to say something.'

'Denby, look, I just want you to know, we're on to them.

'That's good.'

'So I'd rather – we'd rather – that you backed off a bit, went a bit quieter on the whole shebang. We're dealing with it. It's not a party-political football.'

'So you want evidence? It's staring you in the face.'

'Yeah, if we want to do this properly, bring the whole thing to a close, it's got to be handled properly. There's a lot of money at stake, a lot of lives. There's, frankly, the whole peace of the region resting on it. It's not a nest to stir up. The system rights itself, you have to trust it.'

Denby had mentioned it, obliquely, to a few people. A backbencher, in the canteen, people said she was going to go far; deep into development work, always back and forth to Africa. They brought back their trays to the table, and she just nodded and poured salt all over her chips, and changed the subject to some charity for which she was going to run a marathon. He tried again with one of the old guard, an old boy on the Left, a friend of Benn's, bought him a whisky in the Strangers' Bar, interrupting him from his crossword. He'd muttered, 'Plus ça change.' He'd seen it all before. Years without regulation, what do you expect? Crooked bank, soft touch. What infuriated Denby was that no one was interested in doing anything, in setting off the alarm. When would time be called?

'It's business, it's never black and white, it's all a lot more grey than you make it sound,' George continued.

'Iran's under an embargo, right? From the UN?'

George rolled his eyes as if he was dealing with an idiot.

'Not the UN, just the US. They say they are going to shit on anyone who sells to Iran.'

'And we're doing it anyway?'

'We're doing nothing. Who's the *we*? It's *them*, we just keep an eye on *them*.'

'So *they*' – Denby said it in a pitying voice – 'are under our wing.'

'Please stop saying we and us – I don't know who the hell you're talking about.'

'I'm right, aren't I?'

It was like some silly parlour game from school. George didn't look up or answer, which was as good as saying yes. Then he shrugged, and Denby understood that his friend didn't know, and probably didn't care. It didn't seem to matter to him either way.

Over Sunday lunch with Penelope and Zoe the previous weekend, Mark had asked what they thought.

'What's actually at stake?' said Penny.

Trust her to ask the difficult questions. He could rely on his wife for that and it was partly why he admired her. Her surgical precision.

'Well, I think there's a lot of small people, with money stashed away...' He had trailed off, thinking of the men he saw every day on the Cowley Road, their lives, their nest-eggs. He knew nothing, couldn't picture what they wanted with the money. Couldn't they keep it under their mattresses? Saving up for their own taxis? He'd had the same GP for more than a decade – Dr Shah – very precise and no-nonsense in his diagnoses. He lived in a semi on the other side of Rose Hill. Would he have an account with the bank? He had told him once that he wanted to retire to Gujarat, but his kids were still living with him, he had to see them through college first.

'So it affects people in your constituency. Potentially?' Penelope had asked.

'I don't know, I'm not sure.'

'So why else should you care?'

'Because it's wrong. Dodgy. There's a system with standards

to uphold and this kind of roguery breaks all the rules, and it shouldn't be happening in our country.'

'Dodgy Arabs, Dad, huh?' said Zoe, looking him straight in the eye. 'Not quite cricket.'

'That's not what I mean,' he had shouted after her, as she got up and left the table.

'Do you really care, though, Mark?'

George was sucking on the last half-inch of his cigarette, holding it between thumb and forefinger. 'I don't think you really understand how big this is – it's international. Frankly it's out of your league. It's out of *my* league.'

'Are you saying there's a danger, to me? To this?' Mark gestured back to the house; he could just see Penny in the kitchen, at the sink, smashing some more ice out of a tray.

'Don't be a drama queen, Denby. Just stick to what you're good at, what you know about, where you can make a difference. I should think Mrs T will be off in a year or two – she looks invincible, but she can't last forever. They never do. Your time will have to come. And it's safer too, for whoever it is you've been talking to. Think of their safety.'

'Why did you have to come all the way out here to tell me this?'

'Love it out here. Best city in the country. Watching them glide around in those black gowns.'

'The dons?'

'Lucky ponces. Thinking for a living. Imagine that. I should have done a PhD.'

'Seriously?'

'Made for it. Political philosophy. That would have been my thing.'

A memory of the George he'd first met, young and studious in the library, flicking his fringe while he frowned over a page, late into the night, his room piled high with borrowed books. He'd been sharp, the quickest to grasp a problem, sensitive to the nuances of a discussion. The bravest at arguing back with their professors when he didn't agree with a point.

'Why didn't you?'

'Didn't you meet my old man?'

Mark recalled a visit to the village in Kent. The shopfront with the family name and the vast machines out the back, squeezing the mince and herbs from giant tubs into their skins.

George's father believed in practical work, in the rolling up of sleeves.

'He could have stomached medicine, law. Leading some-where. But philosophy? Come off it.'

'We go back a long way, George.'

'I want to see you do well, Mark, You're a good man. I'll look after you, I promise you that.' He draped an arm over him, as they used to do when they emerged from the library and went for a pint. 'Come on. I'm not sloshed enough yet.'

They went back inside, and Peter and George joshed, and Penelope and Peter got into a cheerful political argument, and the rounds of wine were circulated more quickly, and after midnight, when most people had left, and his mother had gone, Denby was in the field force of his own circle of people, his own friends who looked out for him, who knew complicated things, who understood him, and he kept drinking big sweet gulps. He stopped himself at the crucial moment from another glass and he was just going to bed before he passed out on a couch in front of the stragglers at the party, stumbling, woozy up the stairs. He was euphoric in his drunkenness, fuelled with warm wine and the heat of the log fire, as if many things had come clear to him.

And then he saw George put an arm around Penny's waist.

He turned on him.

'Do you know what this little shit is up to?' Mark shouted. 'Do you know?'

George looked stunned. He pulled away from Penny immediately and they all looked up at Mark, who wheeled around wildly in his own hallway.

'They let all sorts of things go on behind your backs, you know. Let's sell! Let's break the embargo. Who gives a shit where they come from? Who gives a shit what they do? We've got a bank here, they'll advance the money, we've got a man here who will sign the papers. We've got clean hands, let others do the dirty work and watch on, like the nasty little voyeur you are, George. Let's just pretend we're good old Blighty, fair play, old chap!'

And then Denby lifted his right arm and pummelled George, right down to the ground. He launched himself at him with such force that their walnut console table was thrown backwards, flowers in a Wedgwood vase tumbled down, and then Denby, in his daft, boyish, soft-handed way, went at George again with his fists, and landed his knuckles around his chest, doing little damage, but yanking at his clothes and knocking off his glasses, still pounding hard, until he felt Peter and Penny gripping his pockets and the back of his shirt with such strength that his shirt collar ripped. Peter held Denby by the scruff of the neck, and then there was an embarrassed silence until Penny gently picked up George's glasses and began apologizing to him, which was really the worst thing of all.

THE FOLLOWING NIGHT WAS SUNDAY. HE HAD TO RETURN TO London in the morning. In bed he could hear owls calling out, back and forth to each other. Penelope was next to him, but apart from him. At least a foot of cold sheet between them and he started edging over, leaning a hand on top of her body, rising and falling, and then removing it for fear of disturbing her. His mind raced forwards and backwards, placing himself in time. The world they were meant to be delivering after the Second World War, the way places were going to get richer and follow in the steps of the West.

Mark had left a message apologizing on George's answering machine. Grovelling, really. Penny had called him a taxi that night and paid for it all the way back to London, and George had been gracious, recognizing his upper hand.

Denby looked at the ceiling, and recalled a news story in October, a fire-ball that rolled out over the sea for half a mile. The Gulf ablaze, a ring of hell, and smoke clouds cracked black and orange as fire coals. The seabirds drifting into shore, slicked stiff with oil.

The next morning when he looked in the mirror he startled himself for a second. There was a man there who looked like him, but was older, with straw hair and grey stubble. A foreigner, a father, he saw the hair in flames, a man running from a bomb.

23

THE FOURTH OF DECEMBER. ALL DAY HE HAD KNOWN IT WAS HER birthday but it was only late in the afternoon that it bothered him; it hovered there, like something that could be tomorrow or yesterday, like something that could be ignored or disregarded. How important were birthdays? Adults had so many of them and his had come and gone without notice. After the launderette, he popped into a pub. In the evening he remembered again and it seemed more pressing, like something he had to act on.

Moving towards the telephone he imagined her in frills, surrounded by helium balloons, and eating cream éclairs.

He drank a couple more tins of beer, and found the Bell's in the kitchen cupboard and had a double.

He dialled.

It was quiet, there was no sound of a party.

'She's almost in bed, Khalid, I've put her in the bath.' Suzie's voice was kind and she didn't admonish him, she didn't want to cause a fuss on Alia's birthday.

'Put her on the phone. I want to wish her happy birthday.'

'She's in the bath. Can you call back in ten minutes?' she said.

'Can I see her?'

'Just tell me the time and the place, Khalid. I've never stopped you.'

He waited, poured another, and rang back. This time Alia picked up the phone. She held the receiver too close to her mouth so he could hear her breath, slightly snuffled as if she was cold.

'Happy Birthday.'

'Thanks, Dad.'

'Have you had a good day?'

'Yes, Dad.'

'I've got a present for you.'

'What is it?'

'I'll give it to you when I see you.'

He vows he will get a present for her.

'OK. I've got to dry my hair now. It's dripping.'

'Do you miss me?'

'I'll see you soon, Dad.'

'Goodnight, darling.'

'Goodnight.'

The fact that he called shifted something along with Suzie, and gave him more confidence to ring again the next day. He called when Alia was at school and planned his words beforehand. He was business-like about it.

THEY WERE GOING TO START WITH SUNDAY AFTERNOONS, every week for a couple of hours. Suzie was mild again. She said very clearly, 'You must keep to the agreement, Khalid. It's very important for her. I don't want you to let her down or disappoint her. Do you understand that? She's doing well at school again, her teachers are pleased, she's in the school play next week, I don't want you unsettling her.'

He went straight to a pawn shop on the upper end of the Edgware Road and found a pair of diamond earrings. The man behind the counter was dressed in black and slid on gloves for handling the precious stones.

'They are actually made of cubic zirconia, a miracle substance. Man-made diamonds – the Russians cracked it first – developed during the space race.'

Small, not too heavy for a child's earlobes, twinkling in the light and reflecting small rainbows.

Too perfect. Worth much less than diamonds.

'There are none of the tints and flaws which make real diamonds so admired.' The salesman warmed to his subject.

Colourless. Did that matter, if they looked so much like diamonds?

Khalid knew how diamonds felt, from his mother's rings, and her nose-piercing, the catch of those things on his body as a child. He could barely tell the difference. Cubic zirconia is the future, he told himself, as he looked inside the little padded box. These will look good. He was about to pay.

But it mattered, it irritated him that these weren't real, that they didn't have the rarity of something traded and unearthed.

'Do you have any similar, in diamond?' he asked the man.

'Certainly, sir.'

And there was a fuss with locks and keys and a glass cabinet. He produced the diamond studs and laid them alongside the first pair. The man was ceremonious, enjoying the challenge. Everything about the diamonds was better, even the size and depth of their velvet pillow, the way they radiated age and gave off a dappled light. The cubic zirconia earrings looked plastic, suddenly, and manufactured, because of their symmetry.

Only Allah is perfect.

'Four hundred for the diamond pair,' the man said, and he clearly thought that Khalid would be able to afford them – he was taking him seriously. Ten times the price of the others. Khalid knew he hadn't got anything to draw on, not a credit card in his pocket, not a stash of notes anywhere to dig into. His hand moved to his wallet. Wildly, a sequence flashed across his mind: taking the only twenty he had to the horses across the road, backing a winner, coming back with the right amount, haggling the man down, doing a deal. For the first time in a long time he saw his own delusion, like looking at himself in a magnifying mirror. He needed a gift for Alia when she came on Sunday.

'Another time. I'll take the first pair.' He paid and left as quickly as he could.

THE FINAL INSTALMENT TO VICKERS NEEDED TO BE PAID BY THE tenth of December. They had been using the branch on the corner of Green Park, as they had been advised, and he walked past Marble Arch purposefully, up to the side entrance of the bank, his polished shoes tapping on the gleaming white steps. The paperwork was filed in a leather portfolio case, carried under his arm.

The bank manager recognized him immediately as First Arabco's London representative and welcomed him with ceremony. The manager led Khalid over to a cashier in a discreet room, and she checked the balance on First Arabco's account using a computer, which showed 1,768,353 pounds sterling. She printed out the balance for him on a ticket so he could study it privately. 'All in order?' She looked up at him admiringly, from under her dark fringe, with heavily underlined eyes.

'Yes, it's all correct. This is the transfer I need to make.' Khalid acted professionally; he had memorized the account number so that he didn't need to fuss around with papers, and filled in the transfer slip with neat, confident handwriting. At the bottom of the page he signed off as Jamal Siddiqui Esq., which was a name they'd coined with Sammy after a few beers late one evening, and which he had practised signing perhaps one hundred times.

There were knock-on consequences, causes and effects, which had to take place. They had put everything in place. It was a game, spring-loaded, like a pinball machine he played once as a child. Once the lever was pulled back and released, each small steel ball bumped against the other, and the thing was to keep it all moving, not to miss a link in the chain, until the final one fell into the hole, and the game was won. The supply chain was something like this. And they had completed the final payment. Khalid felt a wave of relief through his body, almost elation. The cashier printed off the record of the transfer and folded it slowly into an envelope for him, licking the seal, while holding his gaze.

As he turned to leave, and moved through the revolving glass doors, an Englishman in an overcoat came in looking curious, suspicious, with no real business in the bank, and the last thing Khalid saw as he left the building was the manager watching the man trace his fingers over the furniture.

THE MORNING OF ALIA'S VISIT ARRIVED, AND HE WAS UNCERTAIN about where to take her. He had been thinking about the question since he spoke to Suzie. After meeting her at the tube station, should he take her to the shared flat or not? At first he planned to do the obvious thing and take her to one of the restaurants, Chick-King or one of the shisha places, for fried chicken or shawarma wraps. He knew a lot of people, and someone would come and join their table and slap him on the back and chat to them, it would take the pressure off. It would be easier. Less questions from Alia, no fuss; he could take her back to the tube station after an hour or two.

Then Sammy said he was going to be out for the afternoon, the place was all his, and maybe he should do something more homely, less temporary. He would bring Alia to the flat and cook a proper meal.

He spent the morning getting ready. He hoovered, once he got the machine working. In Habarbazaar he picked out potatoes, onions in a net, basmati, a packet of pitta bread and a large tub of yoghurt, little tubs of jeera and haldi. In the depths of the shop, picking from the glass jars, among the sacks of grains and lentils, a woman in a headscarf was shopping with a girl about the same age as Alia, her trolley so full it looked like it might topple over, and he stood aside to let them pass.

Walking home, the weight of the shopping on his arms was heavy and unfamiliar. Back at the flat he peeled the potatoes and put them on to boil, and fried up a paste from the spices.

Digging around in the kitchen cupboards, he found some of the things he needed, a sieve, a blender, covered in a sticky residue, and it took him a while to scrub them, and get them clean enough to use.

He put on the radio, and rinsed the rice so it was ready to cook.

Looking at the time, he realized he should go and meet Alia.

SHE WAS WARY IN THE FLAT, PICKING ABOUT LIKE A CAT IN NEW territory, and he had to encourage her to take her coat off and sit down. Awkward, almost a teenager and not sure how to position herself in the room. She soon stood back up again and picked up things, and paced the place, gave sideways looks at Sammy's bomber jacket on a peg and the files of paperwork by the glass table.

'So this is your office, and you live here?' She quizzed him a bit, without pushing him too much. She was keen not to offend, though she couldn't help asking a little. Her mother would be wanting details when she returned home.

'Yes, we're doing some work from here, for my new company.' It was best not to elaborate.

He said something about communications. He was helping a famous Arab with his communications.

'He's a great man, my boss, he lives on Hyde Park in a mansion, like a rock star. And if things go well with this deal, if it all goes right, I won't be living here anymore. He'll give me anything I want.'

He saw it all for a second through her eyes, the cigarette burns on the carpet and the duvet from the sofa-bed stacked in the corner. He wished that he'd bought something to make the bathroom smell better.

He could not afford to be embarrassed. He was not going to lie. This was where he was living.

'I see,' she said, and she played around with the calculator, swivelled on the desk chair while he carried on in the kitchen.

He asked her to put the pitta breads in the toaster and to take the paperwork off the glass table, and lay out the cutlery. Suzie had taught her how to be helpful and to be polite. She found the salt and pepper, and turned some kitchen paper into folded napkins. She didn't want to offend him and he knew she was trying to appreciate the effort he was making. He showed her how to blitz up the yoghurt with ice in the blender to make lassi and it turned out well.

'Just like a restaurant,' she said when they were eating.

They were sitting opposite each other at the glass desk-table. She was wrong; it had a much more homemade taste, this aloo jeera, far less oily and fresher than anything he had tasted outside – he didn't contradict her, though. She had nice manners, approving the way she placed her knife and fork down, and took small bites.

'How's your mother?'

'She's OK. She's got some weird new friends. Women friends,' she added hastily. The cutlery spun to angles on the glass surface, and she tried to straighten them out.

'Where is she?'

'She's making pots this weekend, in Shepherd's Bush. In someone's garden, they've got a real kiln that actually fires the clay and everything.'

'Pots?'

He'd have liked to ask about other men, if there have been any about. Alia wouldn't tell him anyway even if he asked. As thick as thieves.

He didn't know when to give her the earrings; he didn't want to make too big a deal out of it – not real diamonds, but they were something – and there was the sense of shame, of the embarrassment of facing his daughter squarely in the eye. An uncomfortable intimacy that he had been avoiding.

After lunch, they cleared up together. He dried and put the things away while she washed.

He hadn't wanted to drink, but he cracked open a can of Heineken. Just the one.

He took the gift box out.

She was more interested in the card than the present, though she opened the box and wore the earrings immediately. He had always taken cards seriously. This one was pink with a long rhyming poem in it about special daughters.

He checked the time and ensured that she had her bag and her coat. Suzie was going to meet her at the Hammersmith end, so he just needed to make sure that she was on the Tube at the right time. 'Thanks, Dad,' she said as they walked down the stairs of the flat, and smiled, showing her big white adult teeth.

Outside it was drizzling. Buses went past them, heading towards Paddington, and they dodged the puddles filling up again, left over from a heavy shower yesterday. She walked exaggeratedly, with disgust, around a spot where someone had thrown a cigarette, still alight, as if it was too much effort to extinguish it. Near one of the currency exchanges there was a gold Rolls-Royce, a long, sleek Silver Shadow, parked arrogantly, drawing admiring looks from passers-by. 'Not my sort of thing,' Alia said, refusing to stop.

She was more interested in a shop selling second-hand records and wanted to look in the window. For a second he saw how exciting the city was for her, and how everything was still possible.

They were nearly at the station, on a side-street, just near the tube entrance, when she spotted the big graffiti letters sprayed on the ash-grey wall, in red. PAKIS GO HOME. The characters dead straight, but done without artistry. Khalid must have walked past the spot a hundred times, and had ceased reading it. But Alia stopped and wouldn't move on.

'Come on, we've got to get you there on time.'

Alia kept saying things about these painted words. As if something written by a skinhead in a second actually mattered. She couldn't make sense of it but she knew it was wrong. The words were obviously about Khalid. But where should he go?

'Maybe it means you should go back to Mum?' she said, a child trying to correct an error, clumsily.

'Bloody bastards,' Khalid said. It was the only time he had ever sworn like that in front of her.

They parted at the station and he gave her back her rucksack, which he'd been carrying. He couldn't understand why she chose those things, quite ugly things by anyone's standards, from an army surplus store. The bag had a West German flag stitched onto it, and she was wearing big thick boots, as if youngsters would like to be conscripted and sent off to foreign wars. She could look pretty if she made an effort. He restrained himself from saying anything. Khalid was pleased with how the day had gone. He congratulated himself on conducting himself well. And Alia smiled at him and embraced him voluntarily by the ticket barriers, and turned back to wave too as she went through the lift doors.

'See you next week,' he called.

'See you next week.'

'TURNS OUT,' SAMMY TELLS HIM THE NEXT DAY, 'THE END-USER certificates are going to be the real thing after all.'

'Not up to us to fake them, then?' Khalid asked, amazed.

'Actually from the actual sodding government. Plan's changed. We've got everything in place, it's better that way. Less risky. They think it's dual-use stuff, all above board, Vickers makes engines for cars.' Sammy paced the room. 'What a crock of bull.'

They waited. A few days passed. The certificates were the very last piece in the puzzle, before they could green-light the truckers.

They arrived on Friday in the second-class post, in brown envelopes marked with the logo of the Department of Trade and Industry. Stamped, signed. Flimsy little bits of A4 that could be bills or parking tickets. Sammy ran down the stairs when he heard the post shuffling through the letterbox, and kissed the envelopes as he scooped them off the mat. Khalid leaned over the bannister to see. 'Bloody unbelievable,' Sammy shouted up. 'We are in business, my friend.'

That night Khalid dreamed of passenger ships and small fishing boats, always boats. Mostly, though, it was container ships. He saw the cranes winching the containers up, he heard the crew slamming the doors, the reverberation of the metal. The darkness engulfing the sealed cargo inside. He touched the water, as they glided past, anonymous, barely distinguishable. He saw them as clearly as if he was sailing the ocean on a tiny craft, only water in every direction, vast, alone, unconnected to each other, loaded vessels with their identical blocks, one container no different from the other. And among all those steel crates there was one that belonged to him, loaded with his cargo, making its way from Karachi to Tehran.

Who would care what was inside one or two containers, among all those thousands? What difference did it make in this huge wide world if one was loaded with forklifts, and another was loaded with toys, and another was loaded with engines that might launch missiles? In his sleep he willed his ship to keep moving forward, on its slow, inevitable journey, as if he was moving a piece on a monopoly board. Forward, only forward.

24

It was late when he passed the corner shop on his way back to the flat. The decision was still weighing heavily on him. The streetlights with ginger halos, and the cold air chilling him unexpectedly when he emerged from the warmth of the Tube. He realized that he needed butter for his toast in the morning. The Goodway Foodstore. What a joke. Everything was stale in there. Jesus, if Health and Safety inspectors could see the state of the place. The piles of biscuits stacked on the floor and the cartons of imported juice and soft drinks, fallen from the back of a lorry. A single fluorescent light-bulb lit up the stock; it was uncomfortably bright over the till, yet shadowy in the corners. Did the man spend a penny on looking after his shop?

Denby found the butter in the chiller cabinet, among the random yoghurt tubs and slices of processed cheese. He groped behind flaps of clear plastic sheeting, a substitute for glass panels, and took it over to the counter.

Behind the till, the same man was still there.

The shopkeeper, unshaven, glued to the telephone as if he hadn't moved since Denby last came into the Goodway. The receiver clamped to his ear. Who on earth could he be talking to for this long? What could they possibly have to say to each other? The man was almost sinking behind his counter, piled high with sweets and gum, with cigarettes behind him, and the leftover newspapers heaped and tied in bundles on either side. Denby imagined the man was getting fatter and more unkempt by the day. He remembered an NHS leaflet about samosas and heart attacks.

He only had a ten-pound note and the man still managed to produce the change in seconds, without glancing at him, slamming it down on the countertop. He continued jabbering. Denby bristled, the rage of his day, all the small furies swelling to a place in his throat.

'Thank you would be a decent word to say.'

'Huh?' The man shrugged, held the receiver away from his ear.

'I come in here every day for something or other and you never speak to me.'

The man laughed, a jolly, mocking laugh. It could have been a substitute for not being able to speak English.

'Well, I think it's rude.'

The man gave him a pitying look, and slowly, casually, flicked his front teeth with his thumb. He turned back to his phone call, the sound of a woman on the end of the line faintly audible.

Denby slammed the butter back down on the counter. It was a ridiculous gesture, he knew it as he did it, and left empty-handed. He would eat his toast dry, there was sure to be something in the back of the fridge, some old marmalade or jam.

THE NEXT MORNING HE WALKED DOWN THE LONG GREEN corridors to the Commons Library. Libraries – a good place to make important decisions, a habit going back to his student days. A studious researcher sat at a desk scribbling urgently in a notebook as if she was writing an examination paper, as if it was a matter of life and death. Denby walked past the long emerald shelves of Hansard debates and through the carousels, into the history section. He passed a wall of books on European history and stopped near a shelf labelled Poland. He picked a book, leafed through it, replaced it again with haste, as if it was written in a language he couldn't read.

He walked out, continued moving down the endless corridors, out into the lobby and towards the chamber.

Going through the great oak doors still thrilled him, shaking him out of whatever stupor or fog of indecision he was slumped in. His spine pulled straighter, and his head was held high. The chamber was a steam engine from the industrial revolution, with pistons and flywheel. He was inside the green heart of a mythical beast. He slid quickly onto an opposition bench and touched his head with his order paper to acknowledge a few colleagues. Mostly empty rows, hardly any on the government benches.

Piers Fletcher-Reid was on his feet at the dispatch box.

He was dabbing sweat from his pink face with a handkerchief, and squinting from behind his thick glasses as if he had just emerged from underground.

Denby unfurled his order paper. Foreign Office questions were drawing to a close. He was there in time to hear the end of an adjournment debate on Chile.

He listened to the questions as they swirled around. Much of it difficult to understand fully without detailed background information from the researchers' notes and the lobby briefings.

The final item for the session was Iran–Iraq. He watched a backbencher from Yorkshire stand – a venerable old Tory, with a longstanding interest in peace talks – and ask the Junior Minister for Foreign and Commonwealth Affairs if he would make a statement on progress in attempts to bring about a ceasefire between the two countries.

Piers was sweating again, and blustering. He was a poor speaker, and stuck closely to his notes.

'The UN Secretary-General has had recent discussions on this with emissaries from Tehran and Baghdad. However, there is unfortunately little sign of progress. We continue to hope that the Secretary-General's untiring efforts will be successful.' He dabbed at his forehead. 'The Security Council's Resolution calls on Iran and Iraq to observe an immediate ceasefire, to discontinue all military actions and withdraw all forces to the internationally recognized boundaries. As my right honourable friend will know, both Iran and Iraq have affirmed agreement with the principles embodied in the resolution, and Iran has expressed the need to save life.'

Reid went on a little more. The negotiations were very delicate, a number of departments and agencies were closely involved. It all turned on a knife edge and the Foreign Secretary was moving mountains to help bring an end to this catastrophic war which had devastated the lives of so many.

Someone from his side of the House, another backbencher, asked a pointed question about the restrictions on the sale of arms.

'Our policy is well known. As a direct result of our impartiality in the conflict, we prohibit the export to either Iran or Iraq of defence-related equipment that could significantly enhance the capability of either side to prolong or exacerbate the conflict.'

And with that Piers Fletcher-Reid slumped down on his bench, taking up the space of two men. Some people had started talking about the Cold War ending, quietly, hopefully, as if they were coming to the edge of an old time. The world was flat and now it's round, and they can sail in a different direction.

He watched Piers confer with the man sitting next to him in a three-piece suit. Denby knew his own limits. He had always been good at doing things well when he understood them. There were forces here beyond his scope, beyond his imagination.

HE CALLED PETER. IT WAS DINNERTIME. PETER'S ELDEST SON picked up the receiver and passed on the phone to his dad. Denby felt a long way from a family. He could hear them all round the table in the background, the boys competing for laughs; someone saying something about him lamping George. Well, he deserved it. Peter kept chewing noisily while he talked.

'Christ Almighty, Denby, let it go. It's a waste of your time.'

He'd wanted to discuss options, to work out the possibilities, but Peter kept speaking.

'No one round here gives a shit about it. They want to see you speak up about what you were elected for. The campaign leaflet never said anything about *banking*, did it? That's not what I promised when I went knocking on doors, freezing my bollocks off every weekend.'

'Have you even read anything about it?'

'I don't need to read. I just need to look out my window and see the poor gits on the street in sleeping bags.'

'But isn't it the right thing to do?' He realized that he was longing for Peter's bluff speech, to be talked down.

'You've got a shot at the shadow cabinet. I've spent months of my life getting you here. Let's not blow it.'

'I guess there's plenty to be doing.'

They had just got the permission for the second phase of the leisure centre, and the story was front page in the *Oxford Mail*. Peter was cock-a-hoop.

'If you want to talk international, have a word with some charity folks. I can get you a meeting with the head of Oxfam if you want?'

AEROPLANES STARTED UP OVER THE CITY JUST BEFORE SIX o'clock, tracking down the Thames towards Heathrow. The growls and whines of the plane engines, coming one after the other, releasing wheels or ascending, up and towards the coast. Dawn broke over the city, and the winter light strained through the curtains. He willed himself to sleep, calculating lost hours, and minutes gained, moving across the width of the double bed, which was cold on one side, listening to the sound of running water and a shower starting up on the floor above him.

He couldn't do it.

There was something not quite proper about the question, as if he was trying to jump the queue or unpick the workings of state, or to break the locks on the thirty-year rule.

Of course there are secrets, he is a new boy. He shouldn't start throwing his toys out of the pram. It's not his story to tell. And everyone crowds around him, in the haze of dawn sleeplessness; George with his accusations – he will be better at constituency work – he's right, of course, he will – and his father and the workers from the Cowley plant. Is he making life better for them? Other workers somewhere, making parts, hammering metal. Old lecturers and their graphs. And his mother, on the benefits of secrets. There are admirable things about silence at the right moments, the release of information at the correct time.

Crumpled under his sheet, he recognizes the truth of his decision. When they've got rid of the Tories, when they are back in power, that's the time to tackle these things, systemically, root and branch, that's when they can do it right. Not these cheap potshots. It's clear to him what he needs to do.

A black cab rumbled up to the driveway and waited below his window, and he heard a door slam as someone paced quickly down the corridor past his front door to a business meeting or a committee, and his alarm clock finally went off.

'I'D LIKE TO WITHDRAW TWO PARLIAMENTARY QUESTIONS. MY secretary left them on Thursday...'

The Table Office was quiet apart from the sound of typing. Three women in a row, their fingers moving very fast across the keys. One in pearls was the gatekeeper, like the receptionist at the GP surgery protecting the doctor from his patients.

There was a miniature artificial tree on a table in a corner, draped with some scrappy tinsel. It was out of place. At home the fir tree, the wreath on the door. He couldn't wait to get out of London.

Perhaps he would need a reason for a significant act – he started to come up with an explanation. But the clerk was busy

– she saw questions all day long – they'd just come in on the heating of schools and the arming of the IRA and the drilling of the tunnel under the Channel.

'They'll be chuffed – less work. I'll send a note over to the Treasury and the MoD – early Christmas present.'

She didn't even ask, are you sure? She didn't give Denby time to recant or to turn away. It had been decided, he was as committed as a voter who had placed his paper in the ballot box.

Taking a piece of paper from the file, the clerk shredded it with her fingers into tiny and tinier pieces. The pieces fluttered down like flakes. She was unnecessarily harsh, as if she was determined to eradicate his question from the world.

IN THREE MORE DAYS, HE COULD RETURN TO OXFORD FOR THE recess. That night Denby took a brisk walk along the embankment. On one side ran the river, on the other, the four-lane road. Below the brick walls, the river water was churning. The winter night was drawing in and Christmas was in the air. The string of fairy lights glowing white along Chelsea Bridge as he breathed in the exhaust fumes, the smell of people heading home. Battersea power station blotted out the horizon, a megalith, keeping watch over the river. He gathered his woollen coat around him, quickened his pace. London was working on him, its overpowering scale, and its magnificence. To his surprise, and even though he wanted to get back to Cowley, to everything familiar, he was starting to feel good in the city. Perhaps he might learn to master the place.

And Labour, finally getting their act together. He liked the look of the new shadow cabinet, it was really shaping up. A few of them had bright ideas; Smith was the right choice for chancellor. And some of the younger ones had been speaking out, Blair was shaking off his boyishness. What did George say? She couldn't last forever. They all know it. Their time will come. What had he got into? It was a strange time, all that business with his mother. He was relieved to shake free of it all. Peter had been right all along. England is what he knows, and heaven knows there's enough to do right here. He needs to focus on the job in hand. When he returns it will be a new year.

They've got to take people with them; there's no point being loony forever. They need to understand the psyche of these boys in their open top sports cars.

They have a common ground in this country. There is a centre ground.

Mark Denby had a new commitment to his vocation, and something else – what? He'd never call it patriotism, so what was the phrase for it? He looked out across the leaden depths of the Thames. At one end, its tidal mouth, which for centuries sent merchant sailors out to cross the oceans, at the other, the source, an old ash tree in the country. Twisting and flowing all the way through London's heart. Below him, the mud where the river had receded, like treacle.

25

SUNDAY CAME, AND SUZIE HAD SAID YES AGAIN. HE COULD MEET Alia at Edgware Road station at noon, on the dot. She'd put her on the Circle Line at their end. 'She's looking forward to it — she can stay for a burger — McDonald's or Burger King, she doesn't mind which — then I need her back home before it gets dark. She's got homework she wants to finish up for Monday. Don't screw it up.'

What were the odds? Of course it would happen, it was typical. Despite his optimistic spirit he knew in his bones it would be this way. Is there such a thing as lady luck? If there is, she was a very angry woman that day, hurling plates at him from on high. The telephone rang at twenty to twelve, and he just missed it; he heard the final ring, fading accusingly, as he lifted out the ear piece and levered himself up from reclining onto his elbow. He had been listening to the cricket commentary on his Sony portable and hadn't slept well, and there was a pain somewhere in his body that he couldn't quite locate.

The pager started bleeping, a piercing sound from the other side of the room, but before he could reach it Sammy came in from the kitchen, with a piece of toast in one hand, picked up the receiver immediately with the other and dialled without looking at the numbers, with the firm commitment of memory.

'Yup, all clear, we'll be there.' He slammed it down. 'We're on. It's ready. Driver's on his way.'

'I need to make a call.'

'Khalid, it's on – we've been waiting for this for weeks. Get your stuff together, we're leaving in ten.'

He dialled the number for Suzie's flat, his flat really; dialling that number was automatic, not even a matter of recall. It just rang, and by the time it had rung ten or eleven times his hope hurtled downwards. They must have left already for the tube station.

Sammy was picking up his jacket, and checking over the documents again. He had the movements of a fox that had been woken up, and now felt hungry, and he looked up at Khalid with expectation.

Khalid knew precisely what he needed to do. This was something they'd talked about, and rehearsed in their minds many times, walking through each step, the meeting with the buyers so that they could check the inventory. He unlocked the filing cabinet, took out the binder holding the papers and looked them over. As he rifled through the folders, a sheaf of papers and documents fell out of an envelope, and something slipped down the back of the filing cabinet while he bent to try to pick everything up. He needed to focus, this was the off, they were out of the starting gates. Why was he sweating so much?

Sammy gave him a wary glance as he clicked shut the briefcase, and turned the little silver dials on the side, doubting him. What sort of loser had K matched him with this time?

Khalid rallied himself, collected his wallet, checked his hair in the bathroom mirror, and patted down the lapels on his navy overcoat. The whites of his eyes were a peculiar china blue. The scores from the Test match passed like streaks across his line of vision. He would miss the rest of the innings – both the irrelevance and irritation of the thought bothered him. He gripped the basin to steady his nerves and remembered what they were doing, and anchored himself with the facts, and tasted the money like something salty in his mouth. The pain in his chest was worse, a hand inside his ribcage squeezing hard. He took some paracetamol from the bathroom cabinet and washed down two, then two more, one after the other, splashing his face afterwards with cold water.

'OK, Sammy. Chalo.'

Outside, Imran was waiting behind the wheel of a black Mercedes S-Class. He got out, and pulled Khalid into a firm embrace and then shrugged as if it was nothing, as if he'd just been asked a question and the answer didn't matter. 'I told you, it's for the once. Just a favour. Get in.' It turned out that the photographic business hadn't been all that it seemed. A lot of people didn't pay up when they saw the products. 'There was too much outlay,' was all Imran had said.

'Nice day for the coast.' Sammy slammed the rear door and swung open the passenger door. Imran adjusted his rear-view mirror; a lucky nazar swung from it wildly and, after a slight hesitation, he detached the blue charm and put it in the glove compartment, without looking at Sammy, who was sitting in the passenger seat and staring intently ahead. Khalid could tell that Imran was nervous of Sammy and this increased his own confidence, and helped him to focus. Imran was the novice now, the junior party, and Khalid placed his head on the leather head rest on the back seat and breathed in, letting his eyelids down for a moment. He was sweating, heavily, far too much, and he drew a handkerchief from his pocket to soak it up, patting it over his neck.

They turned out of the road, towards the tube station, where they needed a left to edge onto into the traffic on the Marylebone Road, taking them up and over the flyover. The Westway would give them a good run, a clear road carrying them south.

Passing the entrance to the tube station their car was racing for a green light, and it accelerated just as he thought he saw her. Was it her? He twisted his neck but everything was blocked for a moment by the height of the bus alongside them, and when they overtook it, his eyes blurred from the flashing neon on a shopfront.

Don't screw it up.

'Anything wrong, Khalid?' He had the darting look of a man who has forgotten something important.

'No, nothing, put some music on, will you?'

LATER WHEN THEY WERE DOING SEVENTY ON THE A3, FLANKED by monotonous trees on either side, Imran tilted his head from the wheel, and asked, 'So what you going to do with the money when you get it?'

He was trying to jolly everyone along, like a parent with children in the back seats.

'I've got my plans,' said Sammy, flicking ash out of the car window. 'Need about seven more jobs, and I'm out of here. I'm going to retire somewhere warm, get a little house somewhere, never have to bow and scrape to any chief, or put up with these sodding winters. I'm thinking of going back to Bombay, some people say Spain is nice. Not sure about the food, though.'

'What about Cyprus?' Imran had been trying to ingratiate himself with Sammy, and Khalid found it amusing, taking his mind off his discomfort, though he wished his friend wouldn't get too involved, for his own sake.

'What about you, Khalid? Got plans?' He turned his head a little back towards Khalid in the rear seat.

Plans. Yes, he's had a lot of them, still has a lot of them. When he weighed up the money, his cut, he couldn't think straight. The problem was it was not enough.

'A car, maybe a flat. It doesn't get you far in London.' That place he bought in Hammersmith, with two bedrooms, the wide glass windows. Brand new when he bought it. One careful owner. It must have gone up in value.

The borders of his world have shrunk, they have been drawn around his London patch, from Marble Arch across Hyde Park, up to the Westway. His body resisted leaving its corner of London – looking out the window as southern England rushed past on the A3 – at these roads that looked all the same and at the green road-signs and unremarkable green trees. He was never going back to Karachi, whatever he might have said to his mother and his sisters on the phone.

'What make?'

'A Jaguar, maybe a Rolls-Royce. Gold bodywork, leather interiors,' he said quietly.

Sammy laughed bitterly. 'We're not in that league, Khalid, we're not going to make that kind of money.'

This seemed hurtful and unnecessary, as if he was taking a pin to his dreams, and Khalid wished he could hurt him back but there was nothing he could say. And Sammy went on, as if he was rubbing a dog's nose in it.

'Haven't you got a plan? One job, it's not going to be a bed of roses afterwards. You haven't thought it through?'

'I'm going to make it big. This is just the start for me,' Khalid said, more angrily than he intended, wanting to believe it as he said the words. 'You've got to start somewhere.'

'How old are you, Khalid, forty-four? You *have* started. This is it, mate.' He was laughing again in a way that made Khalid's skin prickle.

'Sammy, you've forgotten how to dream, my friend.' He managed to get the last word in, the final say. Imran tried to smooth things over, turning up the qawwali cassette, as if their tensions could be drowned out with music.

Even as he said these words, a sadness descended on Khalid because he knew he was never going to be Adnan Khashoggi. Sammy was right, he wasn't in the seven-figure game, the eight-figure game. And that's what you needed if you wanted servants, opulence, a sniff of a yacht. He could have been. He had always looked the part, there were nawabs and princes in his bloodline. No one before him, for three hundred years or more, has wanted for anything. Didn't that count for something? And if he wasn't going to make it, what was his future?

His maths teacher admonishing him at school came unwanted into his mind. He had been at a very good school, with starched uniforms and textbooks shipped over in crates from Oxford. He would write the answers to the equations, scribble them out in seconds, rush to show the teacher; he often had the right answer. But he hated showing the stages, working out the intermediate parts of the problem. You must plan your answer, said his school master. He was humble, thoughtful – what was his name? It'd gone from Khalid's mind. He'd been a soldier, in the war, before Independence: once he'd told them about arriving in Sicily and going to Rome. The peaches, and facing the ruins of Monte Cassino. 'So much like hell,' he had said. It hadn't meant much to Khalid then. That old Lahori, he was brave. Perhaps he had a point, about the stages, the planning.

The good days – the ones to come – had been chalked out like the borders of a new country. He thought he just had to cross over. His failing had been optimism. He hadn't seen that the life to follow, the riches, might never arrive. Could life end without a sea-change, without the moment of transformation, without the big win? He had lived a parallel life, of the imagination, in a future that would deliver him from his present. He held the handkerchief to stem the sweat which was pouring down from his brow.

'So THIS IS ALL IT IS?' KHALID FOUND IT HARD TO BELIEVE THAT this was what all the fuss had been about. 'All that, for this.' They were staring inside the back of a container lorry, fifty feet long, the pale sides billowing out slightly in the wind.

Large wooden pallets were stacked carefully, packaged tightly in foam and cardboard wrappings. The contents of the lumpy blocks were impossible to identify through the chunks of polystyrene padding, which had been wound round with thick strips of grey duct tape. It could have been bricks or building materials, or something for dealing with sewage. The lorry wasn't even half full.

'Not that spectacular, is it? Not when you think of all the

damn work involved,' Sammy said, 'but don't judge a book by its cover. These are beauties. Absolute stunners. A few more of these and I'll be putting my feet up on a beach for a while.'

They were in a vast industrial park, located off several identical roundabouts. The place was closed on a Sunday – Sammy had the codes to get past the security gates. High fences stood on every side, topped with barbed wire, CCTV cameras leering in every corner. The place was deserted. Overhead gulls wheeled and Khalid could smell the sea, its wild calling. It had been a long time since he had smelt the sea.

The lorry driver, unshaven and gruff, returned from taking a piss. He was in an anorak, not warm enough for the weather, and he stamped his feet, and swore and his breath floated up like steam.

'On y va.' Sammy handed over a folder to the driver. Everything in it that the man would need to get these things through the port, across the Channel, and on their way. Export certificates, licences, permits, the details of their machine-supplies company, phone numbers, references, everything that he might ever want should he encounter a policeman or a customs official at the borders, across toll gates and through junctions, down the long, smooth motorways to Marseille.

Khalid prayed that all the papers were in order. There was room for error although they had been careful. He had never tried so hard to get things right.

The container would be loaded, break-bulk cargo, fastened with lashing rods and steel plates, loaded onto a French ship which would take seven weeks to edge around the oceans, through Suez, the Gulf of Aden, the Arabian Sea.

It would end up in Bandar Abbas. When it reached there

it would be out of their hands. The shipment would make its way to a warehouse where these engines would be unpacked by grateful mechanics, taking out the rusty old parts, dating back to the time of the Shah, that had ground their Chieftain tanks to a halt, and bolting in these shiny new ones instead. Their caterpillar tracks would start to turn again, their turrets would swing round as they rolled onwards to the desert.

Khalid couldn't think that far ahead; he just willed the container to Bandar Abbas, to turquoise water, to be hauled up by the cranes. His work would be done.

The driver flicked through the file. It was clear he hadn't got a clue what he was looking at. 'God, this driver looks stupid,' said Sammy, banking on his inability to understand English. 'You'd think they'd have sent someone with brains. And where the fuck are they? You'd think they'd be the keen ones, no?'

Sammy was getting irritated. He kept looking around, as if he wasn't sure which direction they'd come from, although there was only one gate. Imran tried to be useful and opened the boot, brought out a multipack of Cokes, cracked open the ring-pulls, and handed them around. He offered Silk Cuts too. Everyone was smoking but Khalid felt nauseous on the first inhalation and stubbed his out.

Khalid had the strangest feeling in his arms, spreading across his back. His chest, as if it might pop, as if it had been inflated to bursting point. He pushed his last two paracetamol from the packet and swigged them back with the Coke.

There was no way he could say anything, he told himself, he was not going to mention how weak he felt. This was not the time to be ill. 'I'm getting back in the car,' he said, although his throat was constricted and he wasn't sure if the words came out.

The gates opened and they arrived, at last, sweeping rapidly around the corner, a black Range Rover with two men in the front. English guys, Khalid wasn't expecting that. They screeched to a stop and jumped out. Close-cropped hair, one of them in jeans and the other, fleshy, but well dressed, in an overcoat, leather gloves and thick-soled boots. A butcher's boy, thought Khalid, even through the fog of the pain gripping his chest.

The man in the overcoat pushed his glasses up on his nose as he approached, held out his hand; his coat rode up on his thick white wrist.

Sammy was gesturing to Khalid to get out of the car but somehow he couldn't. He wanted to and he knew this was not the time for pissing around, but his legs were planted in the back, too heavy to heave out. Instead he saw Imran, standing there in the place where he should have been at Sammy's right. That was good. Khalid wound down the window, so he could hear, so he could breathe. His body was so heavy and he leaned against the inner door of the car, the relief of the chill of the glass on his cheek. He was just going to close his eyes for a moment. He saw men shaking hands. He could hear the hum of urgent talk, a low voice, a louder accent, Midwestern. The voices rising.

'Don't mention that name here. OK. Don't ever mention that name.' The nasal-sounding American, in a patronizing voice.

'Is this some kind of wind-up?' The podgy Englishman, pacing from side to side, impossible to know what he was threatening.

'Imran, what are you doing, shut up, man.' Sammy's implacable tone, a final warning.

THE CHAT TOOK SOME TIME, MUCH LONGER THAN SAMMY would have liked. He was irritated that Khalid didn't get out of the car, although he didn't articulate it as a conscious thought. Imran had put his foot right in it, mentioning Khashoggi by name. Sammy had to smooth things over, dampen down the antagonism, ensure they were on amicable terms again. If he considered Khalid at all, it was with the sense that he would deal with him afterwards.

They had done the usual joshing and intimidation, the checking over of papers, and the scrutiny of the details and of each other. Everything had already been approved earlier in the week, by fax and phone, and so it was simply theatre. Even the hostility was part of the performance. It was an epilogue to the real business, a ritual necessary for everything to proceed with trust. It all took about fifteen minutes.

The men in the 4×4 left. They jumped into their Range Rover and vanished behind the tinted windows, pulling away from the concrete site in seconds.

The gulls stopped screeching for a moment.

A peace descended on them.

Sammy was nervous, though. Something was out of kilter.

When Sammy and Imran got back to the car, Khalid was lying against the window. His eyes were closed and he looked as if he was asleep. There was something not right, his mouth was slack, and had something spewing out of it. His neck was at an odd angle.

Sammy got it immediately. 'Oh no, no, no… Khalid, you stupid bastard.'

He scrambled astride Khalid in the rear of the car and loosened his shirt around the neck, checked his pulse.

But even as he did these things, and grasped for his pulse and compressed his chest, he knew he was too late and he was only doing these things for Imran's sake. It was clear to him immediately that these were daft gestures. The body was already rigid, the heat seeping from it.

Sammy stroked the smooth lapel of Khalid's overcoat.

'Gone and copped it on the job, haven't you?' he said softly, brushing his hand tenderly across Khalid's eyelids, and levering himself out of the car again.

Imran was pacing uselessly outside the car, wringing his hands and praying quietly. He chanted: 'Inna lillahi wa inna ilayhi rayi'un. We surely belong to Allah and to him we will return.'

Sammy shut the rear door.

Imran said, 'Shouldn't we call an ambulance?'

Sammy looked around the barren, grey car park as if a paramedic might miraculously appear. The seagulls were again making shrill calls to each other in the granite sky above. They didn't even know where the nearest telephone was. Imran was visibly shaking and Sammy could tell that he didn't want to involve the law any more than he did.

'We're not dropping the ball now,' said Sammy calmly. 'We'll deal with this ourselves.'

26

THE LECTURE WAS DUE TO START AT FIVE O'CLOCK AND SHE dashed from the library, across the quad, entering the Provost's seminar room two minutes before the talk began, to find it stuffed, with barely a free seat remaining. The room was already too warm, the thick curtains drawn, heavy with anticipation.

The lecture was given every year by a distinguished guest, followed by a four-course dinner. Sometimes a journalist or an upstanding figure in public life, often a parliamentarian. There was a three-line whip for the Fellows and postdocs who turned up in an approximation of evening wear, wrapped around with gowns, sensible shoes peeking out underneath, and were expected to stay for the dinner afterwards.

Alia squeezed past a line of students, to get one of the last seats in the third row. A Fellow in English, one of the elderly stalwarts, patted the empty seat next to him conspiratorially.

'Duty or pleasure?' he asked.

'Duty — though it can't be worse than last year's.'

Last year they had someone from the Environment Agency who was actually very good — he gave a subtle and damning critique of government ecological policy — but his voice was monotonous, and he had gone on for well over an hour.

'This will probably be better,' she said.

'There'll be sherry, anyway,' he winked.

SHE COULD SEE ALREADY THAT LORD DENBY HAD COMMAND OF the room. He had the relaxed ease of someone who genuinely enjoyed talking to complete strangers, as he exchanged a few words with the college secretary. He wasn't here because he had to be.

The crowd settled and a hush fell as he moved to the front. The Provost went first, with his neatly trimmed beard, and gave an earnest introduction, without any jokes and too much biographical detail – verging on the sycophantic – and Mark Denby looked out, inquisitively, at the crowd, taking in the numbers, the range of faces. He ignored the lectern placed at the edge of the room – speakers usually hid behind it, and fussed with the microphone and water glasses and showed pointless slideshows, but there was obviously going to be none of that.

Denby was far more confident. He perched himself on a table and started talking confidentially, intimately, without notes, as if he would not have said these things to anyone else.

'Let me tell you a story,' he began.

He ran his hands over his smooth head, which had become something of a trademark, a self-soothing gesture.

His theme was Britishness.

He told a story about how people might feel rooted in one place again. About how Britain, and more specifically England, had changed – and how he didn't want to lose something. He used football puns, analogies with garden roses. A few comments on the English language and a neat segue into Orwell. The gentleness of the English civilization is perhaps its most marked characteristic. The most stirring battle-poem in English is about a brigade of cavalry which charges in the wrong direction.

Laughter washed through the room.

God, to be able to speak like that. He had just the right tone of formality and authority. And funny. Like the sort of dad you would want to give you away at the wedding. His speech arched into a perfect curve, looping back on itself, not a phrase out of place, not a doubt crossing Lord Denby's brow.

Alia looked about her; a couple of students looked sceptical, slightly confused, but the majority were gripped. He had them in the palm of his hand.

He warmed to his theme and made several more expertly timed anecdotes, no policy suggestions or didactic points. The Provost jumped out of his seat to give the vote of thanks, effusive and gushy, transformed into a more natural speaker himself almost by the effect of Lord Denby of Littlemore.

AFTERWARDS, THERE WAS A RECEPTION IN AN ADJACENT ROOM with oak-panelled walls, and everyone stood talking with flutes in hand, with a large oriental carpet underfoot. As people gathered around Denby, he conducted himself generously, talking at length to a solemn doctoral student, asking his own questions in return, accepting the thanks and the interest of the students.

They were seated on the same table at a diagonal to each other, too far away to naturally strike up conversation. She noticed how moderately he ate, slowly, chewing his food thoroughly; drinking just one glass of white wine and dismissing the waiter's later offers by placing his hand lightly on the top of his glass, while talking, without even noticing. He didn't pour cream on his dessert, and left half of it uneaten. He still had the leanness of a younger man. It seemed to come naturally to him, without effort. When finished he placed his linen napkin carefully to the side of his plate.

He had finished talking to someone at his side and she saw her opportunity to lean across.

Alia stretched herself forward so that he could hear her. 'You were onto the BCCI case early, weren't you, Lord Denby?'

He turned towards her and crinkled his brow.

'Yes, what a rotten state of affairs – I like to think I had a little hand in it closing. I mean, I was among the first who brought it to the attention of the Tories, though they were woefully slow to act.'

'And Bingham?'

'Ah yes, there was a report.' Evasive, as if he'd rather move on. 'We tried to speak up for those who lost out... the Asian businessmen... all those people who suffered.'

'So how bad was it?'

'We put forward Early Day Motions, we kept pestering the Tories with it – it's still in the courts, you know.'

A woman in a nylon white blouse offered coffee from a silver pot, and he declined.

'What do you think the bank was up to?' Alia persisted. Bad manners to stick so doggedly to one question with an important guest, but what else could she do?

'Who knows. There's all sorts of conspiracy theories.'

He looked ever so slightly bored, as if it was an effort to match her level of interest, and tried to change the subject, to lead her towards plays he'd seen in London recently and then pivoted, raising the subject of Oxford admissions policies. But she kept going back to the bank.

'So who is to blame?' Alia swigged the last of her red wine too vigorously as the guests started to stand and clamber over their long wooden benches, gathering their gowns and skirts. Lord Denby stood too.

'Blame for what?'

'I don't know. I mean, the whole mess, the state of the world.'

'Well, that's a completely separate issue.' He looked at her disappointed, as if he was having a rational conversation which had just veered off track, illogicality allowed to burst in. She felt she had committed the greatest sin at an Oxford dinner, an outburst of emotion. And the most frustrating realization was that she didn't know what she could extract from him, what she expected him to say.

'To be honest, I think you have to understand they have a very different way of doing things in the Middle East.' At the end of the table, waiters were starting to stack up the dirty dessert plates.

'But didn't you know about it in 1987? Couldn't you have said something earlier? Come on, people must have known? It had been going on for years. And once you came to power you might have persisted, followed the trail with more determination? I've read all the reports, they seem so... allusive, secretive.'

'It was very complex, very murky. You can read all about it, though I don't suppose you'll get any closer to the truth.'

'Actually, I am going to. I am going to India next week.' She decided it as she said it, her ears inflamed red with indignation.

She pushed the heavy bench away from her to stand, and the dirty plates and cutlery clattered as she did so. She spoke with resolution and in a way which was so emphatic that several people who were leaving the hall turned their heads to look at Alia: 'I am going to find out what happened.'

He walked with her towards the Senior Common Room, where the guests were already passing port and chocolate truffles. 'Something has changed in this country,' he murmured. 'We've moved further away from our sense of ourselves as a nation. Don't you think?' He moved on, towards the Provost's small, tight circle. Their conversation was over.

THAT NIGHT SHE LAY IN BED AWAKE, THINKING OF WHAT SHE had said to him. Of his evasions, and of his lecture. The world kept trying to print something onto their fabric, to cut out patterns. It was painful, the birth of new countries, the price of cheap labour. The paradox. Alia tried to untangle it all, until she fell back on the pillow, unsettled. When she awoke, the room was filled with the stark clarity of an English morning, and she knew exactly where she needed to go.

THEY OFFERED HIM A CAB BUT DENBY REFUSED AND CHOSE THE brisk walk back to Oxford railway station, in time to get the last train back to London, walking with a spring in his step, with the satisfaction of a job well done.

The lecture had gone well. He had said what he wanted to say. The Provost was fulsome. Meeting the students was the most interesting part. They were just the same, just as sharp in their questions and curiosity as they ever were in his day. There was no reason to fear the young.

And that intense woman, who'd recently finished her doctorate, a junior tutor, pressing him on BCCI of all things. That was strange.

It was hard for him to recall all the details now. It wasn't talked about so much anymore. Of course it all came tumbling down, like a tower of building blocks, taking people with it. It was the summer of 1991, just after the end of the Gulf War. The Governor of the Bank of England leapt like a cat prodded with a stick. Code name Sandstorm. Evidence of massive and widespread fraud, and one day, all over the world the branches were closed down – Luxembourg, Cayman Islands, Spain, France. Four hundred and thirteen branches. The one on Park Lane, boarded up. All that luminous white tiling ripped out. It's a car showroom now. Everybody pleaded ignorance, it wasn't me, guv – and it was spun like a fresh scoop, the newspapers played along. Price Waterhouse took a hit, they should have said something sooner, and there were grumblings about the bank that went on and on, the liquidators tried to sue. Still trying and getting precisely nowhere. Millions of small depositors scrabbling for years to get back a percentage, stories still cropping up in the papers.

Some of Denby's colleagues had picked it up, and he had to admit, he'd found it of interest too, while the Tories were still in power. A potential weak spot for them. It was rotten. Bingham's report had made that clear enough. It was trickier once the baton passed, after '97. Once he was at the ministry he had done the right thing, keeping it under wraps, invoking some statutes, fighting back the questions. Anybody would have done the same in his shoes.

Was it the fading of radicalism, the corners rounded and smoothed, youthful enthusiasms mellowing? That's not how he saw it.

He liked to think he'd have done the same at any age.

Some things have to be maintained; trust in the nation, trust in the Security Services, trust in banks. There was no point at all in his view in undermining the public's faith in the Bank of England, raking the Intelligence Services over the coals. Once you're in power you realize that most British people are trying to do a good job, to keep the show on the road. So a few sheikhs had made fortunes, and sailed off with superyachts, and been hand in glove with the Services. They'd run away with the circus in the 1980s. It was a sensitive time, it was a time of war. They had to let it go, what use would it do charging people with Misfeasance in Public Office now, for something so long ago?

He was on the empty platform and looking down the length of the track, waiting for the lights of the last train. It was still warm, a summer evening, and when he reached London about midnight he hoped Penny would still be up. It made sense once he was in the upper house to buy a place in London, so Penelope found a house in Battersea, just south of the river, with big Georgian windows, in an area that was coming up. It was convenient for Westminster, and she sometimes came down mid-week, and they caught something at the National.

The place in Iffley's just been renovated, an extension built on the back, with vast doors and skylights – all Penny's idea – and it must be worth nearly a million, ridiculously.

It's funny, how things build. He's proud of what they've

accomplished – just that day he'd returned to his leisure centre, one of the first things he'd achieved as an MP, and cut the ribbon on a new extension to the playground for the under-fives, with a café for the mums and childminders, subsidised coffee and refurbished changing facilities, access for the disabled. Some people call it the Denby Centre, locally, which brings him much more satisfaction than he would ever admit. The kids, so many different nationalities and languages, tumbling over each other and squealing down the slide.

The train was delayed and he sat down on the metal bench, which still held some residual warmth from the day. All the great journeys of his life had started from this railway station. The first time he ever went on a train was from this platform, gripping his mother's glove as they boarded a steam train for London.

His mother had died, without much warning, it must be fifteen years ago now. Not long after their conversation. He had kept a small shoebox of papers and letters. Evidence of her feelings, unspoken; he found it disconcerting. An abstract love, not rooted in the business of life: mortgages, decisions, taking the rubbish out, or even average-enough sex, in the dark, taking off pyjamas and dressing gowns. He couldn't get rid of that photograph. He imagines that after he dies someone will throw it out, because it will be meaningless without any explanation. The man with the straw hair will mean nothing to Zoe. It seems unlikely she'll piece it all together.

He never quite found the moment to talk to Penny and Zoe about it. And he feels a little foolish, if he ever admits it to himself, because it seems such a minor thing, why wouldn't you share it? With your wife and child of all people. And these days there is a Polski sklep in Oxford. Some of those children on the swings in Cowley today. There's a date on the back of the picture, 1943. Perhaps the likeness is so strong that someone will inquire about it further. Or perhaps they won't be able to see it at all.

27

IT'S A LONG WAY TO COME. SHE'S CALLING IT A HOLIDAY — SHE packed sun–cream and sarongs – although they both know why they are here. Their hotel is in Arambol, white towels and rose petals scattered on the bed, perched on a secluded beach. They have come here together, friends on holiday, with separate rooms. They usually end up eating breakfast in this place by the pool, with its touristy menu, and paper lanterns, so all the waiters and the other guests assume they are a couple. Stefan sits in the courtyard restaurant playing a computer game on his phone, his thumbs moving with superhuman speed. He's wearing a Hawaiian shirt and baggy shorts, and his long hairy legs are stretched out in front of him.

'I cannot believe you are playing a game in a place like this.'

She rocks back on her chair, sees the palms splayed out above, smells the spiced food frying in the kitchen.

He doesn't respond.

'So I'm going to head off now.'

He looks up again, while continuing to play intently. His thumbs seem to move without even knowing what he is looking at, an artisan, weaving something.

'OK,' he murmurs, half-listening. '... Ahh. I nearly had him.'

She stands up.

He puts his phone away in his pocket. 'Right, you are sure you don't want me to come?'

They've talked about this many times. It's all clear.

Then he looks at her properly across the table. He gets up and offers his hand, and raises her from the chair.

He embraces her in a tight, warm hold, for a long time.

It's too humid, and his shirt sticks to her skin a bit, though it's not unpleasant. It is the sort of embrace that dissolves fears.

ANJUNA IS TO THE SOUTH, A BIG SWEEP OF DIRTY BROWN SAND, dotted with cafés that spring up again, year after year. Tourists drink from chopped coconuts and beer bottles, and watch the ocean. All day Alia asks, going from place to place. Repeating his name, following the half-trail. It's approaching sunset and she needs to rest, though she wants to push onwards. She can't doubt what she's doing – she believes she will find him.

The beach café is built on wooden crates over the sand, with plastic chairs and umbrellas, faded by years of sunlight, and a roof of woven palm leaves. Bob Marley plays from the loud speaker.

The boy who's serving drinks looks about fourteen, a day-glo bandana round his head, with frantic eyes and dilated pupils. He takes the piss out of the kids on gap years, and chats with the long-stays – Germans, Israelis, Russians – who live out here for the season. Everything is hazy, and you don't ask too much. Alia knows that much – it's not a place to take out a camera, or to ask questions. The long-stays are superior to the tourists, and they think they understand the place, have seen it through the prism of LSD, speed, sweet clouds of grass. They have war-stories of trains to Hampi, and sicknesses, and bribes extorted. They leave their oversized Rizlas out in front of them, alongside their mobile phones and sunglasses.

The kid comes to take her glass, and to collect his money.

'Do you know someone called Sammy? Sammy Wadia? Lives here all year round?' It's worth asking again.

There can't be that many men in their sixties living here all the time, staying even through the monsoon.

'What's it to you, pretty lady?' The boy puts on a Mancunian accent – improbably – although his parents are still back in Pokhara, running a tea-shack.

'I'm an old friend.'

She is self-conscious sitting here on the beach in her new sandals, her flesh too plump and well fed on meat, compared to these scrawny folk, wired from bouts of dysentery and manic dancing.

And before them the extravagant sun, preparing to bow down right in front of her, too big and too fast and too red. She drains her mango lassi noisily through a straw.

'Not police lady, are you?' He looks at her. These kids have years of practice, at reading faces and body language, they can tell when someone has money in their pocket, when they work for the law. He can suss her out in an instant; an innocent, not exactly telling the truth, but no trouble either.

'Sammy the Parsi?'

'Could be him.'

'He keeps himself to himself.'

'Do you know where he lives?'

'Past the German Bakery, last house out of the forest on that side.'

She has found him. She has almost found him.

There's a wide open space behind the beach front, a farmer's field taken over by the weekly flea market, where traders from as far as Rajasthan come with shawls, and bags and trinkets, piled as high as their waists, and stand all day haggling with tourists.

Today the field is empty, though, not a soul in sight, and she steps over the cracked dry mud, and burned crop stumps, following the path towards the forest on the other side. The mosquitoes are emerging in the dusk and she wraps a thin scarf over her bare shoulders. Set back from the beach dunes, the path is thick with coconut and bamboo, and dotted between the thick forestation are clearings, where foreigners have set up makeshift cafés since the 1960s and made homes for the season in old Portuguese mansions, rented from local fishermen.

Through the dense green foliage, she can see Tibetan prayer flags and paper stars suspended from the porch of a small house. A moped passes her, precariously balanced on the thin dirt track, with a man and a woman riding pillion, their hair flying behind them. Their clothes are all the colours of the rainbow.

Although it's dusk the earth gives off an unholy heat, and she's sweating. She feels more and more that she might be lost and clutches the Swiss Army knife in her pocket.

Then the electronic pop beating, and a sign for the German Bakery. The roof is made of palm fronds and a sign is painted on a whitewashed wall: Tofu, Wheatgrass Juice, Pancakes. There's a dirt path running past it, and she knows she has found the right place.

Handsome in its day, faded Portuguese glory, blue shutters and peeling plaster walls. There's a man sitting on the verandah of the bungalow, in shorts and T-shirt, on a cane chair. There are fairy lights woven into the trees above him, and he seems unbothered by the mosquitoes. His whole body is the deep brown of a man who has lived here for a long time, his legs pockmarked with lines and old scars. He draws deeply on a hand-rolled cigarette. He doesn't notice her. He's flicking through a local newspaper, squinting as the light fades. At his feet there's a pye-dog sleeping on its side, roughed up, as pocked and worn as him.

'Hi,' she says.

He looks up. 'Hello,' he says and lowers his newspaper to his lap. 'The moon is going to be good. It's a full one tonight.'

'Mr Wadia?'

'Long time since anyone called me that. I'm Sammy.'

He looks at her, and his face is hard but not unkind.

'My name is Alia Quraishi. I think you knew my father. I'm Khalid Quraishi's daughter.'

'You're not? God almighty!' He laughs out loud, amazed at her, and slowly gets to his feet. As he laughs, it turns into a long choking cough, and he reaches for a handkerchief. She can see from his hunched posture that he's not as young as he'd first appeared, that he's battle scarred and bent out of shape, the lithe muscles of a younger body still prominent in his sinews, and in the grip of his handshake.

Sweat has soaked through her armpits, and her head thrums with residual jet lag, the effects of the heat. The sight of him has released her from fear, and she will see this through. Emboldened by the strangeness of it all, by the sight of Sammy Wadia.

329

'How smart of you to find me. Come on up.'

She joins him on the deck and he pulls up another wicker chair.

'Did you even know I existed?' she asks.

'Of course. I saw your picture in his wallet. Your father was very proud. So many years ago. All dead now, aren't they? – all the boys. It was another time.'

'What do you do out here?'

'I've been here for years. I've gone soft in my old age,' he says. 'I help out with the Israeli kids.'

'Some of them come out here after their military service, they're twenty-one, twenty-two, they've done two years and they flip, lose the plot, take a lot of drugs, grass, LSD, and they can't deal with the freedom, after what they've seen.

'They can't handle it – they've been in the army and then they come here and they end up dancing naked on the beach or sick in the hospital in Panjim– sometimes the parents come out. I help, I lend them money, I let them use my phone. I call the parents if they can't face speaking to them. And I talk to them – they just want to talk. A counsellor if you want to call it that.'

He talks at length about the young people. How they've had their heads shaved so long they've forgotten the colour of their own hair, and how they are sick of uniform and sick of drill, and they start dancing here. Some of them have trauma, PTSD is the buzz word. And Jerusalem keeps sending rabbis out, but they are too far gone, and they need someone local who understands it from their point of view.

'I had one the other day. And when he gets stoned he just starts crying and he curls up on his front – you know, that thing they do in yoga – the child's pose? – they don't know what happened, and, I ask you, does it matter?'

'So you're not doing deals anymore, whatever it was you were doing?'

'The export business.' He smiles. 'That was another lifetime.'

'My father's lifetime.'

'We were small fry, darling, little minnows caught up with the big sharks.'

'I want to know about Khalid. I've been trying to find you for a long time. I've got questions…'

'I had discipline, I was never a gambler, you see – ten times – I promised myself – ten deals – and out. And I stuck to it. Made my money and got myself here. I saved myself.' He doesn't answer questions head on, but talks onwards, steering his own course.

'Was it arms?' She needs answers.

He nods.

And for all that she already knows it, for a moment she imagines wriggling arms, severed from the shoulder, piled high in containers, like some grotesque massacre of the Hindu Gods.

Now the image is of men with suitcases of prosthetic limbs, standing under dark railway arches, exchanging fake body parts.

'It's more complicated than it sounds, wasn't cruise missiles, more like washers and bolts, spare parts, stuff to keep it all moving. It isn't like you send a crate of rocket launchers by DHL, it's more complicated, a hell of a lot of paperwork, a front company. You have to hold your nerve. Ah, it was a pity. He was too young. Heart gave out.'

'It was a heart attack?'

'Do you want a beer?'

He goes off inside the house, through swinging wooden doors, and she can hear the sound of the forest all around her. The whirring of crickets and the high whine of mosquitoes. Unfamiliar bird calls. The moon has come out, brassy and oversized, rivalling the sun.

Sammy re-emerges with two syrupy brown bottles of Kingfisher in one hand, a rusted bottle opener and a pouch of tobacco in the other, places them on the low glass tabletop. He sits down with another hacking cough, the phlegm rattling in his chest.

'So let me tell you, Alia. That day, we had a big deal going on — we'd been working on it for months. Unusual case it was, actually had the shit in front of us in a lorry — that doesn't always happen — much more risky, crapping ourselves we were, of course. And we had to go down to Portsmouth — we'd driven out from London, Khalid, his mate and myself, to meet the sellers, to do the deal and sign it all off.'

'For Khashoggi?' She speaks tentatively, saying out loud the names that she has read a hundred times. Sammy's existence means this isn't a story. He exists, they all existed.

'For Mr K. And the exact damn moment that the sellers have turned up in their Range Rover, your father got back in the car... We tried to resuscitate him, but there was no pulse, nothing, he was cold within minutes.'

'So why was he found in the water? Why not take him to the hospital?' Alia has been picking the label off her beer bottle, but now she looks up at him.

'Look, it wasn't my finest hour, but what was I meant to do? We were there, in a strange city, with the shipment, biggest gig of my life to date — and Khalid was stone cold dead. There was nothing any of us could have done for him. And I had Imran crying on one side and I had to make a quick decision. I couldn't turn up at the police station or the hospital – ah, here's my mate, he just died on a day out in Portsmouth. Your old man was the director of the put-up company, it would have been too obvious. I couldn't answer any questions, couldn't even explain why we were living together. So what was it going to be?'

'So you just threw the body in the sea?' Her voice has gathered some strength.

'I was going to have a bloody cardiac myself if we didn't get him out of the way. We tried to take a bit of care. His mate was upset about it, insisted that we needed to follow the rites. Fair enough. We waited until it was dark and drove to a place further out along the south coast and pinched a dinghy. Washed his hands and feet and his face, and said prayers.'

And then they threw him overboard. He doesn't say it but the knowledge hangs there between them both.

'So he wasn't killed? It wasn't murder?' Her voice is raised now.

She looks him straight in his pale green eyes.

And very slowly he says, 'I am truly sorry if you thought it was.'

She leaps up.

'I can't believe this, after all these years. I *wanted* him to be murdered. He must have been murdered! It's the only thing that makes sense.' And she shakes off her flip flop and beats it on the side of the wall, hitting the bricks as if spanking the building, as if beating with all her might will make him dead in a different way.

'Why did you want him to have been murdered?' Sammy

leans forward, giving a wheezy chuckle, as if she is amusing. He's misjudged this visitor.

'Because otherwise it's just sad, it's not tragic. It's not anything, other than a sad lonely man who couldn't even stick at the job long enough not to die.' Sweat and tears and mucus all stream as one down her face. Her shoe is still in her hand, and the verandah's wooden planks burn through the soles of her feet, releasing all the heat of the day. 'If he wasn't murdered, who the hell is to blame?'

Murder would have been poetic, that was what she had expected; she wasn't prepared for anything else.

'It didn't last. It was all drying up by then. Once the Iran–Iraq war ended, the good times stopped rolling for K. They locked him up for a while, but they couldn't get rid of him completely, kept him on a shorter leash.'

'Did you still get paid?' she turns and asks him.

'Yeah, of course. They reached Tehran. We pulled it off.' He shrugs, a small glint of pride.

And then she is seized with the force of something else, the injustice of something that needs amending, the cheating and the merry dance. And she understands Khalid's fundamental goodness and his silly mindless search, all as something that is part of her, that she will never shake, and that knowledge doesn't help at all. She gasps as if she has been mugged in the street.

'I want the fucking money! It's mine! It belongs to me! Where is the money?' she roars, and she is lunging at him with the beer bottle, and spitting with rage. She screams out so that the sounds of rage echo throughout the forest, and the pye-dog runs and slinks under the deck. She hurls the bottle

– it flies past Sammy Wadia and explodes on the corner of the low table. Decades of anger in her ribcage, relishing the brown glass splinters breaking everywhere, the crash of the bottle, the way the beer foams and drips all over the tabletop. She takes the other bottle and throws it with full force, to follow the other, as if a sport, all her muscles charged, as if her target is finally found, as if she knows what she must hit.

And as she does so, a langur in the neighbouring tree sets off the alarm, whooping. And then, in answer, a thousand starlings lift, and swirl above the trees beyond the house, like black powder sprinkled over the sky.

Sammy dodges the flying glass, stands flat to the side of the exterior wall, with his hands behind his back, full of respect. The earth reeks of the beer swirling at his feet.

'Where is the money? I want my fucking money.' She says it quietly now, as the charge seeps away, and leaves her with a clearer mind.

She is as alive as she has ever been, without future or past, only needing and desiring with the certainty of someone who has been cheated.

Sammy has seen threats over the years and stands with the shattered glass all around his verandah, in great clear brown hunks and splinters, and she can hear him inhale. He looks at her, assessing her case. Waiting it out.

He stands very still.

'Look, can you come back tomorrow afternoon? I'll have something for you.'

'That money is mine. My father sweated over it. It cost him his life. I want that money in my hand. I am not going to apologize.' She can see her own mania now, coming into focus.

'No, nor should you.'

'I am not saying sorry.' She puts on her shoes and crunches across the broken glass towards her bag.

'I wouldn't expect you to.'

'I want the money. I don't want any bullshit talk about helping people out here. The cash matters. And I want my share.'

'I understand, you don't need to explain.'

'It's a reparation. Do you know what I mean?' She shakes her bag to emphasize the point.

He nods. He seems like he is in complete agreement. As if they are on the same side.

The next day she rents a Yamaha, and drives it at speed along the inland road, feeling the wheels lift over the potholes and surfaces, the heat whipping off the motorbike, overtaking couples and families on their scooters, and trucks loaded with bamboo canes. The bike accelerates on the paved road from Vagator, and the makeshift shacks with packets of cashew nuts, and crisps, and soap powder, and the scarlet Kingfisher adverts and restaurant hoardings all merge into a furious loud blur as she speeds along the road.

Sammy is waiting for her, already standing and looking out across the forest and watching as she approaches.

The verandah has been neatly swept, there are no remnants of the previous evening. The place looks shabbier in the daylight, battered by the sun. The sleeping dog, back in his spot, stirs and scratches his side lazily with his back leg. She holds her crash helmet under one arm.

'Come inside. I've got something for you.'

She should be frightened of entering the house, but the anger is still coursing, not the same explosive rage as the previous day, but now a rolling boil, and she follows him inside. The fury of the previous night is diluted, by the bike ride, by the intervening night, but she is still ready for a skirmish, ready to protest, a hand resting lightly on the penknife in the pocket of her baggy trousers.

The room is shady, and her pupils adjust from the whiteness of the afternoon light.

From the haze emerges a mattress on the floor, a cane chair with faded cushions, a hard floor the colour of the Goa mud. The wooden shutters are half closed. An old electric fan above them turns frantically, a running heartbeat, as if the blades might detach and propel across the room. Or lift the house and carry it up into the air.

There is no offer of beer.

Sammy goes inside an inner door and emerges again with a bag, a jeweller's bag, made of deep blue velvet.

'Take one,' he says, offering the bag.

Alia places her hand inside, like picking from a lucky dip.

Diamonds, each one brought up from the deepest reaches of the earth, each one as hard and intimidating as a mountain. Beauty, not wealth. Refracting light on each side, a shard of rainbow in the air, catching the infinitesimal dust particles of the room.

'They are yours. All of them.' He hands over the bag, without ceremony. 'Have this too.' A bundle of rolls of banknotes in a hessian bag, the sort used for vegetables on market day. Rolls in cheap brown rubber bands. She lifts one out and the rubber has disintegrated so the band snaps in her hand and the fifties splay out like a deck of cards. Her Majesty, in a tiara, mouth set in a disapproving line.

I promise to pay the bearer… for the Governor and Company of the Bank of England. Signed by the Chief Cashier.

The wadge of notes is thick. She has started making some calculations, but before she can finish, he says, 'The rocks will bring in about two hundred K. And there's about twenty grand in the bag.'

Yes, this will do, she thinks. This is about right.

'Here's an address in Holborn. He'll exchange them – not all in a day, they aren't that easy to shift. Got to beat inflation, you know. And the fifties are a bugger with taxi drivers.' He pauses. 'You'll need to get the cash out of the country, roll it into clothes, inside socks. You look sweet as pie. They'll wave you through.' As if he knows what she is going to ask, he says, 'It's no good to me. I've got enough to keep myself in morphine. The nurses here are angels. They'll look after me.' He drags on the cigarette in his fingers insistently, in a death-defying way, taunting the reaper. 'I've got about six months. I've taken care of other people. This is yours. You are right. It should have been yours. You've got to desire. We need to want. It makes us human.'

And as Alia held the diamonds, Khalid was as real to her as he had ever been, smiling in his inscrutable way, standing before her. And she was back in London, the rough fabric of the Tube under her skin, and rushing through a tunnel of green endless suburban trees, and prising open a small velour trinket box.

'Listen, your father got back in the car, and he lay down across the back seats, with his coat under his head, and he held his chest, and he fell into a sleep. I knew as soon as I saw him. His eyes were closed and his mouth was open. It was quick, Alia, very little pain, he can barely have known what was happening. Best way, to be honest. He wasn't a bad man.'

And then she hesitates. Somehow there needs to be an exchange, the transaction is not complete.

'I've got something for you.'

From her bag she offers Sammy the lighter. That burnished gold lump.

'You smoke. I've given it up,' she says, as she hands it over.

They shake hands, for longer than necessary, in a way that says many things. A handshake that is better than speaking of any of it.

She goes down the steps to rejoin the mud track, heaves her motorbike upright, pulls her helmet back on.

He stands against the railing looking outwards.

'Watch out on these roads. You want me to come with you?'

'I'll make my own way.'

As she gets closer to the beach she can hear the sound of a full moon party. The thumping bass line coming through the amplifier, turned so loud that even the ground seems to be quaking, the music competing with the sound of the sea. Down below her on the beach she can see a party of people dancing, in a trance, mostly high, or wasted, or mad. They've been dancing constantly since the previous night. Day-glo paint on their faces, skinny men without shirts and wild hair, women whirling in sarongs, their tattoos blurred by their movement. Things hang from them, necklaces, ropes, beads, and they dance with fevered energy. Hippies and freaks.

She parks up the bike, runs down onto the beach, kicks off

her sandals and joins them. Entering the crowd, the smell is syrupy, of sweat and joints. A woman welcomes her, smiling and opening her arms as if to a lost friend, and the bodies part to make space for her. They all have a little orbit, their private euphoria.

She wants to dance, she's not drinking and she's not high. Her whole body feels lighter, and the music – repetitive and electronic – runs from her feet into her legs, up her spine, into the crown of her head. She grips the straps of her backpack, and feels the slight, immense weight of it shifting. Alia lifts up her hands to the daytime moon, and the music pulses at the same speed as her own ventricles. She dances and dances, springing from foot to foot. Above the horizon the moon rises, pale and slightly transparent, like tissue paper, and the sound of the waves crashes into the beat of the music.

THEY HAD BEEN IN THE AIR ABOUT AN HOUR, AND THE MAN IN front had kicked out his footrest and levered his chair down low, so that she was pinned against the window, looking out on the wisps of clouds. Seatbelts were clunking as people started to become restless, as the plane steadied out. The air was still sticky with the warmth of the land she was leaving.

She thought of the zeros. Smiley faces, hula hoops, omegas. A lot of zeros.

She would volunteer with the theatre. Spend a year travelling. Her future was a fantasy parading in front of her, as unreal as the paper it was written on.

'Are you sure they're real, you're not being conned?' Stefan had asked.

But there had been something so conclusive about Sammy. There was no doubt in her mind at all.

It wouldn't change anything at all, and it would be transformative. It was power. She had been given power, in the form of zeros. In the form of rocks.

And down below she saw the size of the country, as the plane hummed over the thousands of pockets of cultivated land, and somewhere there was a crack in that land, somewhere there had been lines drawn which couldn't be seen from the sky, there were layers of ancestors' bones laying down deep in that beige soil, tombs and shrines, men who had knelt together in rows, with the sun reflecting on their backs, somewhere there was the place of origins that couldn't be known. A large river, drifting by, gold heavy on the wrists of new brides, the crisp white cotton of Eid, the sugar cane in thick green tubes, all moving towards market, towns where kites darted from roofs, and poetry was declaimed until dawn.

Somewhere, as she craned her neck against the deep sill of the window, down there, was the place that was no longer hers, and somehow she knew they were inside her, the lives that she came from. And just as she knew it, the plane tilted to one side and up rose the mountains, triangular shards of rock, the Himalayas, hard and endless and crusted dazzling white.

And the view of the plains was gone.

EDGWARE ROAD, LONDON

15 DECEMBER 1987

28

UNDER THE FLYOVER, HARDLY ANY TIME SINCE THEY'VE LEFT, he says, 'Hey, Imran, bhai, stop would you? I need to go back to Edgware Road station. I just need one minute there.'

Sammy looks at his watch.

They all know that they have time. Nothing's going to happen until they get there, but they want to crack on. Sammy feels vulnerable until the deal is complete.

'It's important. I'll be one minute.'

Imran takes his foot off the pedal, and slows the car, torn by his loyalty to an old friend, and the new paymaster. The red light gives them a few seconds to decide. 'Should I stop, boss?'

Sammy shrugs; he trusts Khalid deep in his soul, knows he's not going to run off, and he's committed to seeing this job through. They can spare a few minutes.

'Crazy fuckers,' he says.

The car makes a wild U-turn in the middle of the road, turning across the box at the traffic lights. Car horns beep from both sides, a cyclist throws them the finger and bangs on the back of the car.

They go back past the shops that they've just passed, the sign for Church Street, ZamZam, Azmar's Kebabs, the big high-rise office blocks, and weave back under the thick traffic on the road above them.

It feels like a long time to Khalid. It's probably only a minute.

What's he going to say if he finds her?

He'll just say sorry.

He'll say that he wants to see her and that she could come next Sunday – if she wants to, and if her mother lets her? He might cook – it's been a long time but he could try a pilau. Has she ever tried his pilau? It's not bad. Peas and lots of butter, that's the secret. He used to make it for Suzie.

He'll say he can't take her with him because he's going to do something very important today, and he'll tell her about it next week. It's big, it's going to change things for him.

They pull onto a double yellow line, on the wrong side of the road. 'Be quick, Khalid, OK?' says Imran.

'Bloody amateurs,' Sammy complains but gets out and opens the rear door for him. Khalid steps out and smooths down his overcoat and steps out into the road, dodging across three lanes of traffic, making his way diagonally in between the cars that are crawling forwards. He's focused on the red tile archway at the front of the station. He runs in.

He's out of breath when he reaches the other side of the road. It's hard to breathe. This is a stressful day. He must start taking it easy soon. He needs a break. He can't today – they've got to go to Portsmouth. There are important things they need to do in Portsmouth. Portsmouth rings in his ears, the ships waiting there, and the grey sea before him.

He knows that she has gone as soon as he enters. The ticket hall is empty apart from a man in a London Underground uniform, sitting in a plastic chair by the barrier with a newspaper in front of him. A gust of wind rumples the sheets. His head is wrapped in a sky-blue turban.

Khalid circles the ticket hall as if he is searching for something.

'You alright, mate?'

Khalid looks at him. His name badge says he is called Harbinder Singh. The badge is round, with the logo for London Underground, and he wears blue overalls that also billow as the wind rolls through the hall.

The man reminds him, unexpectedly, of his own father, who he hasn't thought of for so long. Something about the depth of the lines around the eyes, and the wisp of the beard. Khalid sees his father, sitting with the same half-moon glasses, in a wicker chair in their drawing room, in the evening light, reading the *Friday Times*, peering over the top of his glasses, looking at his teenage son before him, disapproving of his long hair, his brightly coloured shirts, asking when he last prayed.

'I'm late for my daughter. She's about ten, I mean, she is eleven. Long black hair. Probably had a backpack.' He opens his wallet to show him her picture. 'She's younger in this picture, you can still see...'

In the school portrait, tucked in his wallet, she beams out, smiling, in her school jumper and matching headband. She is scrubbed clean as if she's just been pulled out from the bath. She looks eager to please. She looks like a girl who is going to do alright.

'She went home.'

Something lurches in his heart.

He looks around and towards the lifts, which are sealed tight, as if he could prise them open with his will and summon her, and bring her back. She will be sitting in the carriage by now heading west. Underneath his feet he can feel the tremor of the trains; the floor rumbles, like an earthquake, and he feels unsteady on his feet.

He'll make it up to her.

There'll be presents galore after this. He will take her to Hamleys – is she too old for Hamleys? Maybe the Savoy. They can go and have high tea, cream cakes. He'll get her anything she wants, and she can choose something for herself. She's becoming a young woman now, probably something sparkling, it's time she had some proper jewellery, like his mother and his sisters. The way they used to prepare themselves, the shine at those weddings. Real diamonds, sapphires. That's right – she should have something like that, a ring, earrings, she won't be in those stompy boots and jeans forever, it's surely a phase, there'll be a time when she wants the same things as all of them.

'I'll make it up to her.'

His chest is hurting ridiculously. It's so taut inside his ribcage, beating painfully. He must take some painkillers. He knows what he needs to do. He feels inside his jacket pocket, and there's a packet of paracetamol, nearly empty. He pops a couple out of the packet, swallows them hard, without water, pushing them down his throat with saliva.

He needs to get back to the car. There are men waiting for him. He has a deal to do. Container ships are waiting on the sea.

As he turns to leave, the man on the station looks up, and makes a strangely formal gesture with his hand to his head. He tilts forward a little, and almost brushes his forehead with his fingertips, his palm facing inwards.

'Adab, brother.'

The gesture of greeting and farewell.

The way the servants motioned, as the family saw him to the airport, for that PIA flight when he set out for Heathrow. Heads bowed, someone had garlanded him with a string of pink roses, like a groom, scented with rosewater. Standing outside the house with the gates wide open, the car ready to pull away. The way his family clasped him that day, and the servants stood in a line and gestured their respect.

'Adab.'

Palms turned inward, his body recalls the gesture, the light touch of his own fingertips.

I offer my respect to you.

Khalid places his hand on his heart in response, and leaves the station.

THE APPENDIX

THE RIGHT HONOURABLE LORD JUSTICE BINGHAM SITS IN HIS room in Gray's Inn. Tom Bingham, scratching his head, lowering his tortoiseshell-rimmed glasses, and cleaning them slowly, turning the desk lamp on as the evening light fades over the cobbles in the quadrangle below.

He believes in the rule of law. He's devoted to it, to this secular religion of which he is a high priest.

The files on his desk are heavy. Bursting at the seams with the weight of depositions and claims, minutes and interview transcriptions, letters and scribbled notes extracted from various ministries, from the liquidators, and from Price Waterhouse. And this is just a fraction of the papers. They fill a room. It has taken a whole team of shorthand writers and secretaries months to get to this point.

He can smell the aroma of gravy coming from the kitchen. Soon dinner will be served downstairs in the wood-panelled hall, where Queen Elizabeth I peers down on the judges and barristers, querulously, in her lace ruff and drop-pearls. Some of the wood in that hall was carved from the beams of a Spanish galleon, captured from the Armada, marched through London's streets and held aloft in a victory parade in 1588.

Bingham would like to finish drafting this section of his report before he eats. He will sit with his fellow benchers and say nothing, and take meat and potatoes and a little wine. Although they pretend otherwise, they will be itching to know about his ruminations, but they respect him too much to pry. Afterwards, it will be back up the mahogany staircase to the files. He'll be back in his office, perhaps until midnight.

It's a swamp: the choked weeds of the banks, the depositors and shareholders, the footsteps washed away in the silt. It was a dreadful bank, run by a lot of third world chancers, full of vanity and a fair amount of low cunning. They had ripped off all and sundry, and managed to dress it up in fine language and noble ideals.

And people knew. Of this much he is certain. On Threadneedle Street, in Whitehall, they knew for years and they said nothing because it was a useful portal, a parallel financial system which granted them access to the inner sanctums, allowed them an invisible place on the white sofas, it gave them knowledge — and power, to hand over brown packets of cash that were spent on machine guns and lined pockets and bought limousines, all to push back the Soviets. The CIA said 'jump' and London asked 'how high?' Running men like that Khashoggi fellow as their arms mule. Those fools in the Services had thought they were waging a war for civilization. Maybe he had believed it himself too, for a while, but it is over now. The West has won.

But there was a high price along the way. They didn't keep to a neat party line. Sometimes they just sold arms willy-nilly. Keep everyone fighting, bog them down, like some neverending mythic war. Take that show between Iran and Iraq. It's clear what monkey-business people got up to, and he has names. And a pretty penny some of them made too.

But what is Tom Bingham to do? How much can he say without bringing disgrace to many? He's an honest man, yet he knows the limits. They were whispered to him, as ice was stirred into a drink, in this very room. Not that it matters, he told the fellow to sod off. It's his Inquiry, and he's not one to be easily frightened, God knows. Justice is my guide, he told him.

Bingham wears the law like a protective cloak. He's sixty next year — there are still many things he wants to achieve. He is famed for his judicious nature; it's in the fibre of his soul; his dexterity with words and his ability to see where the balance of truth lies, to weigh up, to write judgments which gently coruscate — for those who can read between the lines.

He can't risk looking like a whitewasher. And he's bound by the terms of the Inquiry. To inquire into the supervision of the Bank of Commerce and Credit International under the Banking Acts. That's a conundrum. He's meant to assess the Bank of England's role — not more or less. It ties his hands. He inspects the signet ring on his little finger, rotates it around. The guilty faces of the deposition, that fellow from the Bank of England's Supervision Department with a fancy watch. He's good at spotting the way liars look away, something in the shift of the pupil within the iris, which says it all. Those before his Inquiry had taken the oath; he can only work with what he has heard or what's down on paper.

And what a lot of paper there is. So much to go through. He's more tired than he will admit to himself.

He picks up his fountain pen, and refills the barrel from the pot on his desk. Some things could be said in an appendix, the most sensitive conclusions, dealing with the role of the Services. They might get through if he tucks them there. And if not, posterity will be on his side. If they block publication, he'll have set the record straight and the Inquiry will wait patiently for its historians. After all, it will be his name printed in gold on the spine of this report.

He begins to write:

'The Bank did not pursue the truth about BCCI with the rigour which BCCI's market reputation justified... the degree of alertness and inquisitiveness shown by many of the Bank officials who dealt with BCCI was not high...'

He looks for something more metaphorical, perhaps a touch of poetry is needed.

'If a sail has to be changed, it is better to change it before, not after, a storm has blown up.'

And the storm blew up, by goodness, it blew.

The pen drops a globule of ink on the paper which spreads out, mercilessly, obscuring his writing and spoiling the work. 'Damn them,' he says, and takes a fresh sheet.

ABOUT THE AUTHOR

YASMIN CORDERY KHAN was born in London and is a historian and broadcaster. She is the author of *The Great Partition: the Making of India and Pakistan* (for which she won the Gladstone Prize) and *The Raj at War*. Her books have been longlisted for the Orwell Prize and the PEN Hessell-Tiltman Prize. She has written for the *Guardian, Times Literary Supplement* and *Prospect Magazine*. *Edgware Road* is her first novel.